Praise for

'A compelling voyage into a little-known diaspora, that of Pasifika peoples in Sydney. Dunn has crafted a loving, yet challenging, portrait of her Tongan-Australian community, with plenty of laughs amongst the grit. I especially enjoyed reading about the lives of women and girls in their too-full Mount Druitt houses crammed with footy-obsessed brothers, sodden nappies and hard-working parents who only glimpse each other in the brief moments between day and night shift work. At times hilarious, this is truly groundbreaking fiction – to my knowledge *Dirt Poor Islanders* is the first novel ever written by a Tongan woman. Her queer characters are brilliantly realised as well as deeply embedded into everyday community life. A wonderful debut!'

– MELISSA LUCASHENKO

'I couldn't put it down. I laughed and I cried and I could smell the food and picture the places. Groundbreaking. Powerful. Brilliant. Masterpiece.'

– SELA AHOSIVI-ATIOLA

'A fresh and vital new voice. The language dances on the page and creates vibrant characters alive and dripping with life.'

– FAVEL PARRETT

'Dunn's voice is distinctive and magnificent. In *Dirt Poor Islanders* she defiantly explores Tongan-Australian life, something we've never seen in Australian literature before. Her debut is ferocious and tender, tracking her protagonist's journey towards self-acceptance with audacious honesty. No one is spared and so much is revealed, including the complexity and power of being Tongan.'

– SHANKARI CHANDRAN

Dirt Poor Islanders

WINNIE DUNN

hachette
AUSTRALIA

This project has been assisted by the Australian Government through Creative Australia, its principal arts investment and advisory board.

Published in Australia and New Zealand in 2024
by Hachette Australia
(an imprint of Hachette Australia Pty Limited)
Gadigal Country, Level 17, 207 Kent Street, Sydney, NSW 2000
www.hachette.com.au

Hachette Australia acknowledges and pays our respects to the past, present and future Traditional Owners and Custodians of Country throughout Australia and recognises the continuation of cultural, spiritual and educational practices of Aboriginal and Torres Strait Islander peoples. Our head office is located on the lands of the Gadigal people of the Eora Nation.

 A catalogue record for this book is available from the National Library of Australia

ISBN: 978 0 7336 4926 4 (paperback)

Cover design and illustrations by Alex Ross Creative
Author photograph by Helen Nguyen
Edited by Deonie Fiford, Sela Ahosivi-Atiola & Lee Moir
Proofread by Vanessa Lanaway
Typeset in 12/18 pt Sabon LT Pro by Bookhouse, Sydney
Printed and bound in Australia by McPherson's Printing Group

MIX
Paper | Supporting responsible forestry
FSC
www.fsc.org
FSC® C001695

The paper this book is printed on is certified against the Forest Stewardship Council® Standards. McPherson's Printing Group holds FSC® chain of custody certification SA-COC-005379. FSC® promotes environmentally responsible, socially beneficial and economically viable management of the world's forests.

For Winnie,
the richest gift you ever gave me was your name.

'Remember, every treasure comes with a price.'
– *Crazy Rich Asians*

SOIL

Blood soaked soil as flesh of flesh became full-form. A grounded woman, named Va'epopua, was crying under a toa tree. 'Ah weh, ah weh.' From above, the god of gods watched as his son was emerging, crown first. Fluids flowed from the depths of Va'epopua. Her son was born into earth, covered in kaka and tissue.

When her son took his first breaths, Va'epopua carried him to the edge of a nearby lagoon – a stretch of water that expanded horizon to horizon. Within gentle ripples, she cleaned her son's soft scalp, which was the colour of bark. He wailed and wailed as the grounded woman's thighs, thick as dirt, trembled in the wash.

Va'epopua gnashed at her son's umbilical cord with her teeth and swore silence of her infidelity with divinity. Placing a kiss on her newborn's wide forehead with soil-soaked lips she murmured, 'We make of each other only.'

Alone, Va'epopua raised her son. Taught him the ways of fonua, the earth. Talo, 'ufi and manioke were to always be planted in sets of three. Brown coconut was for milking, whereas green coconut was for juicing. All seafood was permitted for consumption except for turtle; its shell was the sacred mound on which they sailed through the endless moana.

As the toa tree grew ever taller, so too did the boy. From sand to sprout to leaves to fruit — it became clear to him that every-thing emerged from somewhere. So, when his arms became as lanky as brambles, the demi-god questioned his mother. 'What are we made from?'

Va'epopua sifted through shells with her starfish-wide palms and replied, 'Land.'

The lagoon stretched further still and so too did the demi-god. From coral to seaweed to salt to wave — it became clearer to him that everything emerged in pairs. Somehow, he knew that he could not be made of woman alone. So, when the demi-god's calves became as wide as stumps, he questioned his grounded mother yet again. 'I am made from what?'

Slowly planting taro with her stiff knuckles and gnashing inside her cheeks, Va'epopua whispered, 'Different.'

When the earth and demi-god could no longer expand and there was nothing more to know below, Va'epopua pointed sky-wards. From bark to flesh to cloud to heaven, she could no longer hide her shame from her son. In a hollow tone she confessed, 'Majesty.'

The grounded woman watched through saltwater as her son ascended, crown first, upon the branches of the toa tree. The demi-god climbed into Pulotu — the spiritual realm — where the god of gods was awaiting the return of his seed.

1.

Speak English, you savage. That's what the pālangi said as soon as they heard my grandmother's voice. Especially Sharon, the Bogan who lived across from us. An inflatable pool sat idly on her front lawn and shone stark white in the suburban sun. Like a wax-coated skeleton, Shazza stood dripping next to her wheelie bins. The streets of Mount Druitt hummed with heat yet I was shivering behind my grandmother.

Nana yelled back in Tongan, 'Pālangi fie me'a!' This roughly translated to, 'All White people think they are better than us!'

Shazza stared us down like we were a segment on *60 Minutes* and stomped her thongs on the concrete driveway as if she understood what my grandmother was saying. The slap of Shazza's rubber soles echoed throughout the western suburbs before she shrieked at us, 'Pack ya hula-hula crap and shove it! It can't be out on public property like that, ya loon.' Shazza's saggy pale skin was sunburnt in the spots her Australian flag bikini didn't cover. The 'hula-hula crap' was our ngatu – a type of Tongan mat. My grandmother's ngatu was spread out underneath us and all across our front yard until it spilled onto the footpath in front of our house.

Nana and I had spent all morning painting patterns on the flattened mulberry bark as she taught me every shape. Fo'i hea to mark the plantings of taro, manioke and 'ufi. Manulua to symbolise the winged meeting of two birds. Vakatou to illustrate the double-hulled canoe that allowed us to be the first seafaring people of the world. Fakamalu'okatea, which was Nana's favourite design because it revealed the story of a woman who gave birth under a toa tree. Even though my grandmother never said it to me, I reckoned fakamalu'okatea was her favourite because Nana was also born under the shade of fronds, which had spread over the ground of our village, Malapo.

As the sun wore into evening, I looked up at Nana from the ngatu. This close, I saw that the marks on my grandmother's face were like the shapes on the ngatu. A blotch under her left eye, like a rock, was my father. A cluster of beauty spots on the bridge of her nose were my aunties, Meadow, Jasmine, Heilala, Lily and Daisy. In wrinkles by my grandmother's mouth was my uncle Talasi and Nana's husband, Tupou. And somewhere in the folds of her pores were my brother Jared, my sister Nettie and me.

Crows croaked above us on powerlines and the shadows of palm trees grew over us. My fingers curled around the thin handle of a paintbrush, with its bristles coated in thick black ink. The backs of my hands held the weight of Nana's melon palms as she helped me outline the ancient markings of our ancestors. Together, we traced back to a time when Tonga was nothing but earth.

'Ta'e. Ta'e. Ta'e.' I heard these words as if my grandmother was speaking in the broken English she reserved for me and my siblings because we didn't speak Tongan. 'Kaka. Kaka. Full you of kaka!' Nana's puckered brown mouth was curved downwards like an inverted crescent moon. Her afro, a black cloud, waved back and forth.

Shazza banged her bony fists on the lids of her wheelie bins, and started to drag her Bogan trash down to the kerb. But she kept her blue-eyed glare on us. 'This here Ozstrayla dammit, eff off to Fiji.'

Spitting back in full Tongan, my nana raised both of her fists, which were the size of rockmelons. I only found out later that Nana was cursing Sharon for being a dole-bludging meth-head harlot while she, my grandmother, slaved away at Arnott's biscuit factory just to put corned beef on the table. 'Youse fink you pore? Me know pore.'

Shazza shoved up a rude finger at us, as if the gesture could return us to the tiny islands from which my nana came. I shivered again. *But not me, not me. I was born here.*

Shazza was so focused on flipping us off that she forgot about her kiddie pool. Her heels wobbled against plastic sides until she stumbled into the water. The wheelie bins fell sideways and spilled open – revealing crushed VB cans, emptied Weet-Bix boxes and stubbed ciggies.

Nana cackled like a fire was emanating from a deep and righteous place inside her.

Sharon flayed her lanky limbs. 'Watch it, lady! I'll deck ya on that bloody footpath.'

Nana kept laughing, her afro vibrating.

Shazza stomped back into her house with the Union Jack of her bikini bottom disappearing beneath her coccyx bone.

Once more, I shivered behind my grandmother's back. The streets of Mount Druitt slowly closed in around me as if it was a city to be destroyed by God; reverting me to the dirt of my ancestors.

I never painted ngatu with my grandmother again.

2.

4 Avery Street was my nana's first real home. A fiftieth
birthday present from her seven children: my father,
Aunty Meadow, Aunty Jasmine, Aunty Heilala, Aunty Lily,
Aunty Daisy and Uncle Talasi. It was my home too, but only
on the weekends. My dad would drop off his first three kids,
and then he'd go back to his second wife, step-son and my
two baby half-sisters.

Nailed to the front of the heavy wooden door of my Nana's
house was a red and gold plaque that read, 'Fe'ofa'aki',
which meant 'Love one another'. 'My home, as home God,
we luff,' Nana explained, tears running down her face as
she swallowed the gift her children bestowed upon her. The
Home of Fe'ofa'aki was a red and cream two-storey structure
made of cement and wrought iron; flanked by two wide and
blossoming palm trees.

When I first saw my nana's house, I thought it was a castle
right in the middle of Mount Druitt.

'Nah, some Wogs built it in the sixties and then some Lebbo druggos bought it in the nineties and trashed it. That's why we could afford it,' my aunty Meadow clarified.

The night she explained that to me, Aunty Meadow's weight was wrapped tightly in a giant towel. I watched as she patted dry her bare breasts, stomach and thighs – which all fell into each other in fleshy, fair and freckly folds.

'Got my rags!' she lamented. 'All these cramps but I can't have kids because I got the shallow end of the gene pool. What a burden.' There were streaks of red within her towel's fibres.

I shrugged. 'You got me.'

For the rest of the night, Aunt Meadow and I caught a re-run of *The Lion King* on the Foxtel she'd bought five years earlier, back when we lived in housing commission. The little black subscription box was the most expensive tech we owned and it served as a reminder that Aunty Meadow was fulfilling her duties of providing for the family as Nana's eldest daughter and my mehekitanga.

Of all my aunties, I was Meadow. We were the same: both the first-born daughters, both half-Tongan and half-White, and both named 'Meadow'. Aunty Meadow taught me that in English our name meant 'a piece of grassland' and in Tongan we were simply 'grass'. This was the reason we were sometimes called by the nickname 'Musie'. But we rarely referred to each other this way. To me, my aunty was 'Lahi', meaning 'senior'. To Lahi, I was 'Si'i', meaning 'junior'. We even shared our name, according to Lahi, with the daughter of a mobster in some show I wasn't allowed to watch. *Typical.*

Eventually Lahi went on to explain, like an encyclopedia, that for Tongans, the more names a person was given the more important they were. Among all my names, it took me ages to memorise my actual and full one: Meadow Kakala Theresa Fe'ofa'aki Reed. Every distant relative I ever came across took the time to recite each title like I was part of the royal family. But I only liked my last name because it sounded the same as 'read'.

Even though I only visited 4 Avery Street on weekends and school holidays, it was our first real home. The house lives in my memory like a permanent resident. Nana exists on the outside; painting ngatu or tending to her garden along the wrought-iron fence.

One Saturday, I was helping Nana pull weeds. All day we uprooted large clumps of bindis, buckhorn and tiny clusters of clovers. When I wanted a break, I grabbed bundles of roots and ran over to the storm drain just past our house and stuffed the weeds in the gutter. There, I peeked a glimpse over at Sharon's house.

I hadn't seen Shazza since the incident with the wheelie bins. The Wogs next door – on our side of Avery Street – said she had become a recluse after her son died of a meth overdose. I stared at Shazza's dilapidated bungalow, with the grass of her front lawn grown to knee height, until I noticed her blinds moving. I rushed back to my grandmother.

'Pālangi fie me'a,' Nana reminded me through a breathy laugh. The tanned soft-firm skin of her upper arms shook like clipped bird wings.

Nana paused to rip an aloe from its stem and showed me the thick clear sap oozing from its open wound. She explained in a mixture of Tongan and English, 'Put open on pala me show me show.' She brought the aloe vera flesh to an old graze on my knee, which I had gotten from tripping while playing footy with my brother, Jared. I was so unco for a Fob, probably from being half-pālangi. The aloe vera cooled the fresh whitish skin of my scab and left a sticky sheen. The tickly sensation made me giggle. From a thin, still-growing tree, Nana plucked nonu, white-yellow fruit, which reminded me of the grubs in Pumbaa's mouth.

I had watched *The Lion King* one hundred and twenty-seven times because Mufasa's death reminded me of my mummy, Le'o. Mummy died and crossed an unwinding path into heaven months and months ago. With each re-run, I sat with my nose pressed up against the bulky TV screen just as Mufasa fell from the cliffside and into the stampede below. 'Nooooooo,' I whispered along with Simba as I remembered how my mummy was placed in a box and lowered into a dark, dark hole dug out of the mud at Rookwood Cemetery.

With her melon palms, Nana crushed the fruit until its juice ran out from her clenched fist. 'Drink from tha nonu an' no mo' pala in hea.' My grandmother pulled back her full brown lips to reveal bark-coloured gums and gold-plated front teeth. In the back of her mouth were dark, dark gaps. I drew my own lips down and swore to gee-oh-dee that it was the nonu which made Nana's teeth fall out.

When my grandmother saw my resistance, she scoffed and bit into the nonu herself. She warned, 'You puke, you get big sick, no come me.'

Mixed in with these medicine plants were rose bushes of every colour. Nana's first husband, Liam, who was English-Scottish, had introduced her to roses.

Liam left our family when my dad was still a boy. He went back to England and then back to Scotland and then married an Irish-Welsh lady. Or so I heard when my aunties serious-talked. Apparently Liam became dead to our family when he didn't show up for the birth of his first granddaughter: me. We carried his pālangi last name, Reed, like a tombstone. Lahi, who knew more than any wizard at Hogwarts, once explained to me the meaning of our leftover last name. 'British and Scottish origin. Means someone with red hair.' Then she tightened her black low-ponytail with a grimace.

Despite all that, I knew Liam was the only reason my nana was able to bring our family to Australia. I pieced all this together from years of overheard serious-talk between my aunts, who believed I was too young to understand.

Nana was forced to leave Tonga as a teenager because she fell in love with a poor village boy – 'poor' as in 'worth less than the dirt on his feet'.

"Ikai', meaning 'No', was all my nana's father, Great-Grandpa Palisi, needed to say in his Catholic preacher voice to end the relationship. Hours later, Great-Grandpa Palisi shipped Nana off to New Zealand. There, she stayed with her aunt Hina, who was my great-aunt.

Named after an old god, Great-Aunt Hina taught my grandmother how to dress in flared pants and loose floral button-downs – a world away from Tonga's plain grey dresses, ta'ovala and sandals. As Nana grew into adulthood, she came to love her aunt so much that she even denounced the Catholicism of her father and converted to her aunt's Wesleyan church.

It was at the Wesleyan church, while trimming a bouquet of roses for the minister's podium, that Nana met Grandpa Liam. Tired with his life in England, Liam had travelled to New Zealand by boat and then joined the church for a bit of fun. (He was also bored of his own Catholic upbringing). Upon witnessing my nana's melon fingers gracefully cutting rose stems with a rusted kitchen knife, Liam bent on one knee.

"Io', meaning 'Yes', was all Great-Aunt Hina needed to say, in her Wellington College of Education studies voice, to secure the relationship. As mehekitanga, Great-Aunt Hina knew too well that her teaching degree could not bring the remainder of our family to New Zealand. Only a White man held such powers.

Shortly after their marriage, Liam and my grandmother migrated to Sydney. Their move was made easy, firstly, because of Liam's British citizenship. And, secondly, because Grandpa Liam lied and said my grandmother was Māori, who were the only Islanders exempt from the White Australia Policy.

By the time Liam and Nana's first son, my father, was born, the White Australia Policy had ended and my grandmother had already listed tens of tens of tens of family members ready to immigrate. Shortly after my aunty Jasmine's birth in the early 1980s, my grandparents were divorced, but by then all of our family had obtained permanent visas. Yet, even with so many more empty mouths, Liam left an empty bank account and a 'no return' address – swearing he'd given enough charity to our family and our culture to last several lifetimes.

Being one of the first Tongan women to marry, bear children with, and then divorce a young White man, my grandmother ensured we were among the first Tongans to live in Australia as 'Australians'.

From Great-Grandpa Palisi, who shipped his own daughter away from her land. From the pālangi, Liam, who left his Tongan bride better yet worse off. To Tupou, the Tongan man Nana married after all this, who did nothing but piss his wife off. 'Da old god come bird. Swoop-swoop an' snip-snipi da worm. For make man. Si'i. Memba. All man kai tha dirt. Disgust! But no-no dis. Dat paku days. Tēvolo timi.'

I knew kai was 'eating' and tēvolo meant 'devils' but as if I could know-know everything my grandmother was saying. Instead, I just rubbed at my temples and watched as she tended to her flowers – spraying extra water on the petals purple in hue. Maybe all Nana's history was predetermined by a higher power. After all, my grandmother's Tongan name was Losē, meaning that her English name was Rose.

3.

*O*nly my grandmother's melon hands could open the House of Fe'ofa'aki. Her palms were plump and pleated by the years she worked at Arnott's biscuit factory in North Strathfield. Even though we didn't live at Nana's, we spent so many weekends there that I knew the house like it was my own.

The front of Fe'ofa'aki unlocked to a small hallway made of wood. On the left was a massive archway that marked the entrance into the living room. On the right was the flimsy door to my aunty Jasmine's room.

Aunty Jasmine was the third-eldest child, born after my father and Aunty Meadow. She was the biggest woman in our family. Her full tummy fell down in one lump all the way to her skinny knees. 'Changerooms in Target call me an apple like the forbidden fruit,' she once explained while rolling her body around like a swollen snake. In Tongan, Aunty Jasmine's name was Sesimina, which is why we sometimes called her 'Big Sesi' instead of her full English name. In the days I spent within the House of Fe'ofa'aki, everyone knew each other in both English and Tongan because it was what we were made out of – whiteness and dirt.

Hung beside Aunty Jasmine's bedroom door was a framed picture of the Virgin Mary standing in a field of clouds surrounded by light. Virgin Mary's orange-brown hair fell in waves from underneath a white cloth while her pale feet floated forever above a crescent moon. To me, Big Sesi was just a fatter version of the mother of God; both women were of the same light-bright skin and both women wished for an immaculate conception.

Across from the portrait of Mother Mary was the living room. Fibres of a lilac rug filled the spaces between my toes as I flexed my feet. Behind a rickety wooden sliding door, Nana was clanking pots. She was usually in the kitchen when she was inside the House of Fe'ofa'aki. Thud thud thud went the footsteps of my brother Jared and my sister Nettie on the ceiling above her as they played footy upstairs.

In the centre of the living room, the lilac rug stretched under a violet claw-footed couch. On every inch of wall swirled gold frames, all filled with pictures of the messiah. I curled up in the middle of the velvet-seated couch and inhaled silver specks of dust. Above me weren't just pictures of Jesus but a statue of Jesus as well. He stood stoically near another open archway, this one covered by a stapled bedsheet, which led into Nana and Tupou's room. I stared back at Jesus' glass-blue eyes; long, straight blond hair and marble-white skin. Everything I knew about Jesus, I knew because of Nana: Jesus was a shepherd. Jesus was the son of God. Jesus was a healer. Jesus died on the cross for our sins. Jesus rose again as the Holy Spirit. Jesus came from England. Jesus used our bodies to perform miracles. Jesus only let us into heaven if we gave all our money to the church. Jesus loved us with his blood. Tongans loved Jesus. Tongans loved Jesus extra-much to make up for the millennia we didn't know Jesus. Tongans gave up tātatau, meaning tattoos, for Jesus. For Jesus, Tongans gave up our hair instead of our fingers when those we loved passed on. Tongans gave up our land for Jesus. We gave up eating each other for Jesus, thank Jesus.

Whether a statue or a framed imitation of Leonardo da Vinci's artworks, Jesus looked the same: light-skinned, light-haired, light-eyed. As a child, whenever I looked at the son of God, I believed that the pālangi were the holiest of us all.

Directly opposite the couch were Nana's special display cabinets with golden handles. They were actually three single plywood cupboards stuck side-by-side in order to create the illusion of one giant glass case. I thought the handles were made of real gold before they started bubbling and peeling in the summer heat and revealed plastic the colour of chicken bones. Tongans were always trying to show off how rich we were even though we were poor as muck – *because* we were poor as muck. The small incomes Tongans made working on farms, in warehouses and on countless nightshifts went into our churches, our large families, our larger extended families, and our endless cycles of weddings and funerals. The little that remained, if any, was sent overseas to our distant, distant, distant relatives – which was basically any Tongan living in Tonga.

Even though I grew up on canned bolognaise and tinned beef, my nana always spared enough money for her display cabinets. She filled the shelves with porcelain teapots and teacups, commemorative plates with the face of a princess named Diana printed on them, golden trophies from all the football games her son and step-son won, and first-place blue ribbons from all the school singing competitions her daughters and step-daughter won.

Scattered throughout each treasure were faded photographs of when my nana was not Nana but a young girl in grey dresses with a frond's shadow over her freckly face. Prominently placed at the front of the glass panels were glossy school pictures of me, Jared and Nettie. My siblings and I shared the same brown-black eyes, black bushy brows and dark green Whalan Public School uniforms. The only difference between us was our skin tones. Jared and me were brown like the top of the ngatus our nana painted all day. Nettie was as sun-bleached as the underside of the ngatu.

While Dad left this half of his family with Nana, he was getting busy cementing the second half of his family. Also on the glass panels was a picture of the woman dad remarried, Camellia, her sprouty spud son, Corey, and two newborns, my littlest sisters, Lani and Lav. In the background of the photo was our family church, Tokaikolo.

But we didn't talk about that side of my family in the House of Fe'ofa'aki. Instead, everyone just said how Nettie was prettier than me. 'So fair, so fair,' Aunty Jasmine crooned once as my younger sister slept on her lumpy lap. 'So like mummy Le'o, eh?' A wave of heat washed over my cheeks as I yelled out that Nettie might as well be adopted since she was so pale. That was one of the few times Lahi told me off, explaining that it was a sin to make my sister cry because she looked so much like our dead mum.

Our dead mum, Mummy Le'o, was also half-White and half-Tongan – just like our living dad. I used to get confused when I tried to tell the kids at school that both my parents were mixed-race. Sometimes I said I was full-White and full-Tongan. Being bad at maths, I thought that anything with two halves made two separate yet full wholes. Only as an adult did I realise the reason for my ignorance: despite the Anglo genetics that contributed to my slim waist, narrow nose and light-brown skin, I grew up with absolutely no White relatives. Everybody who raised me was Tongan. Everybody who loved me was Tongan. And that made me fully Tongan.

Mummy Le'o died of cancer when I was four, when Nettie was two and when Jared was just six months old. Neither of my siblings remembered our mum's funeral but I went back there whenever Mufasa fell to his death – when all I saw was my mother in her coffin with her marble-white skin all covered in dark blue veins.

Whenever we visited Mummy Le'o at Rookwood Cemetery, I read the Bible verse on her tombstone over and over again: 'The Lord is my shepherd I shall not want.' Without the semicolon between those two phrases, as it actually appears in the Bible, I interpreted the verse to mean I couldn't want God, so I could never want my mum. Translation: 'Suck it up, buttercup.'

Back in the House of Fe'ofa'aki, past Aunty Jasmine's room, was the base of the carpeted stairs. To the left of the stairs was a blue-tiled bathroom. It was the only bathroom in the whole house, so it was shared by all of my aunties (and us three kids when we were visiting on weekends and school holidays).

No matter how many times I saw my nana scrubbing away in the tiny bathroom with an old sponge, elbow deep in the toilet bowl, the dunny was forever cacked with a fresh kaka stain. From the tiny blue tiles, all the way to the ceiling, were clusters of stubborn black mould. Flecks of toothpaste freckled the vanity cabinet and made it hard for us to see our reflections.

Before Christian missionaries, Tongans lived in open fales, pooed in tropical foliage and only showered when it rained. Two hundred years later, Tongans were still getting used to the idea of walls, flushing porcelain and unseen plumbing – let alone having to clean it all.

From morning until evening until morning again, my aunties fought over the bathroom. Lahi took too long towelling her fallen-over folds. Aunty Heilala took too long picking at her face. Aunty Jasmine took too long mopping up her monthly reminder that she wasn't pregnant. Aunty Lily took too long dyeing her black strands to blonde-red streaks. Aunty Daisy took too long slicing herself up with a razor blade.

Aunty Lily and Aunty Daisy were the youngest and darkest of all my aunties. This was because Nana swore to never let a pālangi man touch her again. So, when she felt it was time to remarry in the late 1980s, my grandmother went back to Tonga. The man she found was named Tupou and he was from the village of 'Afa, which was known to produce offspring immune to shark attacks. Tupou's skin resembled the 'uli of the most sacred and blackest-inked ngatu. That was why my nana chose Tupou, because he was dark as earth and imbued with predator repellent. My siblings and I called him Tata for short – a nickname Jared made up because Tupou's round and hard belly made a ta-ta sound whenever my brother jumped on the only grandfather we really knew.

A few steps from the bathroom, just bypassing the carpeted stairs, was Aunty Daisy's bedroom. Aunty Daisy was the thinnest of my aunts, meaning that she was simply overweight rather than morbidly obese. Daisy was only seven years older than me and felt more like my big sister than an aunty. Her Tongan name was 'Seini', which translated to the English word 'chain'. That was why my aunty told us that even in the House of Fe'ofa'aki we were to say her White name only.

Once, in the space between the bathroom and her bedroom, Daisy explained it like this: 'Self'd coz my name the same as something used on slaves. Do I look like a slave to you?'

I furrowed my brows at her dark brown skin, wide-flared nostrils and tightly knotted black curls, and replied without even thinking, 'You do. To our neighbour Shazza, you do.'

My sister-aunt scrunched her flat brown nose and pulled my ponytail, mocking me. The nits in my hair were sucking my blood and having es-ee-ex on my head. 'Yeah, well if your mummy Le'o was alive she'd cut you for being all rude and festy.'

I clawed at Daisy's scratched-up forearm until she slammed her bedroom door into my face, forcing me out.

Superglued on the front of the door was a white plastic plaque that read in bold red letters, 'Beware of the Dog'. Next to the warning were harsh black outlines of a snarling pit bull. I was never really sure why Daisy put the plaque there. Around the House of Fe'ofa'aki there was nothing but stray, white-furred cats all named Angel. They were to keep mice from chewing up Nana's ngatus, which were made from strips of mulberry bark glued together with flour and water.

At the end of Aunty Daisy's bedroom was a dark, dark cupboard under the dark, dark stairs where all her dark, dark clothes were piled up. Once, I heard Lahi and Big Sesi serious-talking that Aunty Daisy cried in her bedroom at night and burnt all her colourful clothes.

The cupboard under the stairs reminded me of a scary story my father once whispered about a dark, dark house in a dark, dark forest where a dark, dark ghost was trapped, alone forever. Me and my brother Jared once dared our sister Nettie to hide in the cupboard. We giggled as Nettie pouted her pink lips and shuffled slowly into the blackness as she tried to prove her bravery; white skin glowing like a halo. Jared and I blocked the door with our bodies and yelled, 'Dark, dark girl!' Nettie screamed her lungs out and banged her Baby Born against the wooden door. Jared and I got a real ear flick from Nana that day because we dared to bring a tēvolo into her home – a devil so bad it made Nettie bite her forearms until she bled. I couldn't explain to Nana that Nettie was seriously durr in the head and not possessed. But I did agree that there was a dark spirit in the House of Fe'ofa'aki. Why else did Aunty Daisy sob in the middle of the night and slice up her skin?

Up the carpeted stairs was a second and smaller living room. This was where my brother Jared was now pretending to land footy tries by using a mattress on the floor as his field. Jared had twiggy thighs, airy arms and sharp shoulders all topped with fizzy-thick hair the colour of an overcooked McNugget. My brother was a short and scrawny kid – smaller than the average Fob boy. But, out of all five of my siblings, he looked the 'most Tongan' with his browner skin, wider nose and well-rounded fingertips. Jared also loved footy like a real Fob. He was always telling us how one day he was gonna be on TV like Sonny Bill Williams. 'Sonny Billz hangs with Muz-lims,' I once said with stiff shoulders and a giant grin.

Jared just mumble-laughed at me. 'There's only Jesus, bro.'

That pretend footy field of a mattress was also where Lahi slept on weekends. Jared and I were both too selfish to properly share our mum-like aunt so Lahi was forced to sleep on the living room floor. This way, she could separate my brother and me with her wall of flesh. The separation between brother and sister was important because it upheld the Tongan values of faka'apa'apa and tauhi vaha'a between us. One night on the floor-mattress, Lahi explained it like this: 'Our culture is based on the relationship between brother and sister. Jared, you are the tuonga'ane, the keeper of your sister's honour, which is our family's honour. Si'i, you will be mehekitanga, the leader of your brother and his children. Teach them how to carry our family into the future. This is why you must never lie down together. This is why you must cover up around each other. This is why you must never be alone together. Vei tapui. Your bond is sacred.'

Thud thud thud.

Crowning the smaller upstairs living room was a street-facing balcony. Those double doors stayed open in summer to bring in the cool breeze that the palm trees caught. In the winter, they stayed closed and acted like a giant mirror.

Next to the balcony doors was a frayed couch where my sister Nettie now sat pressing the pale Baby Born to her chest as if it came out of her. My aunties called Nettie a backwards coconut: White on the outside but Brown on the inside because only a real Fob girl could like babies as much as she did.

Jared and I sometimes wondered if Nettie was all there in the head. She didn't walk until she was two, she was a mute until five years old, and at nine, she still sucked her thumb – sometimes until she bled. And all Nettie ever did was play with that Baby Born. 'Gonna born ten babies,' she once predicted through her thumb. From teenage pregnancies to nightclub knock-ups, I came to understand that Tongans like my sister had subconsciously taken it upon themselves to be fruitful and multiply. Nature gave them no choice: in all of the three island groups of Tonga there were only one hundred thousand of us.

On one side of the living room, nearest the top of the stairs, were more doors. The first door on the left was my aunty Heilala's room, which was just a large and overstuffed bed that stretched from the wardrobe to the wall. Even I needed to shuffle in sideways just to get inside and I was the skinniest person in the House of Fe'ofa'aki. Only God knew how Aunty Heilala was able to squeeze her flabby folds into her sheets each night.

Aunty Heilala was Tata's only daughter from his first marriage. Even though all my aunties were Tongan, Aunty Heilala was the only one of them to be born in Tonga. I figured that's why she was named after Tonga's national flower.

Aunty Heilala was shaped like a kettle pot and her puffy cheeks were covered in small brown holes because she constantly picked at her acne.

Even though my aunties came from different sets of parents, they all looked the same – big like only Islanders can be. Once, as Lahi shuffled into a pair of extra-extra-extra-extra-large boy boxers, my mehekitanga explained it like this: 'No worries for the rest of our fat days. There's a reason why Kamakawiwoʻole can sing "Somewhere Over the Rainbow" like an ocean breeze. All that weight pushes our lungs together and makes our breath cute and fluffy. No one in the world can sing like us Islanders. We be big best!'

It made sense when Lahi explained it like that because her squishy stomach was the best pillow to rest my head against. The aunt I was named after could also hit high notes during Sunday morning prayers that only trained opera singers could reach. Aunty Meadow and all my other aunties carried their weight like a gift too, unlike the Bogan slobs I saw shuffling around Mount Druitt Westfield with their hairy beer bellies hanging out of too-tight singlets.

Right next to Aunty Heilala's room was Aunty Lily's room, which had shag carpet for walls and a tiled mirror at the head of her four-poster bed. Lily's bedroom was so outdated that it felt like stepping back in time.

Aunty Lily was the first child born between Nana and Tata. Her existence was what allowed Tata to leave his first wife. Nana explained that Lily was, 'All part God planning, eh.' But Aunty Lily disagreed when she told me, 'Tongans wanna act holy, cheech, but we just horny.'

Aunty Lily's other name was Swa and I still don't know the English equivalent. Probably because it wasn't a Fob name at all; there's no 'W' in the Tongan alphabet. I reckoned Swa just made it up to stand out amongst her many sisters. Anyhow, Swa's chosen name was neither Tongan nor English, which meant my aunt could be whoever she wanted to be.

On Swa's streak-stained tiled mirror were Blu-Tacked print-outs of Andrew Fifita from the Sharks. Even though she wasn't married, Swa swore to gee-oh-dee that Fifita was her husband because he had also grown up in Blacktown and Mount Druitt.

None of my aunties were married. I reckoned they never wanted to admit how being big, Brown women made it impossible for them to find husbands. Aussies were disgusted by them. Australian-born Islanders only wanted Aussies. Arabs, Asians and Africans were way too foreign to even consider. I did hear that in a somewhere place like Queensland, a fair few Aboriginal people married Islanders. But there was no way my aunties were leaving Mounty County for 'Aussie Texas' – at least that's what Swa called it. The only choice my aunts had were to marry Freshies; Tongans who could love them just as much as they loved an Australian citizenship.

To get to Lahi's room, I passed the frayed couch and brushed past our bulky black computer. The IBM sat on a particleboard desk topped with wires and steel boxes of wika-wika stuff. Everything was covered in sticky syrup patches full of twitching semi-dead ants. The ants were attracted to the Macca's cups half-filled with Fanta that everyone left lying around the Home of Fe'ofa'aki.

The front of Lahi's bedroom door was marked with a wonky heart-shape that I had tagged using her Rexona Ocean Breeze deodorant can. I needed Lahi to know she was loved even when me and my brother Jared and my sister Nettie were at our other home with Dad – because we lived with our father, step-mother, step-brother and littlest sisters in Plumpton more than we ever lived at the castle in Mount Druitt. I reckoned Lahi knew all this because she never wiped my tag clean.

Inside Lahi's room was a four-poster bed like her sister Swa's. But Lahi's four wooden posts were overlaid with sheer fabric, which made the bed look as if it came from a Disney princess movie. On the left side of Lahi's bedroom was a wall-to-wall window overlooking Avery Street. Adjacent to the window was an ornate mirror with a marble benchtop. Lahi's vanity was covered in glass bottles of men's perfume, half-open packets of pads and an assortment of unpaid bills. To the side of the mirror was a flimsy wooden door that led into a walk-in closet. Even though Lahi was a girl, my mother-aunt's wardrobe was filled with suits and ties she wore for her job at Mulctuary Money Management.

I suspected that Lahi's style was related to a video I once saw on the ant-coated computer just outside her bedroom. Late one night, inside a pixelated screen, I saw a website called: www.wetpussycats.com.

For some reason, I knew the word 'lesbian' from a very young age but never the actual definition. That was until my best friend at Whalan Public, Sarah Chamoun, explained it all to me one hot after-school arvo. 'Lebanese,' Sarah said, licking the roof of her pouty mouth on the 'L'.

We were in the empty school carpark standing under a giant gum tree. Our parents were always the last ones to collect us, which was how we'd become friends. Sarah's younger brother, George, was in the same class as my brother, Jared. They flicked a footy between them as they argued:

'Nah, cuz. Hazem the best, cuz!' George bellowed under a bundle of black curls.

'Hand off, dropkick,' Jared teased with a shake of his own fuzzy head. 'There's only Sonny Billz.'

Meanwhile, my sister Nettie sat in a bundle of litterfall, cradling her Baby Born within her own eucalypt-smelling world.

I squinted at Sarah as she played with a golden cross dangling from her neck. Locks of Sarah's thick hair got tangled in the shiny chain. I missed my best friend's bouncy curls whenever we needed to separate for class (I was in Year 5 Kangaroo while Sarah was in Year 5 Gifted & Talented).

'You know about Lebanese, right?' Sarah repeated, flicking her puffy tongue again.

I bit the inside of my cheeks. *Oiya, her kind was a sin in the Bible. Did she know? Should I say sumfing?* Under the sounds of our brothers mouthing off, I cleared my throat and whispered, 'Hold up. What do you mean you're a lesbian?'

Sarah blinked at me for several seconds like I'd thrown sand in her eyelashes. Then she slapped my forearm so hard a sharp sound snapped off our school's scaffolds. I yelped as Sarah flared her nostrils. 'No, you idiot. Leeebbbb-ahhhhh-nnneeeezzz, as in from Lebanon.'

I rubbed the patch of sensitive skin where she'd struck me. *The heck was Lebanon? Sounds like somewhere in Agrabah.*

Sarah sighed and put her hairy forearm around my bony shoulders. She was used to the dumb Fobs who packed out Whalan Public so I suspected she felt sorry for me. Her breath smelt of salty yoghurt and Impulse Romantic Spark when she said, 'Think of it like this: Lebanese are hard kients. Lesbians just lick kients.'

Gulping, I pushed Sarah away as a tingle between my thighs tickled. 'Don't be a grot,' I said as my best friend's perfume of sweetened coconut and burnt coffee muddled my head. Gold cross tangled in her black locks; black locks stuck to the sheen of sweat on her fuzzy neck . . .

Thud thud thud went my siblings as they continued to play with babies and footballs. I sunk into memories within memories.

Back outside Lahi's bedroom, in that dark, dark night, a little hourglass twirled: I clicked on the play button on www.wetpussycats.com. All too soon, the computer's pixels came together to reveal numerous nipples, fair folds and furry lady parts. Women, a bunch of women, were pressed against each other in wet whimpers. I gasped as I saw long hair between thighs, tongue-filled kisses and spines from elongated milky-thin backs bent low. I groaned as I heard screams, low pillow-faced moans and short-breathed cries. My face was hot enough to melt itself. A knot grew between my legs as I jammed my fingers in the power button until the filthiness cut off into a black screen.

Overcome with a burst of dread, I tugged hard on the computer's power cable, pulling the cord from its socket and watching all the little lights drop dead.

What I saw that night made me sprint across the lounge room and out the balcony doors until I was gazing upon the horizon of Mount Druitt, cool wind stinging my eyes.

Mounty County was shrouded in dry, dusty darkness. I saw my fate unravel: *What if my mummy Le'o went to heaven but Lahi goes to hell? When I die and God asks me, who do I choose?*

I never said anything to Lahi about that video. I was ashamed of my aunt's sexuality and afraid of my own. Only then did I recall the most recent and serious of serious-talk whispers. Whispers about how Lahi, the woman I was named after, the woman who raised me, was 'Lebanese'.

Thud thud thud.

4.

'*H*a'u kai,' Nana yelled at us from the kitchen, 'Come eat.' Her shrill voice carried above the grease of baking kapa pulu that sludged through the House of Fe'ofa'aki.

Jared was the first to gap it downstairs. My brother jumped over four steps at a time with a rugby ball stuck to his toned side. Nettie, like a cloud, wafted slowly behind. The pale plastic head of my sister's Baby Born smacked against the railing. Nettie was too hungry to notice she was abusing an infant, even if it was made of plastic. I stomped down the stairs one carpeted step at a time and gripped the wooden handrail so tight that my knuckles turned yellow.

I hated my grandmother's cooking. Her food was made up of manioke drenched in canned coconut cream, kapa pulu swimming in canned coconut milk, vermicelli noodles soaked in a salty soy sauce called sapasui, steamed green bananas in full-fat milk, and imitation crabsticks in lumpy mayonnaise.

If it came out of a can covered in sugar and sodium, Tongans were eating it. But back then, all I wanted was food that came out of a window. Why bother with kai when Lahi could drive me up Carlisle Avenue and get a twenty-pack of crispy McNuggets drenched in sweet 'n' sour sauce with a side of extra salty fries and an icy-sweet Coke? That was as Fob as anything my grandmother cooked anyway.

In the kitchen, steam from boiling manioke ran down the tiled splashback, making the walls weep. Nana's kitchen was divided in half by a wooden benchtop that was cluttered in leftovers hidden underneath damp tea towels. Once, I lifted one of those mouldy cloths and saw little brown maggots writhing in white lumps of cooled fat. I knew right there and then that Tongan meant dirty.

Now, I slumped at the pull-out kitchen table which was protected by a plastic tablecloth patterned with bougainvillea and frangipanis. I sat with Jared, who was still clenching his football, and Nettie, who was kissing her Baby Born on its pouted mouth.

Nana set down chipped plates of creamy manioke and hot trays of kapa pulu with wilted taro leaves bursting from shiny aluminium foil. Her afro was so full of sweat it melted like a marshmallow in hot chocolate. I took one whiff of coconut and rolled my tongue back into my throat. *Yuck!*

The ngatu-like freckles of my grandmother's face simmered as she muttered in Tong-lish. 'Kovi, kovi. Kids so kovi,' she sighed as the kitchen walls continued to weep.

Jared, Nettie and I could never fully understand our grandmother because we were so third-gen. I scrunched my nose and babbled, 'I laugh in the face of Tonga, ha ha ha.'

Nana scoffed at me and continued to tong manioke onto the chipped plates, where the starchy root crumbled in stringy and steamy segments. She pulled up the sleeves of her purple op-shop jumper so that the fabric bunched together in tight folds up her armpits. Nana's shoulders were smooth and muscular even though she was old as. They were the arms of a woman who carried an island.

Jingled keys. Screech of flyscreen. Gas stove fizzed to a stop. 'Children of the Corn,' Lahi sung from the front door. Her voice pulled at my chest as if I was choking on my own heart, but I hated it when Lahi called us the corn kids. I actually caught the movie she was referring to one night when I stayed up late watching Foxtel. It was full of pālangi kids who called themselves 'Amish' and crucified their neighbours in a cornfield. Even I knew we weren't *that* pālangi.

I rushed to the woman I was named from and jumped onto her tummy rolls, sticking to her like a husk. The salt in my nose was replaced with saltwater BO and the alcohol sting of Calvin Klein for Men perfume. I buried my face further in Lahi's sweater vest and tie. I squeezed her so tight, willing my bony arms to find her waist beneath all her flabs; the place I was born.

Standing on my tippy-toes, I pecked her freckly cheek. My aunt's skin was fairer than mine even though I was half as Tongan as she was. At the same time – 'Tackle!' – Jared jumped onto Lahi's back and his football smacked me in the forehead. 'You gronk,' I cried at my brother. Scrumming over our aunt, my brother ignored me. Lahi groaned at us. "Oiauē, I'm too big for this.'

Nettie didn't join us. Instead, she sat cross-legged and straight-backed at the kitchen table with her lifeless doll, waiting for Big Sesi to return home. Aunty Jasmine had claimed Nettie for herself. I knew the exact date when it happened too: On the eve of Nettie's fifth birthday, a hot December night. Big Sesi's hyena-on-steroids cackling filled the House of Fe'ofa'aki. I snuck past the picture of Virgin Mary to take a peek. Baby Born and a Cabbage Patch kid sat between a Woolies mud cake. Big Sesi was cracking up as Nettie squished her baby into the brown frosting. 'Heard happy born, heard happy born.' These were some of the first words my sister spoke, breaking her mutism. I knew then that Big Sesi and Nettie were meant for each other. Both my aunt and sister carried babies in their arms and in their dreams.

Shaking us off, Lahi's breathing came out in tight short puffs. She rubbed at the back of her neck, which was reddened from Jared's grip. Lahi smiled so big she revealed small melted mounds of gold set on her two front teeth. The sacred art of tātatau was banned when Christianity came to the Pacific but Tongans still felt an ancient need to put something on their bodies. The gold patch on Lahi's teeth was curved into the shape of a wave. I once asked her why she chose that shape and she just shrugged. 'We may be called Islanders but we are water people.'

Jared and I clung to the edges of Lahi's sweater vest and started sooking for McNuggets, for books, for a new footy jersey, for stuff, stuff, stuff. Under the weight of our desires, our mother-aunt dragged us back into the kitchen. Manioke steam engulfed us again. An afro emerged like a looming shadow. Even though Nana was shorter than Lahi, she stood over her daughter. Nana held out another oven tray stacked with kapa pulu. The lū pooled with oil and a solid mass of salted fat between its wet wrinkles of baked taro leaves. We all looked up at the woman who made us. She was sweating so much from her forehead that her afro had become completely undone. 'You spoilt dese kids.' My grandmother spoke those words through her full brown mouth, which was set into a line as thin and as hard as a Bible verse.

Islanders must do everything together. We painted ngatu together. We crossed the ocean together. We settled on isles together. We took up Christianity together. We entered into new citizenships together. We became wage workers together. We lived with generations upon generations stacked in fibro houses together. We slept on the same mattresses together. We became half-White together. We got nits together. We sooked together. We stayed poor together. Together. Together. Together. It must be this way; togetherness was what it meant to be Tongan.

I was sitting on Lahi's left thigh while Jared was head-butting her right thigh like he was in a scrum. The wooden table we sat around was pulled out and extended from each side like a Transformer. All the food my nana made was piled before us, still steaming from being reheated in the mouldy microwave. Loads of coconutty bits of manioke and withered taro leaves. Maggots in cooled fat wriggled in my vision like a light aura. I tapped my foot against Lahi's shin, waiting, waiting as Nana and her daughters stuffed their full faces. Still kicking impatiently, I forked my manioke into mushy bits and prayed for Macca's like I'd never see the light of another day.

'Full makes my mut itchy way she follows me around. Like far out I was just having a ciggie, Shazza,' Big Sesi complained, an unlit cigarette between her frumpy fingers. I giggled through my nose. Whenever anyone in my family was upset with someone, we called them Shazza – in memory of the day when our neighbour fell into her inflatable pool after telling us to eff off to Fiji.

Nettie was nestled on Big Sesi's lap. My sister's pink mouth was full of mushed manioke while the head of her doll was squashed under her armpits. Even though Nettie never admitted it, I knew she grew bored of babies just as much as she loved them. Maybe that's why she always wanted new Baby Borns whenever we ran feral through the aisles of Big W at Plumpton shops.

Next to Big Sesi was my aunt Lily, the one we sometimes called Swa. She swung her dyed red-blonde hair and brown cherub cheeks towards her older half-sister. 'Sis, your hooch always prickly.'

Kitchen cracked up. 'Haaaaaaahhhhhhhhh!' Gaps between my aunties' molars were full of mushed mounds of taro leaves as their tonsils lifted to the ceiling. I giggled to myself, again reminded of the hyenas from *The Lion King*. Even Nana joined in, heckling between her gums with bits of corned beef stuck on the dark hairs of her sweaty upper lip. The women in the House of Fe'ofa'aki could only talk about their private parts when the only man who lived here, Tata, was away at church training to be a faifekau – a pastor. Probably in an attempt to keep the home holy.

Next to me was Aunty Daisy, who was still in her high school uniform. Her heavy jaw gleamed with warm oil while her hazel eyes wrinkled into a smile. The only time Aunty Daisy ever looked happy was when she was eating.

'Let us pick ten bucks for a pack of smokes?' Aunty Heilala sighed from across the table. A shiny nurse badge, which was pinned on her pimply chest, wobbled. My aunt Heilala was an aged care worker at a Catholic retirement home in Strathfield. She only got the job because she pretended to love the Pope and went on about how she had a TAFE degree, even though she was still in night classes. Did I forget to say Tongans lied together?

Nana clicked her tongue before licking the grease from her own lips, stabbing up three shiny fingers. 'Haf you money las week an' wut? Git only free smoke.'

'Ummmmaaaaaaaahhhh,' all my aunts whined in unison, high on nicotine. Now that one of the sisters had asked for money, each of them slowly turned to Lahi, whose thigh trembled beneath me. Time for serious-talk, which meant 'wedding' talk – she had agreed to marry a Freshie from the islands. Knowing Lahi's search history, this decision confused me and made me believe that being 'Lebanese' was something we could cure.

All the chipped ceramic plates of lū and manioke glugged together and reminded me of a scene in a Scooby Doo movie where a buffet of sausages came alive and attacked Shaggy. A soggy taro leaf was going to suffocate me: Lahi would soon get married to a man named Lotemi from Popua, and then there'd be no one to take me out for McNuggets.

I was yet to meet Lotemi, but I gathered the Freshie was in and out of Australia on a working visa as a cook. Lahi loved food, so maybe they were well matched. But I wondered why Lahi never spoke about Lotemi to me directly.

Once, I placed my ear in the middle of my wonky love heart tag to listen to Lahi and Lotemi talking long distance. All Lahi did was shout about something called 'feminist-ism' and how she was still a woman even if she cut her hair short, stayed fat and couldn't bear children.

Concerned that some meathead was bullying Lahi, I rushed into her bedroom and snatched her Nokia before she could even see me. As Lahi yelled our name and struggled to hoist herself up, I screamed down the speaker, 'Oi, Coconut. What you saying to my mum?'

Laughing as warmly as baked bread, Lotemi's reply over the loudspeaker was not what I expected. 'You just like her.'

Lahi pulled me onto her bed and I screeched until we were both cackling. Lahi chuckled, 'He isn't dumb. He's just a man.'

At the dinner table, Nana waved her melon palms and rambled in vowels I couldn't understand. While my grandmother set out her rules for the wedding, Aunty Lily ran a pudgy middle finger over the crown of her red and blonde hair. 'Cheeba, I can't wait for ya, Musie. You know what they say about bobos from Popua.' Another hyena crack-up from all my aunties rang out, their laughter ending with explicit moans and groans.

Nettie whined and covered her ears with her hands. How my little sister came to know about those sexy sounds was beyond me. Aunty Jasmine laughed so hard she choked on her own saliva and kept the joke going by taking the unlit cigarette from behind her ear, placing it near her mouth and bobbing her head up and down. She full made sucking noises before lighting up.

'Pumbaa, not in front of the kids!' Lahi warned, snatching Big Sesi's cigarette and stubbing it out on the dining-room table. I gagged on fumes of burnt plastic and nicotine.

Wedding-talk went on and on. Lahi informed everyone that me and Nettie were flower girls, Jared was pageboy and Nana was going to walk her down the aisle in replacement of the pālangi that abandoned us long ago. Nana's afro bounced to a halo. 'God say making da man an' da woman. But make boff in me.'

My brows furrowed into a headache. *Far, what? A mum and dad in one person? Hckh, how? Weh, when?* But something was bothering me more. *Lahi's not gonna let some Freshie get between us, right? We are named the same. She can't change that much for a man, can she?*

Nana waved a greasy hand in Lahi's direction and kept talking in Tongan. I curled deeper into my aunty's pillowy waist and let the family chatter wash over me.

Aunty Jasmine hummed along to Nana's voice as she called relatives and repeated instructions into her fuchsia Motorola flip phone. With Nettie on her lap, and a soulless pale doll on Nettie's lap, Big Sesi ordered floral arrangements, dress fittings and noted each cousin of a cousin of a cousin of a cousin's cousin who owed our family money. In our family, which extended all throughout the Westside, whatever Nana said was Bible. She was the first in our community to make a home in Australia. We owed her our lives and our wallets.

Phone calls went on. Nana's Tongan became so fast that her instructions were just one long slick of mud. She turned and spread her oily palms open and placed her rounded elbows on the table; reminding me of Jesus on the cross. 'Looking all I be do. When I you, haff no one. Now you merry, giff my all. God be happy den.' Nana licked a bit of meat stuck to her plump thumb before she continued. 'Das why we go bank for pig pig money, hmm?'

Sighing softly in my ear, Lahi nodded at everything her mum was saying. The slow breath blowing from the woman I was named after pinched the space between my eyebrows.

All those naked women inside your computer. Did it make you sad to be marrying a man?

Then, in the middle of all the never-ending wedding-talk, my stomach gurgled as if trying to make its way out of my body. Nana blinked up a sandstorm as I wrapped my arms quickly around my stuck-out ribs and gave a tight-lipped grimace. If I was made to eat Fobby food, there was no way Lahi was going to take me for a real feed at Macca's. I knew what she would say, that I already ate and that she was too full and tired to drive.

Nana clicked her tongue at me softly, as if I was sick and needed the plants from her medicine garden to make me feel better. Water sprung onto her lashes when she asked, 'My pēpē, why no kai, eh?'

I held my breath, clenching my mouth shut. If there was one thing Tongans really knew how to do, it was crying on the spot to make other Tongans feel bad. My grandmother's eyes could go from fire to water to fire again. Did I mention Tongans guilt-tripped each other together?

Scratching at the print of frangipanis and bougainvillea on the plastic tablecloth, I shook my head as if Nana spoke to me in full Tongan rather than Tong-lish. When I looked up, her ngatu-like freckles were alight. 'Wut be bad wiff kai, huh? Look me speking.'

Fatty oil cooled into solid mass. Mushed manioke. Teared-up taro leaves. I glared at my untouched kapa pulu and my stomach sounded off again. Like a mirage, salty hot chips and a warm box of McNuggets drenched in sweet 'n' sour sauce floated before me.

In the House of Fe'ofa'aki, there wasn't any food for breakfast and lunch. For povo reasons, Tongans made those meals optional. During the weekends and holidays I spent in the House of Fe'ofa'aki, my siblings and I needed to fend for ourselves with whatever was spoiling in the fridge or placed underneath a mouldy tea towel on the bench. Dinner was the one and only time I could get a real meal. Swore to gee-oh-dee, even Nana wasn't gonna get in my way.

With a light rib-cage nudge, Lahi whispered onto the crown of my head, 'Careful. Your grandmother lives in you.'

When I lifted my lashes, Nana's burning-bush gaze was locked on me. Everyone, both my siblings and all five of my aunts, went graveyard quiet. My skin tingled all over. Nana demanded that I eat, and no one was to leave the table until my food was finished.

Jared gnawed at the little dots on his footy sympathetically. My brother was a picky eater too. Once, he only ate frozen fish sticks for a week until our dad gave him a massive hiding. Our father was complicated: he was scared Jared would get sick if he didn't eat properly, which was why he became mad. But he was also convinced real men ate red meat, which was why he became violent. Nana was complicated like that too.

'Kai, kai, kai,' Nana commanded as she shoved more lū and manioke on my plate. New lū broke over old. Shredded white-brown meat spilled out.

Far, it's eat or be eaten! My chest rose and my throat closed up. If living Tongan meant dirty then eating Tongan meant scum. If I chewed the lū, swallowed the lū, let the salt of the lū burn my tongue, I'd be nothing but a savage cannibal. I had learnt this lesson back in Kindergarten, when a pudgy girl named Dani laughed at me for having powdered parmesan between two slices of white bread until I spat it back up, crying.

Angels meowed inside the washhouse at the end of the kitchen, begging for the food I refused to eat. With a shaky fork, I lifted up a white chunk of corned beef and tried to swallow the meat whole. But I gagged on canned flesh. Somehow the taro leaf dribbled up my nose. Nana wailed as if murdered, 'Auē, auē, auē!'

A ham-fisted grip tightened on my upper arm. Lahi was shoving me off her lap, her breath thick and hot in my ear. 'Eat propa!'

The woman I was named after had never yelled at me before, let alone physically handled me. 'Weeeom,' I cried. 'Meeeow,' went the Angels from the washhouse. And between my sobs, lū puddled on my chest. I whimpered out, 'But this is cat food.'

A palm collided with my jaw. Nana started to shove the lū into my mouth, sludging my face in fat. I tried to move away but she just came closer until her weight was fully bent across the table. With one hand, she held onto the back of my neck, pushing me down so that she could force-feed me with her other hand. 'Mama, mama, mama,' Nana shouted through gritted gums. Mama was the word for mushing food in the mouth for a toddler. My mouth was overstuffed with corned beef now and I was unable to breathe. I finally had no choice but to swallow. This was my punishment for disobeying my grandmother.

Plates plummeted to the floor. The more I strained to spit, the more of the lū I ingested. The more I tried to scream, the more I ate.

My grandmother's grip was too strong. Her doughy waist rolled onto the table. Saggy breasts lumped in front of me; ngatu-like freckles flashing in my eyes. The squeaky sound of our plastic table cover tearing.

My aunts shouted, 'No, Mum. 'Ikai, Mum.' Cutlery crashed to the tiles as I kicked, elbowed, flailed and wailed. All my aunts could do was yell; either at me to stop or for Nana to stop. My siblings hid behind their toys, whimpering along with me.

At last, my grandmother's hold slackened. She coughed down at me as if I was the one who had tried to suffocate her instead of the other way around!

A short tickle up my chest and then I threw up everything Nana had shoved in me.

'No, Si'i . . .' Lahi lamented, sliding me off her thigh, which was now covered in my vomit.

My heart hammered. I hated my nana. I hated her because she was the one who made me like this. She was the reason I was Tongan.

'Fie pālangi. You fink you best me, aye?' Nana scoffed. "Ikai. Me say who you. An' you, you come from my shit.'

Lahi pulled me back over my own vomit and forced me to look inside the flames of my grandmother's eyes. Dropping my gaze, I saw chunks of starch, yellow bile and green flecks clotted in a clump on the line between my thighs. It was an eternity before Lahi let me go and added in a deep voice, 'Meadow, I'm very disappointed in you.' Lahi only saved our name, our real name, for when I was really in trouble.

Taking in the sight of my monolithic aunties, I knew I became a pillar of salt. Nana's words were singed on my brain: 'Fie pālangi' – that's what she called me – 'Wanting to be White'.

And all I could think was: *Why bring us to Australia just to shove Tonga down our throats?*

I gapped it underneath the table, crawling on all fours between the legs of my aunts as if I was getting pushed out of a birth canal.

'Ya hooch,' howled Aunty Jasmine.

'Get flicked,' Aunty Daisy spat.

'Picked little spliff,' Swa and Heilala snapped in unison.

Shaking off their words, I ran through the purple living room, around the side of the carpeted stairs, past the 'Beware of the Dog' sign and barged into Aunty Daisy's haunted room. I crawled past the stacked ngatus and dived into the cupboard.

Falling over my aunt's pile of black clothes, I stumbled on my knees into the dark, dark, darkest corner and sobbed. My aunts were right: I was nothing but a nit who deserved what she got because I was born out of a dying mut and came into this world as the waste of my ancestors. My grandmother, my aunties, my siblings, my mummy Le'o – they all hated me. And I did too. I hated me.

5.

*I*n the dark, dark cupboard, I tried to piece my memories of Mummy Le'o together, but all that did was make me doubt she even existed. No one ever spoke about my birth mother, especially my father. As young as I was when my mother died, I understood my father's silence was a marker of what a man was made to be: Dad was built from stone. The stubble on his bald head was like stalactites and his goatee grew moss-like over his sandstone chin. My father also never talked (almost never) and certainly never ever cried. The only time Dad drank was at family gatherings and it was in those moments that he confessed about Mummy Le'o:

Back in Dad's day, when he was freshly eighteen, Sydney was fast filling up with Freshies and second-gen Tongans. He glimpsed my soon-to-be mother standing against a mural at Mounties RSL. The wall-to-ceiling artwork was a lush green forest full of tigers, peacocks, monkeys and parrots. Nike TNs bouncing across the tiled floor, my father mistook my mother for a swan. She stood against the dark green scenery – so pale and thin even before the cancer. With stinging breath, my father explained to me: 'Youse know what, darling? Swear to gee-oh-dee I fought to myself: "What's a pālangi like that doing at a waterhole like this?" It was that first sight kinda love.'

Later, while my father waited in a buffet line, my birth mother glided up to him. She asked in a feathery voice if they were cousins, which was Islander code for: 'You cute.'

Dad grinned, showing off his naturally straight white teeth. There weren't many hafekasi around then, which definitely meant they weren't related. With a chuckle my father asked, 'Youse wanna name first?' Apparently, my mummy Le'o rolled her eyes despite her reddened cheeks. Dad continued, 'Jared, aye. Where youse from?' He noticed one of her eyes seemed a bit off-centre; only found out later, after they were married, that my mummy hid her exotropia with a contact lens.

When Mummy Le'o said her name was Theresa Mafile'o Kakala Melenaite Tu'itavake Mohuku and that she was twenty-three and from the village of Kolomotu'a, Dad gave a sharp grin.

'She was full older, full noble aye,' Dad recounted to me, marble eyes lighting up as he took a swig from a beer can. 'Far. So said to youse mum: "Why *you* talking to me for?"'

Mummy Le'o smiled, revealing crossed-over front teeth peeking from red lipstick. She swished her heavy long black hair to show off her bony neck – attributes I recognised in myself. Instead of directly responding, she mumbled about bumming a ciggie.

I imagined my father, Jared Senior, a servant from the village of Malapo, watching my birth mother, Mafile'o, a noble from the village of Kolomotu'a, as she took a slow drag from a stick of Long Beach Blues and then coughed her heart out. Dad laughed and patted Mummy's bony back and fell in love with her when she finally confessed how she'd never smoked a day in her life. Islander code for: 'Give us your number.'

Dad handed over his Nokia and admired Mummy's elegant fingers pressing on the worn rubber of his keypad. All the while, my father held onto the crook of my mother's wing-like elbow, inhaling the rest of their ciggie.

Inside my aunt's dark, dark cupboard, turning darker still, I trembled, holding onto the real and only memory I had of my mother: her funeral.

Back in my four-year-old days, I was playing Tips with my cousin, Giselle. We were chasing each other around the low-steel fence of Tokaikolo Church.

Eventually, Dad came to collect me. He was dressed in all black with a ta'ovala, a different type of Tongan mat, tied around his waist by the plaited threads of my great-great-grandmother's hair. The height of a ta'ovala was how Tongans identified the most important people at funerals, weddings and birthdays. The back of my father's ta'ovala towered above his spiked black hair (this was before he went bald) like the golden halo of Jesus. I stopped playing, mid-run, when I saw how my father's thick black lashes were held together in glistening clumps.

Dad choked out, 'Youse. Stop mucking around.' All at once, our game didn't matter anymore.

I waited, shaking at the pillars that were my father's legs, as he devoured a cigarette. After stubbing the butt on consecrated ground, Dad lifted me by the crook of his elbow. His grip locked my little ribs into his stony bicep; as if I'd been wedged into a mountainside. Before we went inside the church, my father pecked my forehead. The stubble on his cheeks pricked my ears. Breathing heavily, I weaved my small arms around his neck in an awkward attempt at a hug.

We stepped through the church doors. One thousand dirt-coloured eyes stared at us from rows of pews. The mourners for my mother's funeral were dressed in an ocean of black and purple. Their bulky bodies were also bound in ta'ovala as a sign of respect. The air around us heaved with sweat and perfume. As my father and I walked through the middle of the crowd, I noticed how the wooden walls of Tokaikolo were peeling and chipping under the weight of our grief.

Dad remained silent and carried me past my grandma Fehia – Mummy Le'o's mum. Fehia sat on a pile of ngatus like they were stacked pebbles. The yellow-brown flesh of her cheeks, of her stomach, of her thighs were spread sidewards like butter. 'Auē, auē, auē,' Grandma Fehia wailed, slamming her fists against her infected kidney.

From what I remembered, Grandma Fehia lived in a two-storey red-brick structure in Liverpool. For the two decades she lived there, Fehia ate, slept and read a worn copy of the Bible on the same weathered red armchair. Over the years, she became moulded into the pleather. The only way to get Grandma Fehia to move was for her daughter to die. After the funeral, I never saw this grandmother again because I knew, even back then, that Fehia died when my mummy did.

Bouncing me in his forearms, my father clambered up a makeshift three-step staircase and onto a rickety stage. We faced the purple-black dirt-brown crowd. I lowered my brow into Dad's pulsating shoulders, sniffling in his familiar Long Beach Blues smell, and hiding my face from the tears on the faces below. *Why so sad? Who was my mummy to them?*

Pews creaked in harmony as the Tongans of Tokaikolo stood up together and started to sing. Their voices were loud and long in hymn. "Oku ai ha ki'i fonua. 'Oku tu'u 'i 'oseni. Na'e 'ikai ke ma'u 'Otua. Na'e masiva he lelei. Haleluia. Haleluia. Kuo monū'ia 'eni – There was a small island that stood in the ocean. It did not have God. They were poor in goodness. Hallelujah. Hallelujah. They are now blessed.'

My nana once told me that Tongans lived in eternal darkness. In that darkness, we existed with cursed ink on our skin and human flesh between our teeth. Then the pālangi came, their skin and creator made of light. We took their god and they tried to take our land. But then our king proclaimed: "Ko e 'Otua mo Tonga ko hoku tofi'a – God and Tonga are my inheritance' – cementing our sovereignty forever. None of that mattered in a dark, dark cupboard thinking about a dark, dark coffin. The only god I knew had claimed my mother all for himself.

At Tokaikolo Church, Dad's chest softened to clay as he whispered, 'Youse should kiss Mum on her way to heaven.'

I felt the callouses from my father's hands on the back of my neck as he sat me down in front of my mother's open coffin. In Tongan culture it is tapu for a coffin to be closed. We needed to see the body, perfume the body, kiss the body. This way, we could commit to memory the body we came from before it was shoved in the ground.

Kneeling before my mother's casket, I leant over and peered inside.

'No, no, no, no,' I whimpered. Dad's cement fingers crushed the bones of my wrist as he tugged me further and further away from the body that bore me. The Tongans of Tokaikolo were busy singing to God, 'Haleluia, haleluia, haleluia. Kuo monū'ia 'eni.' And God was busy cursing me.

In a jolt, I thrust forward, despite my father pulling me back with all his strength. The front of my shiny pleather shoes knocked against the side of my mother's wooden resting place and her hollow chest trembled. My mother's body was bony and blue and bald from the chemotherapy. Her thin frame, so like mine, was covered in white satin. It was Mummy's womb that called to me – 'Everyone returns to the dirt, Little Bib.'

Inside my aunt's cupboard, I saw myself: a dirt-poor heathen with long black hair, black clothes and red eczema on her cheeks scrambling into a coffin, kicking and screeching. 'Mum. Mum. Mum. Mum. Mum. Mum. Mum.'

Tongans from everywhere stopped singing and started sobbing while I pounded my small fists against my mother's empty stomach and clawed at the satin wrapped around her stiff belly button. *Take me back. Take me back.*

6.

It was Aunty Daisy who found me in the dark, dark closet. She snapped me awake. Sighing, I curled limply in my sister-aunt's lush lap. Daisy was the youngest and smallest of my aunts so her tummy was a delicate pleat of icing instead of thick ngatu folds. After a small while, she whispered, 'Wanna see me burn stuff?' Her dull charcoal hands turned to gold as she held a lighter up to a pair of frayed pink undies hiding in a pile of black clothes.

While the underwear singed, I asked my big sister-aunt slowly, 'Being wary of dogs doesn't mean we are dogs, right?'

In the silence, swirls of smoke filled the cupboard. Daisy shrugged. 'Whatever. We've all cut Nana.'

Eventually, Lahi materialised in the doorway of Daisy's cupboard. With blustering breasts, she boomed, 'Aye sook, when I was your age, Nana stuffed canned beef in my mouth too.' Then she squeezed her belly fat at me and added, 'Probably shouldn't have swallowed.'

Later, I was quivering in the front seat of Lahi's busted-down Barina. Neon yellow washed over us – those damned golden arches. I gulped pathetically between hiccups, 'S– sor– sorry.' Kapa pulu oil was crusted all the way down the front of my shirt.

Lahi's sigh was a swell as she rubbed my back and kissed my crown. Saltwater sweat tinged the Big Mac-scented air as I sniffled. Lahi promised she'd help me apologise to Nana because oldest girl meant oldest responsibility. Gold tooth glittered when Lahi smiled. 'Hakuna Matata.'

At the drive-thru, I wiped the last of my tears as Lahi ordered me a twenty-pack of McNuggets with extra sweet 'n' sour sauce, salty-as chips and a large Coke – all from a pimply Asian girl with streaks of blonde in her black hair. I wondered how many Fobs like us this chick had seen through her little window with its 'Area Monitored by NSW Police' sticker.

Under carpark floodlights, the crisp golden batter smacked my tongue and soaked up my sorrow. *Macca's worth a fight.* I washed every crunch down with a sip of Coke. Fizz bubbled into my nose, stinging my eyeballs.

'Slow down or it'll burn,' Lahi explained, as though she was revealing the meaning of life to me. I hoped to be half as smart as Lahi when I grew up. Lahi hoped for that too, which was why she bought me a bounty of books: *Harry Potter and the Philosopher's Stone, Alice's Adventures in Wonderland, Alice Through the Looking Glass, A Series of Unfortunate Events, Peter Pan and Wendy, The Little Mermaid, George's*

Marvellous Medicine, Charlie and the Chocolate Factory, Aladdin and the Enchanted Lamp, The Wonderful Wizard of Oz, The Ballad of Mulan and *The Lion, the Witch and the Wardrobe.* At first, I thought C. S. Lewis wrote the original story for *The Lion King.* When I asked Lahi about this, she just tightened her low-ponytail and said I was too young for Shakespeare.

Chewing on the last of my fries, I wondered: *Oiya, Macca's my Turkish delight?* I was a half-White, half-noble child who betrayed The Great Lion for a McNugget.

We pulled away from Macca's and across Luxford Road to the 7-Eleven to fill up petrol. Streetlights buzzed as I waited in the car, rubbing my full tummy. With a burp, I watched my aunty bounce over to the cash register holding onto a bouquet of limp red roses and an overly-stuffed teddy bear. An Egyptian-looking dude in a turban served her, the collar of his work shirt propped up like a wannabe 2Pac. He tilted his turban, cackling. Lahi must have made some kind of joke. The woman I was named after could make friends with anyone. Her best friend, Uncle Tomasi, was a tubby Fijian-Indian guy who full-liked other men. 'Oh, honey!' he crooned in a high-pitched voice whenever he came to visit the Home of Fe'ofa'aki. Lahi explained how she met Tomasi on Oxford Street all the way in the city. I shrugged and mimicked in response, 'Oh, honey.'

The roses were for Nana but the teddy was for me. Lahi felt the guiltiest about all the bad stuff in our family. She was the first-born girl, which meant everything was her responsibility, which meant everything was her fault, which meant one day everything was going to be *my* responsibility, which meant one day everything was going to be *my* fault.

Police sirens wailed in the distance as we drove back to our love-one-another castle in the middle of Mount Druitt. Just before we reached the two towering palm trees that stood like soldiers, the Barina's tyres hit the kerb and Lahi's hand became a second seatbelt, slapping my stomach and choking my chest.

Lahi squealed and I squeezed the teddy tight. 'That scared me,' Lahi wheezed.

With a quiver in my voice, I said, 'Bet those palm trees were even scareder.'

We laughed and laughed. Lahi and me; we were the first-born girls in our lines, we were the first to share names and so we were the first to belong to each other.

When Nana received her roses, she sobbed, asking why God cursed her with children. Then she smothered me in sloppy smooches all over my crown and down my cheeks. Petals between us, I stood stiffly, waiting for my chance to quickly hug her and then bolt upstairs with Lahi. I wasn't heaps angry at my grandmother but I was keeping a shard in my heart, unable to forget her slippery-strong palms over my mouth.

Standing behind me, Lahi also apologised on my behalf in proper Tongan: 'We are sorry. Please forgive us. Thank you. We love you.' Nana nodded, her afro moving back and forth like a soft cloud. Sticky perfume from the petrol station roses flooded my nose, reminding me of a funeral. Lahi ended our apology with the word 'tulou', which meant, 'excuse our presence'.

The freckles and spots on Nana's face lifted up as she gummy-grinned. The mark of my father, a blotch under her left eye, faded back to its usual dull brown. 'No more angi, ogay. Be kovi me to God if saying no for His flowa of my name, eh? Si'i, ha'u. Mohe wif Nana for night.'

With a scrunched nose, I looked back at my aunt only for her to neatly nudge me into my grandmother's belly button.

I was yet to know what it meant to share a night with my grandmother but I knew fully well what it meant to be bathed by her. In the Home of Fe'ofa'aki, Nana scrubbed me and my siblings every time we slept over.

In the mouldy blue-tiled bathroom, I stood naked as Nana tested the heat of the bathwater with her swollen fingertips. The sleeves of Nana's purple op-shop jumper were rolled up over her broad shoulders again. 'Alu,' Nana said gently, turning the tap knobs until they squeaked shut with rust. As I dipped into the bubbly bath, Nana sat on the toilet seat lid and its plastic creaked loudly under her weight. Buoyed in bubbles, I blew soapsud dandelions until foamy seeds floated into the air and onto the blue-tiled floor by Nana's thickly-socked feet.

The toilet groaned again as Nana stretched out her legs and exhaled. 'Ah weh, Si'i. So sore ev'yweh. 'Oiauē. So sore for be pore an' ol' an' ugly.'

'Ah weh' was the shortened version of the Tongan expression "oiauē", which was close to the English saying, 'Oh my gosh'. While "oiauē" was an exclamation of shock, 'ah weh' was a sigh of relief.

I played silently around in the soapy water, unsure what Nana wanted me to say. We were poor. She was old. Us Tongans were fat and gap-toothed and bark-skinned and wiry-haired. Before White people came to us, we were nothing but creatures of sludge eating each other sick. She knew we were un-pretty, she told me so herself.

Resting my wet face on my curled-up knees, I watched bubbles fall down my shins. A flame in my ears told me that Nana was watching me. When she bent lower to catch my gaze, my grandmother's burning-bush sight cooled into a swirl of mud. 'My girl, wash pipi,' she instructed with a press of her pink tongue between the gaps of her decaying teeth.

Pipi was the Māori word for shellfish. But for my nana, it became the word she used for vagina. I assumed, even as a child, this was because the thing between my legs was shaped like a pipi's shell – a point at the top curved outwards.

Splashing water between my legs, I washed. Nana stood up from the toilet again and reminded me with a heavy grunt the rules Tongan girls must follow: 'No touching. No touchy for onli you, un'stan? You look afta pipi, you look afta Malapo, eh?'

After cleaning down there, I brought my knees up under my chin once more and bent my neck forward, waiting for my grandmother to wash my hair. Nana muttered something about bleeding and staying dry, but I didn't fully hear her. Upstairs, the cries from my brother and sister, Jared and Nettie, about me hogging the bath, drowned out whatever else my grandmother was saying. *Sucked in*, I thought, smirking into my kneecaps.

With an apple-scented squirt, my grandmother started pushing her melon palms through my hair. Her hands were as strong and rough as the mulberry bark the ngatu is made from. The calloused cracks of Nana's fingertips grazed my scalp as she unknotted my tangles and smoothed whatever shard of anger I kept. Every now and then I felt a pinch, my grandmother digging out a kutu and crushing its blood-filled exoskeleton against her thumbnails with a pop. The Bible said that Jesus washed away humanity's sins with His blood because He was the son of God and all that. But I always felt the cleanest and closest to God through my grandmother's worn fingers. She scrubbed me anew, healed me of infestations and grew plants that fixed my scabs. Water trickled down my back and into the bath as Nana cupped some into her palms and let the stream from her hands rinse the shampoo, careful to keep suds out of my eyes.

Over the gentle trickle, I asked Nana if she thought I still came from her poo. "Oiauē!' she gushed with the water and then chuckled out loud. 'My girl, I all that be you.'

My brows furrowed as I tried to understand what she meant, her hands and words were starting to give me a headache.

Nana let me stay in the bath a bit longer as she got my clothes ready. My pyjamas, along with Nettie and

Jared's, sat in a tiny rectangular cupboard on the left of the stairs, which smelt of dead moths. From the hallway, Nana instructed me to put cream in my hair, but what she really meant was conditioner. I rubbed Nature's Way green apple-scented goo gently into the ends of my strands, just as Nana had taught me. Next, I was towel-dried and tucked into a singlet, tights, a long-sleeved shirt, flannel pants and several pairs of socks – so fast I didn't even have time to shiver. 'Fonua momoko, eh?' Nana explained in the same way a dentist might say 'open up' – as if she was fixing something as bothersome and dangerous as a cavity. I didn't know what 'fonua momoko' fully meant but I knew it was something to do with my nana keeping me warm at night so I could make children. She did not want me to become her two eldest daughters, who were barren and fruitless because Nana was forced to take them to the English cold for a month. She went with Liam, who believed *his roots* would save their marriage. He was wrong.

My grandmother's room was hidden behind a sheet curtain, which was stapled over a second open archway in the living room. Inside, a small rectangular window was placed so close to the ceiling that it only caught wisps of purple clouds. At the centre of Nana's bedroom on the tiled floor was a large spring mattress covered with layers of kafu. Kafu was the Tongan word for a specific blanket: a thick and fluffy kind that was deeply dyed with images of peacocks or a single pouncing tiger or a dizzying arrangement of roses and hydrangeas. Nana bought bundles of kafus at Flemington

Markets from Aladdin-looking people who always gave her mad discounts because she had been buying their bizarre wares since the eighties.

In front of the mattress was a wonky black cabinet that held a chunky silver television with a built-in VHS player. On either side of the TV, two small glass cupboards displayed even more commemorative plates of Princess Diana. My nana always claimed that she was obsessed with Diana because the princess reminded her that Tonga was the only ancient monarchy left in the South Pacific. But the real reason Nana loved Diana so much was because she could relate: Princess Diana ran away from an Englishman to an Aladdin-looking boyfriend just like Nana did. That serious serious-talk was only whispered once, by Big Sesi, who reckoned there was a half-brother named Habib somewhere out in the world – given up simply because he was born out of wedlock . . .

Before my grandmother got us settled into bundled kafus, she checked that the door in her room, which led to the back-yard, was locked; shaking the handle so hard that the heavy wood rattled at its hinges. What was my grandmother so scared of? She was a bear to me: tubby, fuzzy and always poised to maul flesh for her cubs. I left my 7-Eleven teddy by her pillow – so Nana had something to protect her.

We crawled under the kafus even though I was already sweating in my layered pyjamas. Nana's stomach was warm like a koala and her Juicy Fruit breath made me scrunch my nose. Nestling into her blooming sides, I whispered how really truly sorry I was for real. McNuggets never washed my hair or enveloped me with kafu right up to my chin. 'Ah weh,' Nana sighed gently. 'Enuff now. All going.'

I pulled off my socks and curled my toes under Nana's thighs. *The Sound of Music* whirred in her VHS player. The tape whirled and Maria twirled and the hills of Austria came to life. I fell asleep to my nana humming along to songs that spoke of peaks where lonely hearts go, to a girl going on seventeen who was unprepared to face the world of men, and to the do-re-mi of having done something good in childhood.

7.

*L*otu fakafāmili. Home of Prayers. I was jolted awake by
Nana's trumpet-like heralding that spread through all
the halls and walls within the House of Fe'ofa'aki. 'Plaise.
Plaise. Ha'u an plaise Sisū Kalaisi.' The blaring way she
called her family to prayer made it hard to rejoice in the
Holy Spirit. It was difficult for me to imagine that even God
was up before the sun. *Wasn't He resting on the Sabbath or
sumfing?* Between the layers of kafu Nana had buried me
in overnight, a pudgy hand rubbed my crown. After some
digging, Lahi's glassy eyes found me. My mum-aunt's long
lashes crinkled at the corners with flecks of sleep. 'We missed
your snoring last night, kernel,' Lahi laughed as I hugged
the first fold of her stomach tightly.

All too soon, I started to sigh and whine about how I
didn't want to go lotu fakafāmili because, after all, I was
still a laupisi – a sook. Lahi patted my back and whispered
that all I needed to do was sit there; I could even go back

to sleep on her lap. Then she lifted me out of the mounds of blanket. My pyjamas clung to my sweaty rib cage and Lahi groaned at my weight because I was in Year 6 and too old for such babying. "Oiauē!' Lahi pulled me up towards the first rays of sunlight that hit the window, carrying me through the embroidered lace curtains, which scratched against my face with the sharper end of clear plastic beads, making me full sneeze.

'Moan for Mary,' Big Sesi mumbled through morning phlegm – a true smoker's cough.

'Drop that twenty-bag brat, Musie,' Swa scoffed. Swa believed in God the most out of all my aunties but only after the sun came up. Lahi huffed as I poked my tongue out at Swa's red-blonde hair from across the purple living room – filled with framed pictures of a blond-headed and blue-eyed Jesus. Swa rolled her eyes and scratched at the back of her tangled bun.

Sitting in a wonky circle on the ornate purple rug were all my aunties, Nana and even Tata. My granddad, who was as round as a carousel, sat under the pale statue of Jesus as a shepherd. Tata's hard and rotund tummy pushed through the buttons of his button-down, revealing tufts of a curly grey snail's trail. This was the man with 'uli complexion and shark-repellent pores. As he scratched at his pancake-like belly button, I wondered how such a fattened male could sit looking eternally pregnant in a house full of plump yet infertile women. It was as if Tata's enlarged stomach held promises of the extension of our family until my aunties would deliver it for themselves; if they ever could.

On the left of Tata was Nana, already showered and dressed in Sunday best. My grandmother glittered in a purple sequin muumuu that put the plastic chandelier above us to shame. Next to Nana was Aunty Jasmine: Big Sesi was dressed in a *Little Mermaid* pyjama set with my sister, Nettie, drooling on her left shoulder. I reckoned my aunt looked more like Ursula than Ariel. And it didn't help that Sesi sat in front of Nana's special cabinets full of thingymabobs.

On the right of Tata was Swa, who was brushing off dandruff flakes from her mushroom waist. Next was Aunty Heilala, whose weight, unlike her father's, fell softly like a blob of sap. Next to me and Lahi was Aunty Daisy, who combed her steady fingers through Jared's fuzzy hair as he slept with his mouth wide-open on her sponge-cake lap.

In a complete circle, my aunts cushioned themselves on their butts. See, real Fob women needed to be big. They carried all that excess chub for their offspring: thighs to steady fidgeting children; guts to entertain toddlers; flabs of dimpled skin to blanket newborns. In this way, God made my aunts the happiest heifers on Earth. I was the exception – a true hafekasi: miserable as Malfoy, skinny as Voldemort's white-bone wand.

Lotu fakafāmili began when Tata blew a chord into his melodica. The instrument looked like something in-between a flute and a baby keyboard but sounded like a whistle in

mourning. The melodica harmonised my aunties' voices into
a language that I was supposed to understand but couldn't.
Big Sesi and Aunty Swa went high while the low vibrations
of Lahi's voice created goosebumps across my sweat-soaked
skin. Daisy and Heilala carried the mid-range. Then Nana
joined in, her singing rose higher and longer than any of her
daughters. Together, their melodies called back to something
greater and older than a plain old Austrian hillside. Together,
their harmonies put to shame every beat from 'Under the Sea'
and 'Kiss the Girl'. Even though I'd never been to the ocean
of my grandmother's birth, I recognised that the heightened
vocals of my nana and aunts were made from the moana
of our ancestors.

Insides of my chest swelling, I tried to join in on such a
sacred sound. 'Ah'eee'men'i.' The broken note escaped my
throat just as Tata's melodica cued for my aunts to end on
the lyric of 'Ameni'. Tone deaf as ever, I elbowed Lahi slightly
in her chunky chest, begging for a certain kind of praise she
offered whenever she caught me reading: 'Good Little Bib.'
It took mere seconds for Aunty Swa to side-eye Aunty Daisy
through her red-blonde hair; for Aunty Daisy, still cradling my
brother Jared, to side-eye Aunty Heilala's weeping red-yellow
chin; for Aunty Heilala to protrude her plain black eyes back
at Aunty Jasmine, who was holding onto my sister Nettie as
if she was Aurora in *Sleeping Beauty*. Nana quietly adjusted a
sequin on her muumuu. Tata held the melodica in a way that
looked like a scalp was crowning from between his folded

calves. It was Big Sesi who finally cracked it. 'God, where do I sign? I'll swap my voice for her bitty bum.'

All of my aunties howled until the plastic chandelier above us shook. With a hot face, I glared at Sesi's pink-brown tonsils and crossed my arms, elbow knocking into Lahi's broad bosom. 'Gimme a spliff and I'll give ya a note,' Aunty Swa chimed in, reaching across our wonky prayer circle to nip at me like a crab.

Far, I'll just stay fie pālangi!

Ever in tune to my laupisi ways, Lahi tickled my waist until I begrudgingly giggled through tightened lips. 'Hakuna matata, Si'i. We joke.'

Yeah, well, being Tongan a joke. I kept my mouth shut but . . .

Nana knocked her knotted knuckles on the mauve pleather binding of her King James Bible – a sound that stiffened and silenced us. 'Aye, no laff.' She pointed her thickened thumb in the direction of a large framed artwork depicting the Last Supper – calling our attention to the many blue-hued eyes of Jesus watching from the walls. 'God lissen eehfing. All sing-sing Sunnyday blessing us.'

It was always my grandmother who could translate my fie pālangi ways, my plastic ways, my hafekasi ways, into real Tongan. With a lilac-toned shimmer, Nana opened the Holy Book once more. 'Hully, lau lēsoni.' Singing was not the only thing with which my aunties could harmonise. In one breath they recited the twenty-third Psalm. I rested against the pillow creases of Lahi, humming to the verse etched onto my birth mother's gravestone. Mummy Le'o sounded better this way: 'Ko hoku tauhi 'a Sihova; 'E 'ikai te u masiva.'

8.

*T*he mark of our father materialised into flesh in front of the House of Fe'ofa'aki. We watched from behind the lace curtains of the upstairs balcony with trembling toes as he stepped out of our beaten-up blue Tarago. Dad: shaved scalp that shone in the setting Sunday sun like sand, biceps that bashed together as he closed the car door, blue veins that coursed like rivers over rock, and chest chiselled to marble underneath a cotton shirt. My father stood statuesque in front of the house that he helped buy for his mother. As my father aged, he became harder than the gelled-spiked hair of his youth, which I remembered whenever I went back to my mother's funeral. Dad looked up to the balcony, finding us – his children. We pulled the curtains back and choked on our breath. Even as kids, we were already aware that the man who made us could also destroy us.

'Ah, scramble!' Jared whimpered, shoving me and Nettie aside like opposing forwards. Nettie stumbled, sucking on a tiny plastic hair comb that came with her baby doll. Our dad had arrived to reclaim us; to return us to our real home; our real home with his second wife; his second wife who was our second mum; our second mum who we simply called 'Mumma' as if she was our first.

Dad silently entered the Home of Fe'ofa'aki. He did not call to us like a lost flock, as he usually did, impatient to leave. Instead, we followed the silhouette of his mountainous frame between the wooden banisters of the stairs. His worn-out TNs headed to the kitchen towards Nana.

From a rickety sliding door, I caught a whiff of boiling taro. 'My son who has forsaken me!' Nana cried in miracle perfect English she reserved only for holy words.

I slid sluggishly down the stairs while my brother and sister nestled behind me. We felt dragged towards our father as if he were the sun. Our father, who was living, yet we wished for our mother, who was dead.

Dad slowly replied to Nana in muffled Tongan and then their talk rose in pitch and speed.

'Oh, is Daddy scared?' Nettie mumbled between plastic and her thumb. My siblings and I looked at each other with the brown-black eyes of our maker and our maker's maker. I smacked the toy comb from Nettie's mouth. *As if!* Our father was a man of stone. My sister snorted at me with watery lashes but stayed silent. She knew that if she sooked we'd all be packed up in that beat-up blue Tarago quicker than a thunderbolt.

"Ikai ha toe 'amanaki,' Nana's thorny voice declared.

76

Unyielding as granite, Dad slammed back, "Ikai toe felave ha me'a.'

On and on my parent and grandparent went and we understood none of it. Jared shifted from one leg to the other, kneeing me in the back. I nudged him with my elbow.

'Oiya, kernels.' The three of us jumped at the sound of Lahi's fabric-soft voice as her rolls leered over us from the head of the stairs. With a wrinkle of her brows, she whispered, 'Don't worry, home is wherever you're loved.' The freckles all over her cheeks sagged like she missed us already. We wailed our protest.

'Fua,' Lahi sighed and then she collected Jared and Nettie in each of her arms and carried them back up. But not me. I ventured further downstairs towards the small closet stuffed to the max with our leggings, shirts, jumpers, dresses, undies and socks. Nana bought us second-hand clothes from Flemington Markets whenever she went Trash & Treasure shopping, while Lahi curated outfits for us from Foot Locker and Target. And Big Sesi snuck in matching sets from Bonds and Peter Alexander she bought on credit. It dawned on me that we never packed overnight bags like the one Stitch takes when he runs away from Lilo. Shuffling through the unfolded piles, I pulled out Adidas trackies and a faded Bulldogs jersey for Jared. Then, I snagged purple tights and a *Sailor Moon* shirt for Nettie.

Out in the kitchen, pot lids rattled as they overboiled; my father and Nana's unyielding voices growing in heat. Quickly, I tacked on moth-bitten jeans and a Pokémon tee for myself.

While I tried to rummage for any socks, even if they were mismatched, I spasmed at the sound of heavy palms banging against a benchtop. 'Me, her, them, him. Nufing, Mum. Just youse, ours, same. Just together.'

Holding onto as much clothing as my arms could gather, I bolted up the stairs while a flurry of Tongan flung through the air. Broken English jumbled in Nana's tirade but her voice was steady as earth. 'Why speaking? Longo. Be me. Who finking you, eh? Only me dat making you.'

Out of breath, I reached the top of the stairs. My brother and sister were melting into Lahi's lumps as they whimpered, our aunty leaning back against her bedroom door. Without a word, Lahi grabbed the clothes from me and started to change my siblings. Sweat beaded on her thin brows as my aunt muttered to herself. I caught words like 'uproot' and 'family tree'. In our clean clothes, we waited and trembled for our grandmother's yelling to stop. *Nana. Lahi. Mummy Le'o. Dad. Mumma. Whose kids were we?*

It was ages until our father's familiar footfalls ascended the stairs. Thck. Thck. Thck. I felt each of his heavy steps in my bones. The gravity of his presence started to crush me. My father was a burning rock, warm from a distance, but dangerous if we got too close. I could not bring myself to look up as he sniffed and declared, 'Youse. Home. Now.' Stuck in his gravity, I couldn't move. I knew it hurt Lahi every time we left her to go home to our new mumma. But I also knew it hurt Dad every time we forgot about the woman who chose him despite having three unfortunate children.

I was stuck. Stuck between a man who owned our bodies, a boyish-woman who owned our souls, and a grounded woman who demanded both.

'Just please . . .' Aunty Lahi pleaded from her puffy cheeks. Even though she was the eldest girl, she was not the eldest child. That was my father, who was the firstborn. That didn't matter though. Tongans followed the first woman of their line and this fonua-given authority informed what Lahi said next. 'Go home to your other kids. I'll bring the kernels back later.'

My stomach flipped at the thought of a few stolen hours within the Home of Fe'ofa'aki – the wrought-iron gated castle in the middle of Mount Druitt where I could stuff myself with all the Macca's Lahi could buy. Dad's stiff form softened. His muddy eyes were dampened with red-rimmed lashes. Nana pounded pots and pans in the kitchen below. The swirls of Dad's goatee deepened as I tried to hold my breath. Like a meteor, my father's voice crashed at the feet of his sister. 'Please? Youse are killing my life. Just give them back.'

Haka-like hiccups meant my brother Jared was sobbing. He was only six months old when our mummy Le'o died – a boy who grew up in a womb filled with spiteful cells; a boy whose voice was yet to break. My brother buried his bushy brows into Lahi's side, leaving puddles of snot and saliva, while his dusty fists clenched to her like a grand final trophy. Nettie, on the other hand, stumbled over Lahi's feet to get to our father – a middle child caught in the middle of this muck.

Tears from Jared, the son who shared his name, triggered something in Dad. Very quickly our father hardened back into familiar form – all boulders of muscles and rivers of veins. In one motion, he crossed the lounge room and pulled my brother from Lahi. Later, I imagined that tug was what an abortion looked like. Jared screamed as if he was sliced in half. Lahi tried to envelop my brother but missed. She cooed with promises of buying him McChickens and a brand-new rugby ball when he came back.

Marble biceps twitching, Dad dragged his son kicking and screaming across the carpet. Without looking, my father snapped back at his sister with his earthy eyes blazing. 'Look what youse done to them. Not my bad youse a lesbian.'

He knew!

Lahi pressed her quivering mouth into a thin line and glared at her brother. They locked on each other with their mother's burning-bush sight.

Finally, Dad flung the squealing boy over his shoulder. Bleating like a lamb, my brother seemed ready to be sacrificed in the name of the Lord. Dad trudged down the stairs as Jared's lanky brown limbs continued to flail. With broken breath, I held Nettie's milky hand as we followed. I turned back only once to stare at my mother-aunt. Lahi was bent forward like a folded mattress as she mourned for the children she could not have and the children she could not keep.

Without another word to anyone in the Home of Fe'ofa'aki, our father buckled us into the blue Tarago. Jared squished his rubbery oval-shaped nose on the window and searched for Lahi through a trail of mucus. Nettie was crying hysterically as she scraped at the passenger window – not for Lahi, not for Nana, but for her Baby Born, which she'd left on the living room couch. Shaking, I sat in the front with my body turned away from the driver's seat.

Back then, I could not understand a father's love for his children. Back then, I believed Dad, with a new wife named Camellia, a new son named Corey, two new daughters named Leilani and Lavender, and another child yet to be conceived, had no use for the leftovers of his first wife. Back then, I reckoned my father did not need us as much as Lahi, a barren woman, did.

Dad forced the ignition. On the grey steering wheel, his palms shook like a rockfall. While our father drove us away from the House of Love One Another, he sighed. He sighed like a man who was widowed too young at twenty-three, remarried too early at twenty-four, and had nothing to show for it but ungrateful children. He sighed all those years out, knowing he was forsaken.

BARK

Lakufā'anga. Throw the fā. Through the dense thicket of toa trees on the island of 'Eua lived the children of Tuakau'ia. 'Eua, the most ancient island of Tonga, was a mountainous yet desolate region where only a brittle and tasteless fruit grew. Fā is what Tuakau'ia and his children lived on. The wooden skin cracked their teeth. The tough flesh splintered into their bones. The core, hard as coral, was thrown over the cliffsides of 'Eua and into the sea. And yet still the Tongans grew. As the fā began to disappear, the full brown mouths of Tuakau'ia's children grew wider and wider. In Tongan they lamented:

Toa, with her bark-rough limbs, cried, 'More.'

Fotu, with his bush-like hair, grumbled, 'More.'

Loi, with her wind-swept eyes, howled, 'More.'

The children's needs ringing in his ear, Tuakau'ia stumbled through the thicket of trees and onto the cliffside where they threw fā cores for all their lives. Tuakau'ia, so reed-like it was as if he'd already been eaten away.

In a dry whisper, Tuakau'ia spoke a final prayer to Tangaloa, the god of gods. 'Come eat the fā that I throw to you.' In Tongan, this sounded like: 'Ha'u 'o kai 'a e fā te u laku atu.' Into the moana, Tuakau'ia leapt. One less mouth to feed meant more fā to eat.

But even with their father's sacrifice there were still too many empty stomachs. Slowly yet steadily, the fā disappeared.

'No more,' Toa admitted, her rough-bark limbs sanded to bone.

'No more,' Fotu sniped, his like-bush hair wisped and splintered.

'No more,' Loi sighed, her swept-wind eyes stuck like roots.

Together, the siblings tumbled through the dense thicket of toa roots and onto the cliffside where their father had jumped so many years before. With a final prayer to Tangaloa, the god of gods, they said, 'Come eat the fā that I throw to you.' In Tongan, this sounded like: 'Ha'u 'o kai 'a e fā te u laku atu.' Mirroring the footsteps of their father, the three children leapt into Pulotu — the spirit realm.

9.

*A*ye, speak Don-gan. Aye, goan. Try.' My brother Jared bashed his bulky elbows into my protruding rib cage. I was eleven bro – already too old for this kaka.

'Faaaar, shove it, Footy Brain,' I huffed. 'I don't speak donkey.' This was what hafekasi kids said to each other when no one else was listening, especially if those half-caste children were cramped into the driver and front passenger seats of a beat-up blue Tarago while their parents inspected their newly-bought house. My brother Jared, my sister Nettie and my new brother Corey; we were all over each other. And yet, as crowded as it might have seemed to anyone walking past, this was the most space we'd ever gotten in here – usually, my baby-lings would be with us. But Nana had been growing increasingly concerned that Lani was too big and Lav was drooling too much, so she demanded they do faito'o fakatonga – Tongan healing. Dad was reluctant but agreed as a peace offering.

The Tarago was parked in front of a bright orange one-storey brick house that had a large 'for sale' poster covered in a shiny red 'sold' sticker: a jewelled plum in the middle of the suburb of Plumpton.

Pressing her chest into my side, Nettie giggled as she forced a hug from me. I started to think she was doing it on purpose because she'd pointed out the little lumps on her chest, even though she was nine, while mine was flat as, even though I was the oldest. 'Baby borning hungry growing,' she'd said.

Now I flicked her off me and she gloated with giggles again. *Swear to gee, she acts like a real mum.*

The other day, my sister also made a comment about my reading too much: Dad picked us up from the House of Fe'ofa'aki and noticed Lahi had bought me a new book, *Grimms' Tales for Young and Old*. Dad started mumbling about how I was filling my head with nonsense stories instead of helping look after my siblings. As one of his bushy brows clashed with the shadow of his deteriorating widow's peak, he asked, 'What youse gonna learn from a book? Book gonna give youse money? Book gonna love youse back? Life lessons learnt by living. Not sitting still and sentencing youse life away.' Stuttering, I struggled to rationalise to Dad that I was currently living *and* reading, so what was the harm in doing both?

Back in the Tarago, Jared puffed his bony chest, showing off his new Bulldogs jersey – all royal blue with a snarling and salivating white bulldog on the left pocket. As if a clump of grass was weighing his tongue down, Jared went on: 'Speakin' Don-gan eeeee-zeee. Like dis. Imma toko and my man Sonny Billz is an uso.' Then my brother grinned, his crooked teeth stained yellow with sugary soft drink, like the rest of ours. 'Try,' he repeated.

Jared was the only one out of us kids who liked being Fob. He blended in with all the other Islander ad-layz at church despite his small frame – rugby made a Fob out of any boy.

'Righto blender,' I scoffed. Me and Nettie steered clear of proper Islander girls when we met them at Sunday school in the halls of Tokaikolo. Those mohe 'ulis demanded we spoke Tongan too, and when we failed, they mocked us. Together, Tongans were always trying to prove how real or fake each of us were. Nettie and me, we were plastic.

With a bang, my step-brother, Corey, barged over my shoulder like a tumbled hessian sack of potatoes. 'Fek it, I gotsda need for speed.'

'Oiya, foul,' Jared tutted.

Nettie squealed until she said in a hoity-toity tone, 'Oh, will dob you in Mumma.'

I took the opportunity to throw my hands back, almost busting my knuckles against Corey's head. Corey didn't even flinch as he sat himself in the driver's seat. Atop Dad's usual throne, Corey slammed his potato palms on the steering wheel while I bit the inside of my cheeks. *Faaar, my step-brother. Taking up my dad's space like he all that.*

Still shouting and stuttering, Corey crunched his knuckles on the gearstick. His brunette-buzzcut and stocky build made him look like a taro. But our new brother was half-White too. Corey's actual father, Darrell Budd, was heir of a family-owned confectionary company somewhere in the city. Or so I heard in a serious-talk between Nana and Lahi. I saw Darrell only once, when he came to pick Corey up for a weekend. His stick frame, dry skin and blooming bald patch reminded me of a withered Willy Wonka. *The money must've been heaps good for Mumma to have once been married to such a Crunchie.*

In pālangi ways, Corey was my step-brother because he was the only child of Camellia, and Camellia was my step-mum because she divorced Darrell and married my widowed dad. But being Tongan meant being together. So, in Tongan ways, Corey and Camellia simply sprouted into my life as if they were always there. Corey was the same age as Nettie so they got passed off as twins despite their different last names: Nettie Reed; Corey Budd. We told anyone who was nosey-poke enough to ask to watch *The Sound of Music* if they wanted to know about our life so bad. It was easier than going around saying our dad remarried because our real mum died. What kinda sad cases outed themselves as sad cases? Not us.

Through the windshield, I saw my parents with their backs to our Tarago. Dad was sweeping his arms across the brown patched lawn and then up over his sugar plum house until his forefinger pointed at the roof – giant arms like a mass of iron. Mumma stood as wide-legged as a stump, which I knew was her way of balancing the weight of her massive baby-factory belly.

'Brrrrmmm-brrrr-fuk-uuummm-brrrrt,' Corey screeched and turned the locked steering wheel as far right as it went. He shook side-to-side in a rush and whispered to himself, 'Fek the eff-bee-eye!' My spudhead of a new brother, like every other boy in Mounty County, fully believed he was Dominic Toretto from *The Fast and the Furious.*

Out of the four of us, only Corey full swore, well, swore-ish. This was because he was diagnosed with ADHD and needed to be treated 'special'. That was why, after buying this Plumpton house, my parents would send him to Whalan Public School with us; the only place in Mount Druitt with 'Special Education' classes.

'Co-fuc-ppers,' Corey screeched. My brother was a regular Dominic Tourettes-o. 'You al-fook-most gotts me? You never fooken gotts me.' Corey's roasted wedge of a fist thrust out through the open driver's window and he stuck his middle finger in the air.

All at once: Jared jumped across the gearstick and shoulder-barged Corey, belting out like a commentator, 'Sin bin.' Corey exploded, 'Ugggghhhfucshicuk.' Nettie stuck the breast buds developing under her décolletage on me again. 'Meadow born oldest but look baby. Born babies before you? So shame.'

With a screech, I kicked back against my brothers and sister until I was with Corey at the steering wheel. Meanwhile, the beat-up blue Tarago slowly started rolling. The outline of my parents – Dad's marble head and Mumma's trunk-like thighs – was growing smaller and smaller. My newest brother, the blight of our lives, was gonna kill us!

I aimed my open palm at the centre of the steering wheel, knocking Corey's carb-loaded forehead into the glass. Beeeeeeeeeeeeeeeeeeeeeep! The honk resounded as I hollered above it, 'Daddy!' My sister Nettie banged on the roof of the Tarago. My brother Jared dragged us all into a scrum, scrawny arms attempting to shield us (Sonny Billz in the making). Still calling for our father, I elbowed all my siblings to keep my palm firmly on the steering wheel.

Beeeeeeeeeeeeeeeeeeeeeeeeeeeeeeeeeeeeeeeeeep.

Then a miracle of muscle arrived. Dad, fully tensed up, stretched and arched out towards us like a bolting boulder. Camellia bounded behind him across the bitumen, rounded belly tugging her forward. She yowled; blonde-streaked strands of her brown-black hair stuck in her mouth. 'The kids, the kids!'

But still, our beat-up Tarago rolled. Corey grunted 'winning's winning' while holding up his rude finger. Shirt flipping over her face, Nettie's grey crop top was in *my* face as she shrieked in a voice beyond her years, 'Oh, we can't die. I haven't even kissed a boy yet!'

The kids. The kids. My mother's words backfired in my brain as we rolled away. For just a quarter of a metre, we were children who belonged to absolutely no one. For just ten seconds, we were free. Free until Corey went flying out the flung-open driver's door, spudhead-first onto the bitumen. My rib cage flew up into my chin, caught within the jagged crook of my father's elbow. Jared and Nettie swirled over each other like runny Neapolitan ice-cream.

It took me a moment to realise that our dad had caught up and hauled Corey out of the Tarago in order to get to the handbrake. My father's mountainous knee protruded at a ninety-degree angle as he slammed the sole of his TNs onto the brake pedal. With a grunt, I was shoved upright and tossed back into the driver's seat. Next to me was Nettie and Jared, cowering in the front passenger seat. Dad seized Corey up from the road by the scruff of his shirt. My step-brother floundered and fought, 'Gerrof-fuc-me!'

Our father roared: 'We. Just. Bought. This house. For Youse.' White spit protruded from his upper lip and the whites of his eyes popped from his head. His pebble-like pupils darted wildly back and forth, booming voice echoing down the street. 'Youse messed in the head or sumfing? Not gonna waste money on youse fullas' funerals and a mortgage – so pick one.'

I shook into Nettie and my sister trembled into Jared and I felt their quivering through the dashboard and into the steering wheel.

Corey was still flogging his taro-arms, shouting, 'Gerroffoffoffoff.' But this time it was to his mother, Camellia, who was pressing her son back into her protruding womb. 'The kids nearly ended up on the wrong side of the blanket!' my step-mum screamed at Dad.

Our father's shouting became muffled from a ringing in my ears. I was wishing that the beat-up Tarago really had rolled off the streets of Plumpton and crushed us to dust. *Why keep us alive only to make us feel kaka about it?* Life would certainly be easier if Dad and Camellia only had to worry about my littlest sisters – the two children that belonged to both of them.

We dared not backchat though; shutting our mouths was the one Islander rule my father made sure we all followed.

Shaking, I breathed in as Dad tilted his shiny scalp up to the clouds and laughed, 'Youse should see youse faces.' His rock-vice grip still over the steering wheel, he flashed a wide, white smile at us.

All at once, I was in the middle of an ancient field, where gigantic Brown men cultivated the soil with their bare, muscular hands, and I was no longer afraid, for they were beautiful.

Pulling each of us from the van and onto the Plumpton cul-de-sac, my father scooped me, Nettie and Jared together, wrapping us between his bulging biceps. A moment later, Corey and Mum were also in my dad's scrum. Our new home shimmered against the setting sun. My father had settled his family in brick and mortar – and from there we grew.

10.

$\mathcal{8}$ Sugar Drive was our first real house: Me, Nettie, Jared and Corey, as well as Leilani and Lavender – my littlest sisters.

My father's house was one storey instead of two, made of brick instead of cream cement walls, and stuck out like a coldsore at the end of a cul-de-sac instead of holding fort just off a main road and armed in cursive wrought iron. In this way, our Plumpton home was nothing but a plum pit in comparison to my grandmother's castle between two towering palm trees in Mount Druitt.

Sugar Drive started with a cluster of pebbles that were melted together for a driveway. A tiny patch of grass and a single juniper tree by a dilapidated metal mailbox was what we were meant to call our front yard. Just like the Home of Fe'ofa'aki, there was a sign in gold letters on the front door. Rather than a print of cursive that delicately displayed a Tongan phrase, this plaque had tin block letters spelling out the name 'Goodlad', meaning 'Good Servant' – leftover by previous owners. I knew a lot of things, way more than my siblings, but in the servant's house there was no prize for wits: when I excitedly explained to Dad that his property held a Scottish name, like us, he glared down at me and mumbled, 'In my house, as in the house of God, there is only my name and there is only my command. Youse understand.' It wasn't a question.

From the front door, my father's small kingdom closed in on a narrow and tiled hallway. There were so many doors down this corridor it was like the rabbit hole from *Alice in Wonderland*, the Disney film. Directly adjacent to the entryway was my parents' bedroom, which was eternally locked. It was tapu, meaning taboo, to ever enter the dwelling place of our parents. One time though, I pressed my ear to their cold door. I heard Dad grumble that he was trying to sleep off a week's worth of overnight shifts. Mumma groaned how she wanted to wash the bedsheets because she spotted all over them. Suddenly, there was shouting and the flipping of a mattress. I ran back to my room and, soon after, the echoes of Dad's steel-capped boots stomped out of the house . . .

The first door on the left side of the hallway was meant to be the entrance to a two-car garage. Inside, however, it looked like any ordinary room except four times the size. With so many babies being born, my parents were lucky that the rich-ish previous owners had decked the garage out into a makeshift cinema. All Dad and Mumma needed to do was place a bunk bed on one side and some half-dismantled nursery furniture on the other, and my two youngest sisters were sorted. The room smelt like wet wipes with a faint whiff of urine.

Leilani and Lavender shared the indoor garage-turned-bedroom because it was closest to our parents' room. I often found Mumma dead asleep on the bottom bunk in her security guard uniform. There, with matching *Dora the Explorer* pyjama sets tattered at the hems, my little sisters curled around their birth mother's stump of a belly like mushrooms. I wondered if it was dangerous for Mumma to be kicking out drunks at the local RSL while she had babies to look after. But my father never said anything and so neither did I.

Next to my sisters' bedroom was Corey's room. For some reason, Corey got to have the biggest, proper-est bedroom all to himself. I reckoned it was because he was Mumma's first-born. My step-brother's bedroom was a place I was allowed to look inside but could not enter. Again, it was tapu to be in any place my brothers slept because of the faka'apa'apa between brother and sister and all that. Corey slept in a lumpy double bed with crumpled second-hand sheets. Off to the side was a rickety black dresser drawer. It was covered in scraped-up Hot Wheels, given to Corey by his birth-dad, Darrell. Like me, Corey only half-existed at 8 Sugar Drive. On weekends and holidays, my step-brother went to Darrell's apartment in the city; right next to his family-owned boutique chocolate shop that was nearly one hundred years old.

When I asked Mumma why she'd given up the riches of a confectionary-owner life, she tutted her tongue. 'What and become some wonk looney? Money can buy everything but the kitchen sink.'

Whenever Mumma spoke, I felt as if she was talking down at me like I was stupid. Even though she was the one forever sprouting terms like 'wonk looney'!

After Corey's bedroom was a set of three small doors that opened up to a vast cupboard. It was filled to the brim with scattered sheets and old shoes – mouldy Nike runners, shiny dress loafers, pointy high heels and mismatched toddler sandals – as if the messiness of our blended lives fell through the centre of the earth and came out the other end upside down.

Mumma lamented the state of her linen cupboard often. Once, she whistled like wind into my bedroom, 'Y'all impassable.' When I tried to correct her, by saying she meant 'impossible', she became as puffy as the Red Queen herself. 'I'm living with mad people.'

Next to the cupboard, on both the left and right side of the hallway, were two bedrooms facing each other. The left bedroom, which was half the size of Corey's, belonged to Jared. The right bedroom, smallest of all, was the one Nettie and I shared. Our room held a bunk bed, a second-hand dresser drawer, which once belonged to Mummy Le'o, and a small cupboard where our school uniforms and Sunday best clung on wire hangers. Nettie claimed the top bunk with her pink 'Barbe' (it was meant to say 'Barbie') duvet. I was relegated to the bottom bunk, which was covered in a Pokémon sheet set that looked legit, even though it was purchased at Flemington's Trash & Treasure Markets (along with everything else we owned).

Across the hall, Jared covered his single mattress on the floor with an authentic-as Bulldogs bedspread, which Lahi had bought for his birthday. The tapu that exists between brother and sister was thinnest here. Jared, Nettie and I always left our bedroom doors open to chatter to each other across the hallway until we fell asleep. Even Corey joined in most nights, camping next to Jared's mattress with a torn-up sleeping bag. For some reason, our nightly arguments about whether a Pokémon would beat a Bulldog in a fight annoyed Dad. He'd stomp over and shove our doors shut while he got ready for work. 'Sleep for school. What youse think I'm working dog shift for?' Every time this happened, we obeyed in silence.

Near the end of the rabbit-hole hallway, just before it opened up to the living room, were another two rooms facing each other. On the right was the bathroom, carved out by a high archway which led first to a vanity area. Shared by all six of us kids, it was by far the dirtiest place in the house. Exhausted toothbrushes lay strewn on the vanity and the mirror was flecked with spit and toothpaste. Mould thrived across the rubbery lining between the sink and the walls and some of it crept onto the ceiling. Endless strands of black-brown and brown-blonde hair floated around our feet like tumbleweeds. Flecks of dried blood dotted the basin from the afternoons that Mumma spent combing all of our heads, even the boys, frantically fighting the kutus and lihas that spread between us. The vanity drawers were filled with half-used or empty tubes of toothpaste, more discarded toothbrushes, plastic brushes with snapped-off handles (our hair was too thick and knotted for Kmart combs) and scrunched-up pieces of snot-filled toilet paper. The towel cupboard, opposite the vanity, was rusted on its hinges with the doorknob missing. This was why we needed to pry open the cupboard with bent butter knives that loitered on the floor. Next to the cupboard door was the bathroom door, which had swelled to an unusual size from the endless stream of six kids showering every night. The bathroom door never fully closed and it was dented in the centre from hundreds of hands smacking the wood as us kids yelled, 'Get out, ya hog.'

Inside the bathroom was a beige bathtub that sat underneath a windowsill. On the opposite wall was a shower with a single glass panel. A toilet was tightly squeezed between. The bathtub was forever filled with astringent grey water. We used it to soak all our dirty clothes when the washing machine broke. The shower dripped constantly. Stars of mould grew on the walls and clustered on the ceiling like little galaxies.

Littered inside the shower were unravelled loofahs, four-litre shampoo bottles and ten-litre body washes from Aldi. Black hair clung to the bottom of the shower drain, which resembled the small strings that were growing between my legs. Splashes of conditioner ran down the shower screen and thin white film covered the drain so our soles were soaked in soap scum after each wash.

Because of the toilet, with its crooked seat and yellow film growing from the u-bend, the whole bathroom smelt of pee.

Even though I knew my parents worked unforgiving hours as security guards in order to keep their six kids fed and washed, I couldn't help but blame them for our filth. No matter how much we scrubbed ourselves up, or how much we scrubbed the house down, we could not remove the dirt.

The space opposite the bathroom was a doorframe with no door. Beyond the bare and rusty hinges was the washhouse. The washhouse was cluttered with floor-to-ceiling piles of sweaty clumped clothes, from which a corroded sink and a dust-covered washing machine poked out. Through the shirts, jeans and mismatched socks covered with dog hair was a paint-chipped back door that was locked shut even before we moved to Sugar Drive. On the rare occasions that the washing machine did work, it was constantly rumbling and knocking into walls so much that it left black scuff marks on the plaster like Aunty Daisy's tēvolo problem. I reckoned that's actually what it meant to be a headcase – some days were just full and loud and wrecking everything and other days were blocked and broken.

On heaps hot days, me and Corey snuck our lumpy English bulldog, Povo, into the washhouse. Our family pet was the only thing that bonded me and my spudhead brother because we both liked animals more than we liked each other. Povo would snooze comfortably on our dirty clothes away from the suburban heat. When we were caught by Camellia, she shrieked about fleas, flies and faeces until angry tears slid down her bark-like face.

Back inside the house, the rabbit-hole hallway opened up to a living room and kitchen that blended into each other. The kitchen started with the sides of a wobbly white fridge, which stood next to a white four-burner gas stove. My dad had hauled each appliance out of a Bogan backyard in St Marys surrounded with discarded tyres, overgrown weeds and bubble-font graffiti. That day, I had gone with him. The only indication it was a store full of used fridges, washing machines and ovens was a hand-painted sign on a bedsheet: '2hand Good Whites 4 $'. Dad and some bulky Wog carried the appliances into our rusty trailer, which was borrowed from a cousin of a cousin of a cousin. Since we could only ever afford used or borrowed or used-borrowed items, I knew being Tongan meant being second best.

From the stove extended one long L-shaped laminated bench, which held everything from a twin sink, a tiny 1.5-litre plastic kettle that was always boiling in order to keep up with sterilising Avent baby bottles, and a worn-white microwave splattered with so much reheated gravy that furry bacteria grew within its unwiped corners.

Scattered on every spare bit of benchtop were Slim&Trim soup and milkshake sachets – a diet Mumma tried to follow in the small windows of time she wasn't pregnant. In the evenings before she went to guard the glass doors of Rooty Hill RSL, Mumma prepared her powdered meals. A fluorescent green vest engorged her plushy frame as she searched for shakers and lamented, 'Bloody musical chairs around here.' I tried to breathe past the migraine that formed between my eyes whenever she said this. *What do you expect when leaving kids to look after kids?*

To the right of the kitchen was the living room. A full three-set bay window took up the whole side of the house so that the glass gazed onto the backyard. The back of 8 Sugar Drive was nothing but shin-high grass, a wonky Hills Hoist knock-off and a splintered wooden fence that looked as if it were made of licked Paddle Pop sticks. The fence separated us from a massive storm drain that cut through Plumpton Park, which was just around the corner from us. Whenever it rained for days on end, sewer rats scraped in our living room walls as they fled death-by-drowning.

Our living room did not have a dining table. Instead, my three sisters and two brothers and I ate meals on a raggedy bedsheet laid on the floor between our four-seater frumpy floral-print couch and an ancient Toshiba television. Dad boasted about finding the lounge and TV set on the side of some random gutter as he pushed the fuzzy mass and the hunchback television down the hallway. It was only later that we found out how roadside pickups were filled with cockroaches; 8 Sugar Drive had been infested ever since.

11.

*S*ooky-la-las sounded off from my two toddler-aged sisters, Leilani and Lavender, as soon as us older kids got home from school. My little and little-little sisters echoed like canaries in a mine as they recited through dribble, 'A-di-oo-dos. A-di-doose.' My baby-lings barely spoke English, let alone Tongan, but they could mouth off the many catch-phrases of their Spanish-speaking heroine, Dora the Explorer. Dad, who usually picked us up from school, would stumble blearily through the front door and, in a jingle of keys, head straight to his room, saying, 'Youse kids get the kids.'

That day after school was no different. Three tiles at a time, I bounded through our rabbit-hole hallway. Jared and Corey followed hurriedly behind me. With a bashing of backpacks and a shuffle of sneakers, I heard the boys shoving into each other, trying to beat the other down the hall. One brother to play backyard footy; the other to play fetch with our dog. 'Pass. Pass.' Jared arced up. Corey spat back in spaz-spasms, 'Pee off but.'

'Oh, Musie. Help me bottle the babies,' my sister Nettie commanded. Chucking my brandless canvas bag into our bedroom, I skipped to the lounge without responding to her. Instead, I clutched my dog-eared and spine-creased copy of *Alice Through the Looking Glass*, which was one of the books Lahi gifted to me before we left the House of Fe'ofa'aki. *Let Nettie look after the kids*, I told myself. *Reading is more important than babies.* 'Oh, gosh. You're so useless,' Nettie scolded.

On the couch, my toddler sisters started scrambling over me. Leilani, the oldest of the two, squawked as if she were stuck in a TV, desperate to be heard. 'Imdamap, big girl, damap,' Lani said in a sing-song voice. She was reciting the lyrics that Dora's helper, Map, sung whenever the little heroine needed directions. With her straw-like brown hair cut in a bulky bowl cut, Lani's head looked overgrown for her face. I pecked the button-like beauty spot at the corner of her mouth as a hello. She tapped her bottle on my shoulder, demanding, 'Off. No say kissy.' Mumma's favourite way to describe Lani was 'too big for her boots' because she was always trying to do and say things above her two-and-a-half years of age: with ease she twisted off the tightly sealed teat of her bottle so she could drink from the lip like a cup.

While Lani was all light brown, our littlest sister, Lavender, was her drooling shadow. 'Do-do-do-do-doorah,' Lav dribbled in my ear. Her mahana hair, which meant frizzy, was as black and as thick as Scar's mane.

Over the Spanglish screaming, I could still hear my brothers scuffling in the hallway. I rolled my eyes as I tried to open up my novel above all the noise. Eventually, Nettie's milky face leered over the top of my book as she took our sisters off the couch for a shower, a nappy change and a feed. 'Oh, absolutely no help. Can you just watch one for a little bit? Tevita gave me his number and I want to call him, he's the hottest lad in my class don't you know.'

Nettie sounded more and more like Mumma these days – like an adult.

I stared at my sister. Her light hair was standing on end as if a lioness had licked her. The messiness of her do was a sign that she was already frazzled from school, let alone all the babysitting that came after. But her dark, dark pupils shimmered at the thought of flirting with boys, already more interested in males than her nine-years-and-eight-months-old self should allow.

Since I was turning twelve, and only interested in reading, I just smirked and took pleasure in saying, 'No.'

Nettie groaned at me, deliberately sticking out her developed chest and bumping my book into my head. She ran off with the babies before I could slap her back.

The days when the only babies were Nettie's dolls with hollow heads were moving behind us. Mumma went and birthed the real thing and Nettie went and stuffed her own chest like she was already full-grown.

Thirty minutes of reading and I found myself searching for the remote. It was no longer enough to imagine Lewis Carroll's Wonderland – I had to see it. By then, Nettie and my sisters were back on the couch smelling like conditioner. Our second-hand TV was still hunchbacked even though we were far into the era of flatscreens. Burnt into the pixels were the purple stripes of The Cheshire Cat because I had watched *Alice in Wonderland* ninety-nine nonsensical times.

As I searched for the remote, Lani, with her too-big bowl cut, started to climb on me as if ants were in her nappy. 'Find 'mote on damap. Find like you like big girl.' Lani's stumpy legs slid through my armpits as she leant her weight on me. I realised that her second toe was growing past her big toe. 'Damap, damap,' Lani repeated, her voice deeper than a toddler's should be. Giggle-grunting, she grabbed my foot with a crab-like grip until I kicked myself free. 'Can do!' she snapped, raising her fist.

Finding the remote in between the crevices of the couch, I zoomed into TV pixels until I could no longer hear Lani's yelling or even feel her tugging at my hair. Animated daisies bent in an imaginary wind as I waited for a blonde-haired and blue-dressed Alice to appear and start singing about having a world of her own. In the corner of my eye, Jared and Corey returned to the living room, each had their fill of footy and fetch. Smelling like dog slobber, Corey ran at me – me, nestled comfortably and innocently on the couch – and started swearing about changing the channel. 'Eff-and-eff. Put on eff-and-eff. Friggen seen this sh-sh-shiz yesshday.'

So what if I watched *Alice in Wonderland* yesterday? I wanted to hear her question: which way this girl ought to go, down the rabbit hole, or up Sugar Drive? Behind me, Jared sat on the kitchen bench stool bouncing a footy on the tiles over and over and over – thck thck thck.

All the while, Nettie was sitting next to me on the couch, tussling with Lavender, whose all-day dribble made a trail down her puffy belly button and into her already-soaked nappy. Lav blew raspberries.

I stared and stared as Alice fell and fell, bidding farewell to Dinah the cat. I whispered along underneath the ruckus of all my siblings, 'Goodbye, Dada, goodbyyyyyye.'

'Do-do-do-do-do-Dora,' Lani drummed on the couch cushions, her bowl head bouncing. 'Doob,' Lav slobbered at my knee, kicking Nettie's chest, arching her backside away from the straps of yet another clean nappy. 'Oh, stay still,' Nettie ordered, shoving Lav's droopy bum back down. Thck thck thck went Jared's ball. When Alice cried giant teardrops, I felt little drops in the corner of my eye, but my teardrops were brown instead of blue.

On the furry armrest of the couch, a speck of muck with six legs scurried up. I gulped, half-holding my breath. Quickly, I shut my eyelids tight and blindly squished the pest on my palm.

'I'm not all there myself,' The Cheshire Cat explained to Alice through the TV as I hesitantly lifted up my hand. Between my fingers, two long antennae twitched as white mush oozed from a reptilian-like exoskeleton. With a grimace,

I wondered why cockroaches couldn't be like the vibrant-patterned grubs that Pumbaa tusked out from under logs for Timon and Simba to eat. Those bugs were pretty and fun, ours were poo-coloured.

Gagging, I wiped the roach's guts into the fabric of our couch – slimy yet satisfying.

Then my step-brother's voice called out, 'Faaaahhh, didn't your muffah ever tell ya not to play with ya f-f-uc-food?'

Corey was standing at the side of our bulky Toshiba, full grinning.

'It was an accident,' I tried to explain, still wiping my palm against the couch.

Corey wiggled his eyebrows. 'Corn-fuk-flakes, corn-fuk-flakes.'

The inside of my head felt like an oven as I said again, 'It. Was. An. Ac-ci-dent!' Stifling a scream in my throat, I jumped off the couch and into the kitchen just to put space between us. As far as brains went, I got the lion's share in this family, but my step-brother could make a mad hatter out of me real quick.

The 'accident' Corey was referring to made my stomach tickle, tickle, tickle as if twitching antennae were stuck in my bowels.

Corey wriggled his spuddy fingers and teased again, 'Corn-fuk-lakes?'

I had backed myself onto our wobbly white fridge, which was easily shaken because it was so empty, and Corey started to corner me. He savoured his next words like fresh hot chips wrapped in butcher's paper. 'Bug-eater, bug-eater, bug-eater!'

Thck thck thck went Jared's football along the tiles for the hundreth time as my brother from the same mother whistled, 'Time out, bro.'

Through my wobbly vision, an eternal stack of dirty dishes encrusted in dried gravy and bottles caked with formula grew larger as water dripped from the leak in our kitchen tap. The stench of stagnant dishwater smelt like half-used chicken noodle sachets and curdled cow's milk. It was the blots of mould in the grooves of the sink splashback that flooded me with the memory:

A school night last week. It was late but I had snuck out of bed anyway. My stomach grumbled as I slowly opened the squeaky food cupboard. I stood on my tippy-toes, reaching for a value-pack box of Cornflakes larger than my own torso. My pyjamas still radiated warmth as my fingers clasped cardboard edges. Bringing the cereal towards me, the shreds of gold rattled inside. Hoping no one else heard all the noise I was making, I placed the big green rooster logo slowly on the kitchen bench and rummaged around for a bowl. We weren't allowed to eat extra if food was gonna last us until next pay. Pirouetting slowly, I rustled out a half-empty four-litre plastic carton of milk, with its lid crusted in flaked cream, from the fridge.

A whine from my belly button. I started to pile the bubbled sugary shreds up to the brim of my bowl. My tummy curled itself into knots as I thought: *Stuff the stuffing and bread slices we only got given for dinner.*

I plunged my tablespoon down into a white sea and dug up cereal like sunken chests full of gold. The first bite was always the coolest and crunchiest. Smiling to myself, I sucked milk into the back of my throat. I munched and munched and munched like a Munchkin from Munchkin Land.

It was after my third mouthful, when my crooked front teeth grazed the steel of my spoon, that the big budget cereal box rustled without my touching it.

Trying not to choke, I watched wide-eyed as, from the edges of the torn soft plastic and onto the ripped cardboard flaps, the darkest cockroach I'd ever seen emerged. The six-legged monster glistened like it was dipped in oil. Its antennae, which were as long as my pinky fingers, convulsed while it shook off cereal crumbs. Cornflakes still in my mouth, I shrunk two sizes too small. I couldn't decide whether to swallow or throw up.

The engorged roach slowly crawled down the side of the box, a single flake clinging to its prickly hind leg like a golden scale.

'Ghk, ghk, ghk,' I started to splutter. On my tongue, between my teeth, along my gums, down my gullet, coating my stomach was everything the cockroach had ever touched. I imagined how it had crawled from our overflowing wheelie bins, to the waste from our dog, along our flea-ridden laundry and into our value-pack box of Cornflakes.

'Ghk, ghk, ghk,' I stammered again and, all of a sudden, my larynx lolled and forced me to swallow. 'Gaaaaaghk!' I gasped, spilling milk from the chipped bowl still in my hands. When I looked down at the shaking cereal, the soggy carbs spelled out a single letter: 'Y'.

Y not stay sleep for? Y so hungry for? Y my brain rot for?

From the shadows of our rabbit-hole hallway, Corey's voice pierced the early-morning air. 'Faaaaahhhk, no way you ate roach-cock.'

Now, with my back to the fridge, Corey pressed his palms into his throat and sputtered like a whoopie cushion. Holding my tongue, I bolted past him, pulled open the sliding door and flung myself out into the overgrown backyard. Plumpton's storm-drain air cooled my inflamed cheeks as I took several heaving breaths, 'H-h-h-huph.' Snot coated my top lip like the white mush wiped on the couch, like the white mush of soggy Cornflakes. 'H-h-h-huph.'

From nits having sex on my head to maggots wriggling in lumps of lard to cockroaches crawling in cereal boxes and cushion crevices, I asked, 'Y'.

A tickle, tickle, tickle up my throat and into the gutter. Bending forward with my forehead scraping against the splinters of our Paddle Pop fence, I vomited.

Y were us Tongans so festy?

12.

'*O*i.' It was the only two letters my father ever needed to put the fear of God in all six of his children. Dad's voice was so deep it cracked mountains; reverberating from the kitchen straight to my bedroom. My crown crashed into the exposed metal grating above me – the prison bars that made up the bottom of my sister's top bunk. A bump sparked down my spine and white dots floated in my vision. 'Shugah!' I hissed, rubbing my itchy scalp. In a twirl, my sister's straw-like strands of hair fell over the railing of her mattress. Swaying upside down in mid-air, Nettie's soil eyes sifted. 'Oh, we can't swear. If I don't dob you to Mumma, what will you give me?'

'Far, I said "shug", durr for brains, so don't even try to rort me,' I retorted, flinging off my Pokémon doona. It was another day after school and I had spent the afternoon reading in bed, still in my clammy uniform. All the while,

Nettie stayed on the top-bunk, practise-talking to Tevita, her wannabe-boyfriend, on a toy mobile phone. Since Dad was awake past 3 pm for once, she was able to take a break from babysitting.

We didn't have time to argue if sugar sounded enough like shit for me to get in trouble; the banging of a wooden spoon drumming haphazardly against metal was calling to us like an alarm. The cooking pot sounded full – we were gonna have us a real mean feed.

My skull throbbed as I gapped it through my bedroom door. My fingers remained interlaced in the worn binding of *Alice Through the Looking Glass*.

I knocked into my brother Jared, who was charging out of his own room. His budding bulk bashed into my side like I'd been smacked with a classic Sonny Bill shoulder-barge.

'Ooof,' I exclaimed, stumbling backwards, dropping my book. Even though he was a head shorter than me, Jared was shaping up into pure muscle from all his footy training. He was the only one of us to be out of uniform, preferring his worn Bulldogs jersey and Blacktown Workers U10s shorts. Placing his rounded fingertips together on his full mouth he mumbled, 'Offside.'

The taro forehead of my other brother, Corey, rose up over us. What my brother from another mother lacked in muscle, he gained in height. 'Faaaahhhhk,' Corey puffed, pulling at his school collar stained with pen ink. 'Move it slow fu-olks.'

Dora the Explorer's mop of hair bopped between us. 'Vam-nose, vam-nose. Big girl hangus.' Little Leilani stunk of stale pee, her nappy drooping as she passed me. She stomped with her too-big-for-boots feet as if she was determinedly following a map.

Little-little sister, Lavender, crawl-followed Little Lani and recited in a series of spit bubbles, 'Ya-mmmm-ya-mmmm.'

Jared and I hovered on our tiptoes, not wanting to squash our baby sisters but desperate to get to Dad in the kitchen. Even with the warning call from our father, Jared and I were still reluctant to pick Lav up, lest we got stuck with the babies for dinner. Tak tak tak went the gas burner followed by the clunky hum of an ageing range-top.

Nettie squeezed past to scoop up Lav from the floor. Lav's breath always smelt like formula. Clucking her tongue, Nettie cooed while wiping drool on her forearm, 'Oh, silly billy.'

Bouncing on my toes, I rolled my eyes impatiently at my five siblings. 'Walk a little faster?' If Dad called on us again, we would be struck down into granules.

Steam hung in the open space of the kitchen and living room, the bay windows and sliding door overlooking the backyard glossed into mirrors. Smells of bubbled-over tomato, baked oregano and stretched-out wheat made my tongue swell from the saliva in my mouth.

With a grunt, Dad shifted a steel pot, which was the size of our English bulldog, over an exposed flame. My father's shadow was made of boulders stacked on boulders. From the fog, Dad's gruff as gravel voice boomed. 'Are youse off youse head?'

We were a flurry of feet. Jared side-stepped back to the linen cupboard to grab a bedsheet. Nettie gripped Lavender on her left hip as she pulled off Leilani's soaking nappy with her right arm in one swift rip. 'Swipe no swipe.' She was quoting from her favourite character in *Dora the Explorer* – a mask-wearing fox named Swiper who liked to steal friendship bracelets. I reckoned that's where Lani was learning cheeky from. She giggled, her bare behind running straight for the festy floral couch. Corey's shoulders slumped as he searched silently for spoons and forks. I went straight for the upper cupboards closest to Dad.

'Tulou,' I muttered as I passed my father, keeping my gaze lowered to the sticky tiled floor. My knuckles trembled as I tried to make sure my touch didn't come near the halo of Dad's granite head. Nana taught me that the only thing more disrespectful than wearing a skirt above my knees in front of my brothers was to knowingly touch Dad's scalp. Nana's broken English wriggled itself in my ear, 'Top off head head off famili. No daughta effa, effa be abuff tha fatha. Understand.' It wasn't a question.

When Dad stirred through thickened bolognaise, I pulsed on my tippy-toes as if there was an earthquake happening. When Dad lowered the temperature on the stove with his pebble knuckles, air skipped in my throat. When Dad slurped up a sample of sweltering spaghetti, as if he were a celebrity chef on TV asking viewers if they could smell what he was cooking, my stomach rose into my chest. I wasn't used to being this close to my father – it was unsettling.

Quickly, I sifted through scratched shakers without lids and pushed past spare parts for Avent bottles. Pressing my lips into a tight line, I ignored the small black dots littering the bottom of the shelves and tried not to think about cockroaches pooping. My breath eased at the sight of fluoro-coloured plastic mugs – glass cups were too delicate for our household.

In the living room, Jared set a holey bedsheet footy-field-wide across the tiled floor. The fabric was ridden with moth bites that reminded me of fo'i hea, the ngatu pattern I'd painted with Nana only once.

Lav giggled through spit bubbles as Lani, now in a fresh nappy, struggled to carry her little sister like a backpack, screeching, 'Lesh go, lesh toots it.'

Nettie's pale skin was strawberry milk as she scolded the toddlers. 'Oh, let's hope when I have babies they're not as bad as the two of you.'

Having finished his part of the pre-dinner chores, Jared squatted on the sheet and used his rugby ball as a seat. His thick neck was stretched into an obtuse angle as he stared through the burnt image of The Cheshire Cat and into Channel 9's live sports coverage of Canterbury Bulldogs versus Parramatta Eels. In Sugar Drive, there were no framed photos or statues of the Son of Man. Instead, television was our Jesus and football was our god.

Stacking the empty plastic mugs on the TV unit, I ducked out of the way of the television screen before Jared could tell me to side-step from his view. I looked for *The Looking*

Glass, which I'd lost in the hallway scrum. Through an oily haze of oregano, I hummed under the noise of shouting siblings: *Where oh where oh where is Alice? Where oh where oh where is Alice? Where oh where oh where is Alice? Which way could she be?* I found the mirror-world at the head of the rabbit-hole when Dad called to us like a flock once more. 'Can youse smell-el-el-el-el.'

Feet again a flurry, my siblings and I stammered over each other's thanks. Being Tongan meant eating together and being grateful to eat together. One by one, Dad served us our full. I felt my pupils cartoonishly stretch as strings of wheat glistened in saucy ground beef, actual minced meat clung to the pasta like jewels. I started to slabber like our dog, Povo. If Macca's was my Turkish delight, spaghetti was my stolen tarts.

While being served, Jared yammered on about how Sonny Bill's shoulder-barge against Jarryd Hayne got them both in the sin bin. Dad barked, 'That bloody Sāmoan.' My brows furrowed together trying to determine if there was any real difference between Tongans and Sāmoans; it seemed to me we all came from the same crap-hole.

'The girls are extra hungry today. Is it true I can make milk myself for babies one day?' Nettie crooned as she pushed in front of our kitchen line. Without answering, Dad piled extra spaghetti in her bowl. Nettie was Dad's favourite because she kept the household together. If it were physically possible, Nettie would be the one with all the time in the world to breastfeed our little-little sisters since Mumma was too busy working. Then there'd be no need for Dad to buy four forty-four-dollar cans of formula every week.

Slowly, Dad replied to Nettie, 'Youse will soon. I reckon youse almost a woman.'

'Pipi pusher,' I huffed.

Dad's rumbling throat made me shiver despite the warm kitchen steam still lingering. 'Musie. Youse got my uniform?'

I kept my mouth shut as he poured spag bol into my bowl. The older I got, the more I realised that, even if a sentence ended with a question, Dad wasn't truly asking me anything.

'Got overnight shift aye. As soon as the shower is off youse better have my uniform ready. Otherwise, I'll be late for work and youse really don't want to know what will happen after that.'

With only a peek at my father's slate-like forearms, I gapped it to the living room as soon as I felt my bowl was full, stammering, 'Yep, Dad. Sorry, Dad. Love you, Dad.' Without looking back, I squished myself between my siblings on the laid-out bedsheet. A pipe rattled in the ceiling, which meant my kai time was spaghetti-slim.

Calves tucked up, knees perched under my chin, I balanced my bowl of pasta. Despite the cool hard tiles against the bones of my bum, I curled my forearm around the bowl's base so none of my siblings could spot my serving. Under the fluorescent twitching from our hunchback Toshiba, I lowered my head so that the tip of my nose touched the top of the warm wheat. I licked my dried lips as little lumps of beef twirled in gold bubbles of diced tomatoes on my fork.

Blowing softly, I watched the heat swirl and then widened my gob as far as it would go and sucked down spaghetti in a single swallow. As the oregano coated my tastebuds, I shut my eyes so tightly that Sugar Drive swirled away.

Pasta went down my gullet before I even knew to chew and the tops of my gums burned. Tongans don't say 'real mean feed' for nothing – there was always a punishment for eating this good. My throat a furnace, I kept shovelling saucy spaghetti into my mouth. Grease coated my lips, making them moist, which turned each slurp into a satisfied squeal. Psckq psckq pscccckq. My bowl was so close to my chest that bits of fattened tomato juice dribbled down my chin. My stomach stretched and stretched until my belly button rubbed against the waistband of my school shorts. Forkful after forkful until I scraped through a deluge of olive oil for scraps. I belched like a full-time horn in satisfaction.

'Argh, c'mon loose head,' Jared mouthed off through his own mouthful as he rolled his backside forwards and back-wards and forwards on his football. Eventually, he jumped up to check the pot for leftovers. There, he groaned again. 'What mulligrubbers.'

I laughed to myself: *Know better, Footy Brain.* When real mince was involved, there were no seconds. Miracles were miracles because they happened once. I burped again.

Corey was stuffed on the couch, cramming his mouth even though we weren't allowed to eat on the lounge. Acting as if he were the exception to every rule, Corey's taro-forehead locked onto the analogue clock above the TV. 'Fu-fork.

Big spoon down soon.' My step-brother was counting time until his mum came back. With six children between them, Mumma took the dayshifts and Dad took the nightshifts. The only time my parents got to see each other was when Mumma walked in the front door and Dad was walking out.

Belly bursting, I placed my empty bowl beside my ankles and opened my frail-spined copy of *Through the Looking Glass*. I started re-reading the part where Alice became queen simply from a crown falling on her head. My skull ached sympathetically because I reckoned it hurt as much as a thump from the bottom bunk. Anything to connect me to Wonderland.

Supposing every punishment was going without supper: then, when the miserable day came, I would have to go without fifty suppers at a time! was poked out of my sight as Lani puffed her bare chest at me. Shaking her too-big bowl cut, she shoved a fork in front of my face. My little half-sister's clammy brown fist tightened on the metal handle. 'Lesh gettu it. Know can dodo it.' I stifled a giggle as Lani blinked through her Dora-inspired fringe in a concentrated effort to feed herself. Her chubby knuckles wobbled like one of the three little pigs until the utensil prongs were headed straight for her cross-eyed pupils.

With a swipe, I snatched the fork away. 'Enough. Mama. I mama for you.' I went to grab at Lani's leftover spaghetti to mush in my mouth, spit out, and feed back to her on the fork. Mushing food for babies was the Tongan way of keeping their bellies warm. For Tongans, cold was the worst fate possible; if we got cold, we got sick, and if we got sick, we died, and if we died, we could not have more babies.

Because our mummy Le'o died, it was Nana that mama'd me, Nettie and Jared. But Dad's second wife never offered to mama the two little babies. After a swig of her Slim&Trim shake, she would say, 'Mama'ing makes babies constipated – eating solids too quickly.'

Like her mumma, my little sister wasn't having it. Lani's fringe puffed until she was rojo in the face. 'Swiper, swiper.'

Watta laupisi. Coldish spaghetti spilled on the holey bedsheet as I yelled, 'Smaaaack? Smaaaack?'

Lani's puffy cheeks deflated as her teardrops fell thick and slow. Then she stomped her feet and scurried off towards her garage-turned-room. 'You smack!'

A threat of violence shuts up any Fob kid real quick. I had the scars to know: One time, Dad couldn't work because he had the flu. To make up funds, Mumma took extra shifts and was gone twenty hours out of the day for almost a week. Nose running and with a heavy chest cough, Dad groaned at me from the lounge room. He was sitting on the roach-bitten couch, cradling Lani, who was still a newborn. He asked me to make her a bottle before she started crying, worsening his migraine. I was in Year 3, so I heaped too much formula. When the kettle boiled, I straight away poured the water into the Avent bottle instead of waiting for it to cool first. I rushed over with the drink and gave it to my father. His fever meant that he couldn't feel the temperature of the formula. But Lani sure did! As soon as the rubber tip of the bottle touched her mouth she screeched in pain – her pink mouth and tongue purpling and swelling. 'Aggghkk!' Dad roared and coughed. The sound froze me to the tiles of the living room floor. As Lani screamed, Dad grabbed my wrist, spun me around, and began slamming his open palm into my back, backside and ribs. Ever since then, my spine always burnt in his presence.

'Ummmm, check the scoreboard?' my brother Jared commented as he rocked back on his football. Right on cue, the shower pipes shuddered to a stop. *Fork, forgot to iron Dad's uniform!*

I grabbed the ironing board from the washhouse, its metal legs mashing together as I tried to unfold it. Behind me, Povo scratched at the window pane of the back door, whining to be let in so she could lick our saucy plates and slobber on our unwashed clothes.

I plugged in our iron (which was missing its triangle tip because we'd dropped it so many times), and slid it up and down the ironing board, as though this would make it heat up faster.

Nettie sing-sung a snicker, 'Oh no, you are in so much shug-ary.' Little-little Lavender spit-giggled along.

With bile bubbling through the pasta in my stomach, I sprinted up the hallway in four strides to grab Dad's wrinkled security guard uniform, which clung to a wire hanger by the handle of my parents' closed door. Without stopping, I bolted back down the hallway in three bounds. Hyperventilating, I pounded the iron's heated plate every which way – down the button sleeve, up the front shirt panels, clipping sides of the plastic buttons and squiggling over each pant leg. My lashes flitted between the ironing board and up along the hallway towards Dad and Mumma's room. Singed cotton stung my nostrils.

'Meadow.' It only took my real name, ricocheting off the tiles like thunder, for my father to hurt me.

Hot iron crashed. 'Shii–' Nettie's nosey eyes shone and I hovered my vocal cords, '–take. Shiitake.' A red welt formed on the inside of my thumb as I rushed in the direction of my father's wet footprints. Tears and a wrinkled security uniform flailed before my eyes.

Dad's bedroom, the beginning and end of Sugar Drive, had deodorant mist swirling from the gap under the door. My burnt hand pulsed rapidly in time with my heart until the tapu door creaked ajar. Keeping my gaze down on my trembling toes, I didn't dare look into the gates of heaven.

'Were you bloody reading again.' Not a question. Father's deep and resounding voice bellowed like a chorus of trumpets. I held up his security uniform in my right hand and opened my left hand to reveal my seared flesh. Grunting, my dad snatched the clothes from me.

The low rumble of his throat hit me like The Big Bang. 'There's what God says. There's what I says. Youse know nothing.' Knuckles of stone, my father held a mighty fist under my nose, a gesture that made me buckle out of breath.

'If my daughter wants to keep wasting time with nonsense, I'll show youse real nonsense.'

At last, his fist disappeared and the light from his bedroom dimmed as he slammed the door. But when God closes one door, another opens: Arriving back home in a jingle of keys, Mumma slid aside the front flyscreen and rustled off her black puffer jacket. The only sign of age on Camellia's wooden face was the purple-black bags under her eyes. Before I could say anything, babies bustled under my legs and pounced on their mother.

'No mama. No mama,' Little Lani demanded into Mumma's thighs, which were made bulky from all the pockets in her cargo pants. Mumma slowly wrestled against her daughter's bubbly arms, and replied, 'Yes, Mumma. Mumma back now.'

Little-little Lav was dribbling and drooling onto Mumma's steel-capped boots and she struggled to wobble herself upright.

Fumbling with the many limbs of her offspring, Mumma stepped into the walls of Sugar Drive. The purple layers under her eyes darkened when she called out, 'Baaaabe. Jared. I need to tell you something, so we better bite the bullet.' It took me a minute to understand Mumma was calling to Dad directly. Technically, just like me and Aunt Meadow, Dad was a lahi and my brother Jared was a si'i too. Did I mention Tongans kept a tight vocabulary together?

'Mu-mu-mu-muck-Mum.' Corey wrapped his mum into a hug as wonky as sweet potato. Mumma kissed her son's crown, still pushing back her babies, while asking how the teacher's aides were in his SPED class.

Pressing his wide forehead into the hollow of Mumma's wooden cheek, Corey crooned, 'Bashed the maths in my fricken head.'

Turning my face away, I sneakily rolled my eyes so Mumma wouldn't see. *Bro is such a peel.*

Camellia, used to her son's stammered exaggerations, simply hummed her approval. Mumma and I agreed on one thing at least, 1 + 1 = 3 getting shoved into Corey's starchy skull was better than 1 + 1 = 0.

It was then that Mumma caught me sucking on the welt on my thumb. The whites around her irises widened, which made her sagging maroon eyelids even more pronounced. 'Meadow, what a sore sight for eyes. Come on, plant one on your mum.'

My jaw stiffened automatically at the flick in Mumma's tone, which was left over from her New Zealand upbringing. As the only one of us to be born in Tonga, Mumma's voice always meant she was asking for something: a vaccuum of the house, a cup of tea, a massage of her pouchy belly or a kiss on her cheek.

I'd memorised Mumma's history so that I could trace myself back to her, if anyone asked, like an umbilical cord: Camellia's dad, Misi Mäkelä, helped to build the famous Dateline Hotel in Tonga. Then Grandpa Misi moved his wife, Grandmumma Sela, and their daughter from the village of Kolonga to New Zealand. This was because, in the late seventies, the pālangi men were still calling, as they had been since World War II, for island-muscle to build their cities. It was Misi's jandalman skills and Finnish last name, which was passed down from some distant eighteenth-century traveller, that allowed his daughter to live in the land of the long white cloud as a citizen.

Soon after moving to New Zealand, Grandmumma Sela was diagnosed with early-onset dementia. From what I understood, her mind went grey as soon as she saw a silhouette of police officers in a sunrise. The invasion against us was called The Dawn Raids – sanctioned when the New Zealand government no longer needed the cheap labour of men like Pa.

Grandmumma Sela's dementia meant Camellia was the only Fob in Aotearoa without any siblings. That's why Camellia needed a big family – she was filling Grandmumma Sela's spotless mind with sunshine.

Now, back in the rabbit-hole hallway, I slunk through my siblings and picked up Little-little Lav by her spittle-soaked stomach. Slowly, I pressed my cheek into Mumma's cheek. She smelt strongly of wet gum leaves and nicotine from all the hours she stood in the Rooty Hill RSL parking lot. Mwahk went our faces as they knocked together, thrusting me like a snapped twig.

Before Mumma could say anything more, Nettie sauntered between us. My milky-hued sister embraced Camellia as if she had come out of this woman instead of the woman she resembled down to every cell. 'Oh, Mum. You wouldn't believe the day I had looking after the babies all by myself. I'm wiped as.' The front door flung shut behind Mumma, who huffed and flayed her elbows in an attempt to squeeze us all back down the hallway.

'Bless you, Nettie. You're my perfect bun from the oven.'

Her hair a halo, Nettie kissed Mumma on her bark-rough cheek and then sauntered away from me, her smile as perfect as plastic.

Camellia pressed her roughened palms into the purple swells of her eyelids and hissed at us like strays. 'All right, get lost, you lot. Go on.' Then she turned to our dad, emerging from their bedroom, and added, 'Babe, we need to talk so wrap your head.'

My siblings trundled to the lounge-kitchen, following Nettie's lead. I pretended to follow, slowly balancing a blubbering Lav by bouncing her on my hipbones in slow mini steps. I never missed a serious-talk; curiouser and curiouser.

Lavender's drool soaked my shoulder. In the corner of my eye, I saw my father dressed in all black with reflective silver block lettering, which formed the word 'Guard'. The sleeves of his button-down were slightly crinkled. The air quickly stunk of Brut Original and mint toothpaste. Jared Senior stood two heads taller than his wife and mumbled as he looked at his watch. 'Yeah?'

Not wanting to be noticed, I quickened my pace towards the lounge-kitchen so my parents thought I was too far away to hear. The way Mumma said her next words shook the tiles beneath me. 'My period late. Late all the way to never and never being the next nine months. Understand.' It wasn't a question.

My father responded in an avalanche of grumbles. Little-little Lav's cold spit ran down my gaunt chest and I felt those hairs, like the ones that clogged the shower drain, scrape against the inside of my thighs. Even back then, I knew that a period was not just the end of a sentence. It was bleeding. It was birthing. It was babies. More babies. *No room but.*

Lav kicked my rib cage and blew a sprinkler of raspberries with her tongue, breaking my stream of consciousness. When I turned back to face my parents, it was like looking through the wrong end of a telescope. Mumma was wide as a deck of cards; Dad was as droopy as a wilting rose. Behind me, I could hear Povo whining from the washhouse like a dormouse. Dishes clanked in the sink as the kettle boiled over and a ref whistled full-time on the television and Jared yelled, 'Up the Dogs.' Lav, my soon-not-to-be littlest sibling, weighed a brick ton in my arms.

With a quick peck on Mumma's forehead, Dad rushed out the front door and towards our beat-up Tarago – the eight-seater van which would no longer be big enough for our family.

13.

*O*n an analogue clock, between the number twelve and the number one, was a fly. Laminated copies of *The Elephants*, *The Burning Giraffe* and *Meditative Rose* were pegged on strings, tacked from wall-to-wall throughout the classroom. On the ceiling was *The Persistence of Memory* – the clocks melting over my head.

In the second term of Year Six, I was chosen to attend Gifted & Talented by my previous teacher, Mrs Palmer. She recommended me after she saw the notes I was scribbling on the edges of my maths book: *1. Cats domesticated themselves by hunting mice on farmlands over 10,000 years ago. 2. Copernicus proved that planets revolved around the sun – then he died from a brain bleed. 3. China's Great Wall is over 2,700 years old.*

'I didn't know you owned an encyclopedia!' Mrs Palmer's chirpy voice pealed as she crouched beside me. But no such books existed in the House of Fe'ofa'aki or 8 Sugar Drive. The only encyclopedia I knew was called 'Lahi'.

'What is a story?' Miss Indigo, my new Gifted & Talented teacher, asked. Standing in the centre of the classroom, flicking her waist-long hair over her shoulder, fiddling with her paisley cardigan; she rotated to look at her students one-by-one.

There were only five of us – Warami, Sarah, Bruce, Emma-Jane and myself – and our square desks were arranged into a wonky semi-circle instead of individual rows so we could all see each other. Sarah, the school captain, sat on the left side of the semi-circle. Then there was me. Next to me was Bruce, whose family had come from a place in West Africa called Togo. On our first day in class together, I jokingly asked Bruce what 227 × 722 was. He ran his thumb over the tips of his fine fingers for a few seconds and replied, '163, 894.'

In the middle of the semi-circle was Emma-Jane. Her dad was the local member for Mount Druitt while her mum was a journalist for *The Blacktown Advocate*. Emma-Jane had light brown hair cropped into a short bob, a minty-scented bell-like pitch, and a lean frame thanks to her afternoons playing netball. I envied Emma-Jane: anyone with educated parents and two names for one was automatically special.

And lastly, on the right end of the semi-circle sat Warami, who had a chiselled face and permanent frown. Warami was a recipient of AIME – the Australian Indigenous Mentoring Experience.

Each school day, Miss Indigo taught from the middle of our semi-circle, reminding us that the arrangement was important because it created community and communication. She stood barefoot; every digit decorated in silver rings, which matched the ones on her fingers. There were no questions off-limits when it came to Miss Indigo. She was the type of teacher who encouraged our curiosity; said it fostered critical thinking skills. Once, Emma-Jane asked Miss Indigo if she had children: Emma-Jane was planning on becoming Australia's first woman prime minister and wanted to know if babies would help or hinder her campaign. Miss Indigo hummed as she wrote fractions on the chalkboard before she said, 'My kids are furry, have four legs and woof.' Another time, we were discussing a concubine named Empress Dowager Cixi, who helped launch modern China. Bruce blurted out in a thick accent, 'Many wives but one husband? How does this add up?' Miss Indigo replied, 'My partner and I are just as weird.' And on yet another occasion, during quiet reading time, Sarah quipped, 'Miss, why be a teacher?' Miss Indigo looked up from a worn copy of *Don't Take It Personally* and replied, 'Actually, I wanted to be a writer, but those who can't do, teach.'

Flicking her paisley cardigan enthusiastically, Miss Indigo repeated, 'Come on folks, what's a story?'

'A story equals entertainment,' Bruce finally responded, twirling a lock of his twisted black hair with long and nimble fingers.

'Hmm,' Miss Indigo mused. Her sun-soaked cheeks were filled with the finest of lines, like the crackle in a glazed vase. 'That sounds more like the *purpose* of a story. I'm asking what *makes* a story.'

On my right, Sarah fiddled with her gold cross necklace. 'Emotions?' she guessed with a bubbly drool. 'The sound of the narrator?'

Of course, the school captain, who also taught me the difference between 'Lebanese' and 'lesbian', was in Gifted & Talented. Sarah hugged me tight when I first joined the group, pressing her bosom into my flat chest and screaming out: 'Sick! I knew you weren't dumb.' Then she looked me straight in the eyes, our noses touching and the down-there feeling between my legs tingling.

Clanking her silver rings together, Miss Indigo replied, 'That technique is called "literary voice".' Automatically, I scribbled down 'sounds like = character'. When Bruce peered at my notes, he grinned widely, revealing perfectly straight white teeth, and nodded. Miss Indigo went on, snapping her head from one student to another: 'My question again is, tell me the *structure* of a story.'

'What, like events?' Emma-Jane asked, her high voice clipped with frustration. She hated not knowing an answer; convinced good politicians knew everything. Through the window above her head, the silver gleam from the bubblers and the bright crooked path of concrete leading to the front office blinded me.

Bouncing on her calloused heels, Miss Indigo beamed. 'Close! What kind of events? Meadow, Warami – any thoughts?'

Pressing my lips together nervously, I turned to Warami, who was sitting at the opposite end of the semi-circle. The permanent scowl etched on his chiselled chin reminded me of the most depressed friggen kid I'd ever seen on Foxtel – Huey from *The Boondocks*. Warami was the same confusing not-quite pale and not-quite tan colour as my sister Nettie.

It was under the school flag poles that Warami first revealed his history to me: seeking shade one hot summer recess, I stood under the shadows cast by the flags and read *The Slippery Slope*, the tenth instalment in *A Series of Unfortunate Events*. 'The government's a friendly enemy, give us bibles, take our lands,' a deep and mournful voice lamented. Standing before me was a lanky boy with defined calves, shaking his head as he strode out of the front office with a folder in the crook of his elbow. Although I wasn't really interested in boys just yet, I found this one stunning – an ancient sculpture polished new. Nervously, I clutched my novel. 'Warami the name,' he said smoothly. 'What mob you from?'

Gum leaves rustled as I blinked back at him. 'Mob?'

The boy arched his brows, knitting them together. 'Oh, Islander.' When I asked how he knew, Warami grinned crookedly. 'We first people know all our guests.'

'Must like that then?' I smiled, pointing skywards. Above us were three flags. The first and highest had red lines, white stars. The second was blue and green with a single star. And the final was black and red, held together by a yellow sun.

My juvenile attempt at flirting fell short when Warami's plump beige mouth turned downwards. 'Nah,' he muttered. 'There's no point if we don't have Treaty, Native Title, or even just Acknowledgement at this school.' Then he revealed the folder in his elbow, which had the words 'The Australian Indigenous Mentoring Experience' emblazoned on the front. '*Australian* is a lie. Bet you don't even know what land you on.' Glaring at my confusion, Warami chuckled hollowly. 'Dharug, bub.'

Back in Gifted & Talented, Warami was sharing a similar lesson. 'Don't care much about Whitefella story,' he shrugged. 'But in Dreaming, we always think of past, present, future and then future as past.'

'Beautiful,' Miss Indigo whispered, placing her hand to her spindly chest. 'Remember kids, we have everything to learn from First Nations knowledge.' Something about her response made me squirm in my seat; it sounded sweet but in a forced way – like putting too much honey in porridge. Tying her purple hair in a ponytail, Miss Indigo turned to me directly. 'Meadow, what's another way to define a narrative?'

I stopped tracing a spiral in my notebook and bit the inside of my cheek. 'Well . . . past, present and future are events in time . . .' Miss Indigo was nodding enthusiastically so I continued. 'I'm reading these books called *A Series of Unfortunate Events* which are about the lives of three orphans. The first one is called *The Beginning* and then the final book, which is just about to come out, is called *The End*. And in the middle, all this terrible stuff happens.'

'Go on,' Miss Indigo encouraged, wriggling her shiny toes.

'Beginning, middle and end!' Emma-Jane squealed, nearly jumping out of her chair.

'Yes, absolutely,' Miss Indigo chimed. 'The brightest of us overcomplicate things. A story is simply a beginning, middle and end. Well done, Emma-Jane.'

Warami and Bruce both mumbled 'pft' under their breath as Sarah leant into me and whispered, 'Don't worry cuz, I know she stole that from ya.'

Setting ten minutes of silence, Miss Indigo instructed us to each write a three-sentence story. The first as the beginning, the second as the middle, and the third as the end. She called this a 'scaffolding exercise' and explained it would guide us as we worked this term towards writing a full short story.

I began thinking what to write; gazing out the window behind Warami's head. On the cracked concrete path leading up to the office were two Fob boys making car noises as they chased each other with wheelie bins.

The first Fob, who was scrawny and had holes in his green school jumper, called out, 'Recycle deez nuts.' Then he rammed into the second Fob's giant behind, which was stretching out his grey cargo school shorts; stumpy calves littered with scabs. Both cackled and then skrrt skrrt skrrted until they were out of view.

Accustomed to the noise, each student in Gifted & Talented stuck their head over their notebooks. Meanwhile, Miss Indigo walked to the front corner of the classroom and sat behind her desk, which was cluttered with used coffee mugs that featured slogans like 'Always Was, Always Will Be' and 'Make Love Not War', misshapen stacks of paper, bundles of pens and ashes from incense.

Pens scratching against notepads, Miss Indigo lit a fresh incense stick, promising the scent of sandalwood and jasmine would broaden our minds. 'Or at least that's what us groovy kids said in the sixties,' she mumbled to herself.

The clocks above me continued to melt and the sun reflecting off the concrete outside our demountable hummed while the air con clanked. I stared at my sheet of paper until words materialised. Start: Nana shows me how to paint ngatu and teaches me all the Tongan names for plants. Middle: Skeleton woman in a bikini comes out and tells us to tick off back to where we'd come from. End: Punch that pālangi in the face! Suddenly, my hand cramped into a fist and my breathing became heavy. When I looked away from the page, I saw one of Miss Indigo's mugs that said, 'Kindness Rules'. *Hmm . . . okay, maybe I need to come up with a peaceful ending.* Delete: ~~Punch that pālangi in the face!~~ End: Turn the other cheek.

All ten minutes sweated from my pores until finally Miss Indigo clapped her rings together and returned to her usual spot at the centre of our semi-circle. 'Now, read your stories out loud.' The space between my brows strained as I looked at Sarah; who shrugged and stared at Bruce; who shook his chin and turned to Emma-Jane; who had this protruding blue vessel in her pale forehead that twisted towards Warami; who rolled his hazel eyes.

Miss Indigo untied her ponytail so her violet hair flowed down to her waist once more. 'Warami, why don't you go first? The rest of us will use our listening ears.' Miss Indigo's tight pupils darted at each one of us.

Rubbing his small biceps, Warami cleared his throat. 'Didn't write down anything.'

Emma-Jane gasped audibly while me and Sarah giggled at each other. Bruce, who was twisting a blue pen between his whitening knuckles, sighed sympathetically.

'I told you,' Warami went on. 'My people yarn not write.'

At this, Miss Indigo's owl-like gaze brightened. 'Well then, yarn for us.'

Flexing his chiselled joints, Warami grinned, revealing a cute gap between his two front teeth. He spoke to us about a god named Biiami who was the Creator of Creeks, Rivers and Bush. Of Magpie and Crow, whose war cries were heard far and wide until they fell into a fire, and when they emerged from the flames, their colours were changed forever. Magpie was black and white while Crow was black all over.

After Warami finished speaking, we sat with his yarn for a few quiet seconds. *Who is the magpie and who is the crow in this classroom?* I wondered, my gaze once again hovering past Warami to the outside world. At the bubblers, a plump girl with blonde hair was drinking. *Dani!* Seeing her wicked tongue slurp at the metal reminded me of our first week in Kindergarten, when she teased me for having dusty parmesan between two slices of white bread for lunch. I was so embarrassed I vomited in a fit of tears.

'Ah,' Miss Indigo sighed eventually. 'See kids, culture can be a benefit. Even if we don't understand—'

Before she could finish her thought, screaming erupted from the demountable next to ours. 'Weeeeeeeeeeee!' The sounds were from a 'special' class too, the *other* kind of 'special'. Through thin walls, I could hear the fragments of a deep muffled voice yelling back at a student, 'Put! No! Off his! Off no! Core—' I blushed in my seat: the 'special' kid in that class was all-too familiar.

Miss Indigo looked annoyed at the sound outside, but maintained her cool, clamping her lips together and waiting for the ruckus to settle down before finally saying, 'Is it alright if we identify some literary techniques from your yarn, Warami?'

Warami licked his curved mouth in thought and nodded.

'There was a coda at the end, right?' Emma-Jane asked swiftly.

'Sure was,' Miss Indigo agreed, re-wrapping her loose paisley cardigan around her waist. 'So, Bruce, see, not only is a story told for entertainment but also to teach morals.'

Compressing his eyebrows together, Bruce replied, 'Yes, madame.'

'Go'od boy,' Miss Indigo replied, and just like before, her response made me squirm. Elevating her covered forearms, entwining her hands and resting her pointed jaw on her many rings, Miss Indigo continued, 'So who wants to go next?'

'Me,' Emma-Jane said, immediately standing up from her seat. 'So, I actually wrote a speculative speech. Spec-u-lative meaning "future". And it's in a world where the first woman is sworn in as Prime Minister.'

The heady smoke of sandalwood and jasmine started to irritate my nose as Miss Indigo explained that we, as aspiring storytellers, should never preface our work. 'Let the writing speak for itself,' she explained.

Forehead vessel twitching, Emma-Jane nodded. Then, taking a deep breath, she recited what she wrote: 'I, Emma-Jane Julia Gillardy, so solemnly swear and declare that I will well and truly serve the Commonwealth of Australia, the Queen's land and her people. I will do this by recognising the Voices of *our* First people, the Aborigines.' Warami's hazel eyes rolled back into his head, like he'd heard this spiel before, but Emma-Jane was too enrapt in her 'story' to notice. 'I will uphold the magnificence of this sunburnt country, which is founded in the harmony of our cultures girt by land and sea. Through our multiculturalism and my election as Australia's first woman Prime Minister, I will show that this "Down Under" continent has eradicated all forms of sexism and racism for good.' At this, Bruce began counting on his fingers – Bored? Confused? Mixture of both? Meanwhile, Sarah picked up her pen, put it down, and then picked it up again – probz conflicted as to whether she should be taking notes. Emma-Jane continued, 'To First people, may we continue to share our land together. To those from other countries like Africa, Asia and the Middle East, you do not have to be afraid of war, communism or terrorism as long as Australia is your home and you put being Australian first. And to our Pacific neighbours.' At this, my ribs suddenly clenched. I sat straight, waiting. 'I extend a generous hand of financial aid so that you can solve illiteracy, violence, obesity and rising sea levels. Australia is here to help.'

All at once, Miss Indigo nervously whipped her purple hair into a flimsy bun, Warami wrinkled his nose and Bruce nodded as if his sums were finally adding up. Scribbling a few words onto her notepad, Sarah tightened her jaw in a strained smile and flicked back her curly hair. Emma-Jane beamed at us, baring the biggest grin as though she was waiting for applause.

My fists clenched as the memories came pouring in: Arthritis knotting Nana's melon-like hands from the years she kneaded biscuits to keep her children clothed and sheltered; Grandmumma Sela, standing between her sons and police batons; Pa, labouring all day with the shovel for a sip of wine; Mummy Le'o, rotting away beneath my bare feet. Time thawed upon my crown as I stood up and waded slowly towards Emma-Jane. Her eyes shot wide open. Then she blinked. And in that split second, I planted my fist straight into her mouth. My knuckles stung against her teeth as she staggered back and shrieked, 'See, violence!'

'Pālangi fie me'a!' I screamed. 'Why do you get to be better than me?'

Immediately, Warami's strong hands enveloped my chest, Bruce's nimble fingers tugged at my shoulders, and Sarah's flimsy arms crossed over my waist, pulling me back into her bosom, all of us screaming over one another: 'Shi! Khe! Muh! Bah!'

In one motion, Miss Indigo tore off her paisley cardigan and pounced between the four Brown kids and one White kid. 'Stop,' she screeched, swinging her freckly arms like a windmill, pushing us apart with her bright-pink palms. 'You're supposed to be the smart ones; you're acting like a bunch of savages!'

Seething through my teeth, heaving to catch my breath, dissolving as tears filled my eyes, the persistence of time melted away, and in the blinding black light all I could see before me was my nana. *Alright Nana ... alright.*

14.

The flesh between the thighs of boys and men was private knowledge. Yet, in the middle of the kitchen, there was a cake tin shaped like a penis sitting on the bench.

Mumma whisked a bowl full of powdered cocoa – skkt skkt skkt skkt. The kitchen bench was cluttered with used Avent bottles, new nappies, receipts, sacks of flour and stacks of cooking chocolate. Gawking at the two bumps down the end of the metal tray, I started listing all of the names that represented these objects, which I'd learned in the playground of Whalan Public School: Balls. Bollocks. Bawls. Ballsack. Nutsack. Sack. Bags. Beans. Beanbags. Bangers. Cherries. Cods. Eggs. Nuts. Deez nuts. Doon. Goolies. Gonads. Nads. Nards. Avos. Testes. Teabags. Cojones. Boys. Big boys. Dangly bits. Low hangers. Family jewels. Coin purse. Oval office. Knackers. Klackers. Step-kids. Dunns. Exhaling a solemn breath, I finally asked, 'That's what a proper pee-pee looks like, yeah?'

Flicking specks of chocolate in my direction, Mumma clicked her tongue at me. 'Curiosity killed the bat.'

With my cheeks heating up, I sat back, open-mouthed.

Mumma's blow-dried hair, dyed with caramel-blonde streaks, was tied up in a messy bun. Sweat gathered on the brow of her bark-like forehead and her upper arms wobbled as she continued to whisk at a thickened mixture of sugar, chocolate, flour and eggs. Raw sweetness swirled in a stainless-steel bowl, which she balanced on her ballooning belly.

It's curiosity killed the cat, you dingbat.

Mumma poured the fudgy mixture into the rude metal tin. A penis wasn't meant for cake. A penis was for marriage, for making babies, as it was written in the Bible. But hardly any Fobs listened to the marriage part, Mumma especially. Darrell was just her boyfriend when she got pregnant with Corey. My dad was just her boyfriend when she got pregnant with Leilani. And after two shotgun weddings, Mumma kept producing mouths to feed. The cooker that was now baking my little-little-littlest sister was set to six months.

With mitted palms, Camellia shoved the rocket-shaped tin into the oven. I had a sinking feeling that babies were made through a similar heat and violence. Gulping, I asked, 'But what's the thingy for?' Curiouser and curiouser.

After re-checking the temperature, Mumma stood upright with a gusty groan. 'You barking up the wrong tree so . . . don't punch me in the nose.' At the last part, Mumma laughed to herself. Warm sugar wafting between us, I remained quiet, my knuckles tense.

Eventually, Mumma looked me up and down through her leafy lashes and lowered her bowl. The steel bottom was full of melted chocolate criss-crossed over itself. For all Mumma's flaws, from too many babies to too short a fuse, even I conceded that Camellia was an excellent baker. She was the one our forever-stretching family turned to for every occasion: colourful fondant in various themes for birthdays, frosted marble cupcakes for baby showers, thick fudge brownies for twenty-firsts, buttery shortbread for baptisms, and crumbly blueberry muffins for school Mother's Day stalls. However, Mumma never did weddings – the sweetness of newlyweds made her too much of a stress head. Lahi's marriage to Lotemi was the only celebration that was approaching in our family's extensive social calendar, and they were hiring a professional baker, so Mumma was all good.

'Maybe I will tell you. If you old enough to fight you old enough for this. Better late than never.' Mumma sighed, sliding what was left of the chocolate batter in my direction. 'Anyway, eat. A trouble shared is trouble halved.'

'Delisheoo can do-do-do-Dora,' Leilani exclaimed through her overgrown bob, which was as stringy as a mop. She climbed up the bench stool fox-quick and swirled her stubby fingers in the lush leftovers. 'Num-num-num,' Lavender said in dribbles, trying her best to climb up the stool as well but missing her footing every time.

I lifted Lav in one arm and felt dribble dripping on my wrist. Together on my lap, Leilani and Lavender started licking at the bowl. My baby-lings smelt of slept-in blankets and unbrushed teeth. Mumma fiddled with the oven, still leafing at me with her eyes. Her shifting gaze made my legs bounce up and down, which made the voices of my sisters jumble like jelly. 'Nu-nu-nu-nu-nuu-num.'

Pinching my brows, I couldn't stand not knowing any longer. Dipping my own pinky into the leftover cake batter, which was fast disappearing from the two chubby-grubby toddlers, I licked up the chocolate. Remnants of raw egg and granules of sugar dissolved into my tastebuds. Then, I held my moist pinky in the air – a promise to keep the knowledge of forbidden fruit just between me and Mumma.

'Cry for the moon, why don't you?' Camellia lamented. 'Don't go blaming me since you're biting off more than you can chew – especially when you get on your monthlies. What I'm about to tell you is something so rich you're only supposed to know it after your rags.' My jaw spasmed as I opened my mouth to ask what the heck 'monthlies' and 'rags' meant, but Mumma continued without a pause. 'Here's the riches to rags of it, your aunt Meadow is having her hens night.'

The cluttered kitchen started to stifle with the warm and heavy scent of melted sugar turning into gooey chocolate. As Little Lani and Little-little Lav gobbled up the rest of the batter and shimmied down the bench stools, I continued to blink at Camellia's stumpy frame. My siblings waddled back in front of the television to be minded by their actual big sister – Dora.

I shrugged, unable to piece together what chickens and night-time had to do with each other.

Nodding, Mumma went on with a glint in her oak-toned eyes. 'Hens night is the first and last night a woman can be anything: a liar, a thief, a fornicator, a drunk, a hom.' Clasping her hollow mouth, Mumma ground her teeth before continuing. 'Anyways, a hens night is a big celebration for a soon-to-be bride before she's made honest and shackled for life to an old ball 'n' chain.'

In a groan of frustration, I rested my forehead on the sticky kitchen bench, which made the baby bottles rattle. Whatever Mumma knew was too much for my pea brain, which was why she scoffed at me and returned to her penis cake.

She opened the oven and pressed a fork into the tip of the batter to see if it was done. Behind me, my baby sisters shouted back the Spanish word Dora was getting them to recite today: 'Amor'. Not long after, the shadowy mass of my father appeared, stomping slowly down the hallway, making me sit up stiff.

'No peeking,' Mumma giggled, shoving the oven door closed with a snap. She, too, felt the gravity of Dad's presence. However, whilst I was frightened, Mumma was excited. My parents were in their late-twenties, only recently married. Sexual creatures. Humans. Gross. But I understood.

While they embraced, I put my head down and stared at a hole in my sock where my right pinky toe was peeking through. The worn cotton was frayed, revealing the silhouette of all my toenails. The nail of my pinky was especially over-grown and semi-cracked because my feet were too ticklish for clippers. My socks were always filthy, acting as a barrier between my bare feet and the ever-grimy tiles. Trying to ignore a smacking of lips coming from my parents, I wriggled my pinky toe through the tear in my sock until it stuck out like the top of an onion. My deformed and yellowing nail was the only thing I could find that was as disgusting as my parents making out.

Once enough quiet passed, I lifted my head and smiled weakly at my parents, who were now embracing with their arms instead of their mouths. My father's thick shoulder blades protruded as he wrapped his biceps around Mumma's budding waist. My step-mother's knotted fingers tangled within my father's rocky hands like roots. The wooden texture of Mumma's cheeks smoothed out and glowed as she blushed, like the explosion of a brand new rosebud.

Letting go of my step-mother, Dad raised one shaggy eyebrow at me. 'Youse in a punch up again?' My spine stung and my face blazed.

Slapping his wrists, Mumma replied for me in a breezy tone. 'Principal gave her an earful already. So did we. Meadow's been lifting her weight today. She's done her time.' Mumma was referring to the one-day suspension I received for punching Emma-Jane.

A small twitch in my cheeks; that was all I could muster as a smile in thanks. Any time I felt grateful for Mumma, a coffin slammed in my stomach.

Dad locked his shiny shale eyes on me. 'Youse lucky I was a worser kid. But remember, I used my fists so youse wouldn't have to.' Translation: 'Don't let my sacrifices be for nothing.' I nodded meekly.

Suddenly, Dad's phone began to ring. He strolled into the rabbit-hole to answer it and came back to the kitchen a second later with a scowl. 'Work. Offered me an extra shift.'

Heat from the oven smothered us as Mumma immediately went off: 'Jared, I get out once in a blue moon.' Translation: 'You're not the only one making sacrifices.'

Dad scoffed, 'No nothing, woman. We gotta pay bills youse know.'

Mumma twisted the oven dial and yanked out the penis. 'Cut the mustard. Bills will be around forever.' There was no longer any sweetness in the air. My parents went on bickering; Dad's nostrils flaring like steam from a hot spring, Mumma pounding her knotted knuckles into her upturned wrists, explaining how sick she was of their endless cycle of work, sleep, babies, babies, sleep, work and babies. 'Do you want a wife or a storm in a teacup?'

Rolling his shoulders, Dad went on to describe our family's fate if he was to reject even a single shift: 'Live it up lux now then. Soon we'll be bums and youse be full sooking at me for a roof to live under.'

Knowing my place all too well, I bounded into the living room, swiping up Lani and Lav.

Mumma's next words made me fumble my two toddler sisters just in front of the roach-bitten couch: 'That one acting grown enough to cluck.' When I looked up, Mumma was pointing a wooden spoon at me. Baby-lings grumbled in annoyance as I plopped them on the ground at my feet. Immediately, both my sisters began bashing their hammy fists into my shins. I'd shrunk and become two sizes too small.

Dad was pacing.

'Musie and Nettie can babysit,' Mumma was saying. 'Waste not want not, babe. I already cooked the friggen rooster.'

I could feel the blood rushing all over my chest, up my neck and inflaming my cheeks as I watched my parents from the corner of my left eye. The White Queen's words floated into my ear: *What is the use of a child without any meaning?*

Pinching on my shins, Lani was using my legs to stand upright. Her bowl-cut head nearly reaching my hips, she bellowed, 'Not you lead way me. Imda big girl too.'

Nipping at my ankles, Lav drooled on my socks until the cotton soaked. 'Do-do-doba.'

Dad's voice ricocheted against the walls of the house. 'Don't youse let them see nothing silly. Nettie all about kids but she's still too young to have them. And Meadow, she's too smart for her own good youse know; tell her something and it'll end up in a book shaming all of us. My girls, got it!'

My girls. It was the one and only time my father separated us.

Dad's boots stomped their way past Povo's whining in the washhouse, and Mumma's tears dripped over the penis cake, and my little sisters continued to claw at me. All I could hear in my head were two words: My. Girls.

15.

*P*lastic on plastic. Tacky trestle tables tacked in transparent tablecloths patterned with bougainvillea and frangipani – topped with patchworks of foil. By the edge of the back door, which led into Nana's room, sat Lahi's old wika-wika stuff all set up and bumping DJ Noiz remixes. Bongos banged beneath the lyrics of Akon's 'Smack That' as I grazed my fingertips over the knobbly soundboard, freshly cleaned of any sticky Fanta trails. Above my head, strings of fairy lights and multicoloured fluorescent leis hung from the underside of the pergola that covered the backyard. The decorations hid the cobwebs in the pergola's corners, which were entwined with dead flies, mozzies and the occasional twitching cockroach.

Underneath the buggy ceiling, carboard cut-outs of a hula-hula dancer were taped to every pergola pole. The hula dancer was a smiling red-head in a grass skirt and coconut bra who looked like the bully, Mertle Edmonds, from *Lilo & Stitch*; nothing like Nani – the actual hula girl.

Smoke plumed in the furthest corner of the backyard; the bulky shadows of my aunts scurried this way and that as they prepared for the party. Through the smoke's wispy depths I could see a whole pig carcass stuck from anus-to-snout on a metal rod as it rotated slowly above a makeshift coalpit. I walked closer to the blistering boar, so close to that puaka I stared right into its milky and soulless eyeballs. Within its irises, I saw the blob of my own reflection. Bulbous head, missing chin and wiggly neck. The space between my knuckles cramped as the ghost of Emma-Jane's sharp teeth pierced my palm. *See, violence!*

My guts cramping, I walked over to the trestle tables. When I peeked under the foils of aluminium, I saw the classics for a Fob feed: lū in wilted and oily taro leaves, steamed segments of manioke bunching in clumps of coconut cream, soy-drenched vermicelli noodles with strips of fattened beef (which we called sapasui) and pineapples stuck with skewers of cut-up melon and still-wrapped chocolate. Dotted between the crinkled silver trays were red and white pinstriped buckets of Kentucky Fried Chicken along with four-litre bottles of Coke, Sprite, Fanta, Solo, Kirks Creaming Soda, LA Ice, Passiona, Sunkist, Mountain Dew and L&P.

On a separate, smaller table was alcohol. The only brands I was able to recognise were Midori, which turned Fobs into studded cylinders; Jack Daniels, which turned Fobs into glass cubes. As I edged closer towards the liquor, smaller bottles titled 'Cruisers' shimmered in an extra-large cooler bag. With a winged eagle embossed on silver caps, each beverage reminded me of the potions I read about so many times in so many fairytales: Professor Snape's riddle brews in *Harry Potter and the Philosopher's Stone*; the Sea Witch's seafoam in *The Little Mermaid*; Lucy's cordial in *The Lion, The Witch and The Wardrobe*; and George's toothpaste and shaving cream in *George's Marvellous Medicine*. But this was no fairytale. Islanders were about to be poisoned.

Busted bongos, auto-tuned vocals, charred crackling and colourful concoctions – the concrete backyard of 4 Avery Street had been transformed into a lū'au.

'Not your cup of tea, girlie,' Mumma's voice blew, making me bump into the cooler. The ice shifted like shattered glass. Mumma was balancing the freshly frosted cock cake between her baby bump and bursting breasts. 'Pull your weight and 'alu the rest of the kai.'

After a hefty sigh, I bounded through the back door and into Nana's room. Bundles of kafus had multiplied ten-fold; stacked in layers larger than an Austrian hillside. Atop the highest mound of blankets were all of my sisters, Nettie, Leilani and Lavender, who were curled up together like hatchlings in a nest. Boys were not allowed at the hens night, so before we came, Mumma dropped my brothers off to Pa and Grandmumma Sela – all the way in Blacktown. Growing boys didn't affect Grandmumma's spotless mind too bad, unlike babies . . .

My full-blooded sister was swaying our littlest half-blooded sister, Lav, to sleep. Our other little half-blooded sister, Lani, rested her too-big head on Nettie's thigh, scrolling through the Foxtel schedule as if she was old enough to read the words. Lani's stringy and overgrown Dora-cut was spread out in a way that made Nettie's crotch appear full of hair – already a woman!

'Oh, so is there really a dick cake?' Nettie whispered, eyes glazing. 'What did it look like? Tell me!' The spaces between her milk-coloured fingers were covered with Lav's half-asleep slobbering.

Even though I heard Nettie over the reverberating bass of Akon reggae, I refused to acknowledge her question: I had no intention of helping my younger sister become another unmarried pregnant Tongan teenager. Instead, I stretched myself on the bare mattress underneath the blanket mound. It was the same mattress I had shared with Nana that night I spat out her kapa pulu. There was no need for me to help set up the party, especially at my step-mother's request. The only woman in the Home of Fe'ofa'aki with any authority was my grandmother and my grandmother was too proud to ever ask me for help.

Nettie peered down at me. 'Oh . . .' Her usual light voice was low and hesitant. 'Do you . . . have hair on your pipi too? Maybe some little brown stuff coming out?'

Chewing on the inside of my gums, I took a while to respond. *Did she even know what she was asking? But . . . did I know?*

Rubbing my still-flat chest I replied, 'Little bits of black hair. No brown stuff.' Then I giggled. 'What, do you not wipe after you kaka?'

The Colonel, with his triangle goatee and thick-rimmed glasses, was the only man in attendance at Lahi's hens night. Unable to sleep amidst the ever-heavy bass, I watched between my siblings and the party from the doorframe of Nana's room. It must've been after 12 am because Adult Swim, the Cartoon Network for grown-ups, was flashing images of a Claymation robot on Nana's ancient television set. Curled up within the threshold of that back door, my toes arched over the sill: the adults partying behind me and the children wheezing in front of me.

Nettie slept wide-mouthed, our little half-sisters under each of her armpits. Lani was spiralled in on herself like a backpack, bowl-cut fringe full of sweat. Lav, with her chunky limbs, was drooling a river, murmuring 'de nada', or at least that's how it sounded. The crook of Nettie's pale elbows cupped our sisters' bottoms like a chicken sitting on eggs.

Turning the other way, I saw all five of my aunts, my step-mother, my nana and three chunky pālangi women I didn't recognise – all gathered for Lahi's last days as a single woman.

My aunts stuffed their faces with puaka; shredded pork flying in chunks as they teased each other for trying to tipsily pin a cardboard tail to a cut-out donkey wearing a grass skirt.

The chunky pālangi women kept to themselves. All three were freckled and mole-ridden – one black-headed, one blonde-headed and one red-headed. Pālangis were lucky to be pale and multicoloured at the same time. Fobs just came in two shades: brown and browner.

In particular, the red-headed pālangi stood out to me because she kept twisting her tomato neck to ogle at Lahi. Whenever Lahi jolted her hips to the music, the woman would turn away and laugh into her short-fingered hand like a schoolgirl. There was something so innocent in that laugh that I couldn't help but giggle a little too.

My aunty Jasmine was the only bridge between the Fobs and the pālangis. Big Sesi trundled through the gaps of the trestle tables, making jokes about her itchy mut while puffing on a cigarette. A pink sateen sash with 'Maid of Honour' in white cursive groped Big Sesi's belly as she called out through a cloud of tobacco, 'Tap that ass.'

On a separate table, my aunts Daisy and Swa waved their tongues, which were stained technicolour from all the Cruisers.

'Aye give us some,' I called out to my youngest aunts, straddling the sill of the doorframe with the soles of my feet.

'Shut it before I burn your lips off,' Daisy threatened; the slices of scars on her veins gleaming under the fluorescent pergola lights.

Swa chuffed so that her reddish-blonde-black fuzzy bun bobbed. 'Puff-puff-pass, you know-it-all.'

Together, my youngest aunts cracked up at me. I glared as they took more swigs of hypnotic liquid.

'Aw, real smart coming from someone who dyes her straw-filled head!' I retorted over the doof-doof beats.

The air stunk of charcoal and petrol. Mumma, ever rooted on her feet, waded her budding belly between her sisters-in-law, offering them cupcakes she'd decorated with eggplant purple icing.

Trying to pin the tail on the donkey, Aunty Heilala, with her picked-apart face half-covered by a blindfold, squealed as she wobbled off balance. Pinning the tail right in the donkey's wide black pupil, Heilala removed her blindfold and squealed again, this time at her lack of aim. For some reason, this made my nana laugh until her afro puffed up like a plume of ash.

Sitting next to Lahi on a plastic outdoor bench, Nana slammed her melon fists into her thighs, trying to catch her breath. 'Das why no pēpē, this mohe 'uli no no wea stick.'

In a large Hawaiian print button-down, which came from Lowes in Mounty Westfields, Lahi sat silently next to her mother. I could tell my aunty was grumpy from the way her throw-cushion arms remained folded over each other and how her freckled cheeks were tinged red.

Every now and again, I spotted Lahi staring at the pālangi woman with the red hair. My mother-aunt made a big show of fidgeting with the laces on her Converses and the pockets on her cargo shorts. Then she flicked her eyelashes up and down like a moth heading towards the light.

The red-head sharply turned away from Lahi's gaze. She looked as stiff as the cardboard cut-outs of the pale hula-hula dancers that decorated the backyard – pink nose up in the air. What was going on between my namesake and this fiery blotch of a woman?

Red Head, having lost her girlish giggles, was the only woman at the hens night who looked more unhappy than Lahi. She rested her fiery mop on the shoulders of her friends, blinking her short lashes so slowly and heavy it was as if she was trying to get something out of her eye. *Probz drunk too.*

I reckoned the pālangis were Lahi's colleagues at Mulctuary Money Management. Each weekday, Lahi headed for work at the bank with her suits doused in Calvin Klein; the only place on earth where I didn't know her. Where else could she have found such posh-looking pālangis; nothing like our Bogan neighbour Shazza!

Suddenly, Red Head rose to her feet and glided towards the donkey cut-out, closer to the backyard door, and therefore me. Unlike her companions, who each wore a coconut-bra over their tank tops, I liked how Red Head conducted herself: a single purple lei draped across her spotted maxi dress. Unsticking the donkey's tail and flinging her fiery strands, Red Head sung out in a bell tone, 'Alas, ladies. Have you not all seen me hit my targets at work? Is it really so far-fetched to conclude that I always get my way, at least eventually?'

Gosh, she spoke so posh too!

Then, as if in slow motion, Red Head pivoted to stare directly at Lahi:

'How sad I wasn't able to pin you. Calamitous honestly. Don't accept your apology.'

This was followed by a heavy silence from the two other pālangis, my nana, my step-mum and my aunts. Big Sesi chewed at the end of her ciggie. Daisy and Swa took fresh shots of Jack Daniels. Heilala picked a gaping hole in the centre of her eyebrows. Camellia balanced cupcakes in her arms like a twisted tree. And my grandmother's afro thrummed like thunder as she grumbled under her breath in Tongan.

Breaking out of a trance, Lahi squished her neck to look back down at her Converses.

Eventually, Camellia whistled like wind through the leaves, 'Maybe we knocked back too many drinks, ladies?'

The pillow-faced moans from www.wetpussycats.com echoed in my head and, as I squatted on the sill of the back-yard door, I clenched my fists under my knees and prepared to pounce.

If Lahi truly was *Lebanese*, she'd be cast out like a leper and separated from us forever. I could see it now; in the fire that was flickering in my grandmother's eyes as she gripped Lahi's cargo shorts tightly; in the drunkenness of Aunty Swa and Daisy, which was their attempt to escape; and in the hunched-over shoulders of Big Sesi and Aunty Heilala, who relied on their eldest sister for sharing secrets and getting extra cash.

With my breath pulling at my tonsils, I shook as the familiar scent of salty yoghurt and Impulse's Romantic Spark taunted my senses. If I could push away the tingle that girls gave me, so too could Lahi.

Before I could process my thoughts a second longer, a mass of oil-slicked muscles in blue uniforms emerged from the shadows and broke the silence. 'Knocked back or knocked up? Sorry, ladies, there was a reported disturbance. Party's over.'

Under the pergola light, the mass revealed itself to be two men. The first was a burly blond who was as jacked as Triple H from WWE. The second, slightly shorter, was all long black hair from neck-to-wrist, like Gaston in *Beauty and the Beast*. The sharp shiny faces of both men were shielded in tinted aviators. A crest on either side of their short shirt sleeves said 'Serve & Protect'.

Police. I only ever saw their crisp blue uniforms and leather boots pounding the tiles of Mounty Westfields during the after-school rush. One time, an Asian officer with beefy knuckles paced the front of Si-Seng Mart. 'Chinkoppa', as the local hood-rats liked to call him, was a stocky bodybuilder. His muscles looked like bubbles as he gripped the handle of his taser, which stuck out like a boil on his hip-holster. 'Powers beyond mortal imagination,' Chinkoppa yelled in a high-pitched tone at the red plaid skirts of Loyola girls and at the worn-out Nike trackies of the Chifley College boys. 'Citizens, I own firepower. I'm your worst nightmare.'

I had cowered into my father's tensed thigh as we tried to side-step around Chinkoppa in order to get into the turnstiles of Si-Seng Mart. One blonde-headed Loyola chick stuck up her rude finger, French-tipped acrylics and all. Chifley boys made quick grabs at the saggy crotches of their trackies.

I never forgot one frumpy Fobbo who looked like a soaked sausage roll. While strumming a ukulele, he yelled out, 'Go eat dog, cop kient.' It was the one and only time I saw Dad laugh out loud in public.

Back at the hens night, the officers that notified all of my drunk aunties of a 'disturbance' were different. Triple H's skin was as shiny and tanned as rotisserie chicken. Gaston smiled with a fine pearly set of teeth shining underneath his crooked moustache, which looked taped on. The women in my family and the add-on pālangis were rooted to the spot. As the police came closer, their dark-navy uniforms began to crinkle. The badge on their chunky chests, where curly hairs sprouted, was embossed with an eagle. The eagle was the sign of an American officer; I knew this because I watched late-night re-runs of *Cops*, where white hands put brown hands in cuffs.

Confused, I swivelled as the women in my family started to cluck and cheer. Tanned Triple H ripped off his navy shorts in one bicep curl, revealing glittery pink undies. He blew on a whistle attached to a lanyard. 'Now which one of you ladies wants to ride the back of this cruiser?' On cue, the gassed-up Gaston also ripped off his shorts, showing off fluoro yellow undies. Techno beats started to play from a portable speaker that he dug out from his pulsating crotch. In unison, the two men stripped off their shirts, revealing tummies so tight they looked like cemented bricks. Together, the police officers thrust their hips in rhythm. The forbidden thing between men's thighs suddenly exposed itself: shafts of flour and sacks of sugar jiggled in too-tight underwear.

My heavy-set aunts became undone, tumbling towards the dancing ding-dongs like a rugby team. Shaking out her messy blonde-red bun, Swa called out, 'Hash. Bhang.' Big Sesi pulled off her sash and swirled it in the air above her head, pushing her apple belly between the men. Her bobbing tummy rubbed up against Triple H's abs. Nana watched on from the trestle tables with a frown, shaking her afro vehemently as Aunty Daisy attempted to drag her into the dance. Meanwhile, Aunty Heilala poked at Gaston's stiff sides with a sharp fingernail as if she were jabbing at her own craters. Even pregnant Mumma joined in, shimmying that blossoming baby bump between her infertile sisters-in-law. The blonde-haired pālangi pulled off her coconut-bra, tied it around Triple H's veiny neck and pulled at it like a leash. The black-haired pālangi pulled off Gaston's crooked moustache and thrust it between her own coconut-bra. Both called out over the doof-doof beats, 'Yeeeaaaaaah.' The dancing d-bags kept up their routine; eyes hidden under reflective aviators so they were nothing but bodies shuffling. In the middle of it all, I spotted Lahi and Red Head creeping into the darkest corner of the yard.

Curiouser and curiouser, I followed, desperate to escape.

Lahi and Red Head were stomping towards a side gate. Sticking her pink nose in the air again, Red Head's single purple lei fluttered across her quick-rising chest. Lahi hopped to catch up.

I peered through a slit in the side gate's wooden slats. A small concrete lane rested between the House of Fe'ofa'aki and Nana's garage full of ngatus. In the dark, dark laneway were silhouettes of wheelie bins and Lahi and Red Head's shadows . . . hugging. My ears swam in the whistles, catcalls and doof-doof music, on-top of the faint mews from stray kittens, birthed by Nana's feral felines.

Red Head's voice tinkled like a bubbler. 'Just say you love me, just once, just say . . .' Then her jaw began to shudder and whatever else was about to come out of her mouth became two sets of white teeth cracking against each other.

'Kate. Katie. Honey. Leave me alone to die,' Lahi cried; breaking their kiss. She continued in a whisper, 'But I remember everyone who leaves.' For what was she but a toddler whose pālangi dad had bolted off to England when she was just two years old?

With a hiccup and a swift shift, Red Head, who I now knew as Kate, shoved Lahi into the side of the garage. My aunt's pillowy sides shafted the line of wheelie bins as she exclaimed involuntarily, 'Patooki!'

My muscles tensed and my calves burned at the choice between staying hidden or revealing myself to shield Lahi from such a bully of a woman. But before I could do anything, Kate seethed in hiccups: 'Your effed-up Islander family ruined us. Aren't you better than that?'

Slowly, Lahi's shadow rose from the bins. She brushed at her breasts, which fell into her stomach, fell into her thighs. Silence thickened until Lahi burst. 'Ohana means family and family means together. Life's not fair. I am Islander.' Then Lahi stalked towards the wrought-iron fence that made up the front of the House of Fe'ofa'aki, disappearing into the dark, dark streets of Mounty County.

Through the gaps of the gate, purple plastic petals fell at my feet. When I looked up, the gate was open and Kate's orange hair shimmered like a sunset. Her long lashes were clumped with tears and flecks of mascara. Her spotted chest, now bare, quivered like jelly. Sniffing, she bent over and extended her short-fingered hands, which were as delicate as a sprig. Her cold palm on my upper arm soothed me like aloe vera.

'Little Meadow,' she whispered. 'Please look after her.'

SALT

Tu'utaki. Warrior of great strength. On the edge of a mountaintop, he squatted and waited for a sailing army of men from Fiji. Tu'utaki's enormous frame of maka was known far and deep throughout the South Pacific. Staring over the moana, he felt the enemy approaching – so connected to the moana he was.

The army of Fijians were waging war because Tu'utaki stole a woman, Yasi, from their land without permission. In that theft, Tu'utaki's endless shadow reigned over Yasi's village and slaughtered every man and boy that dared to take up arms.

A great warrior took what he wanted and Tu'utaki wanted Yasi, whose skin was the scent and colour of sandalwood. Yet, even as a wife, Yasi retained the bloodshed of her brothers, especially when it trickled between her thighs with each full moon. So, whispering with the birds, Yasi hatched a way to be released from her husband's stronghold.

While Tu'utaki continued to wait upon the cliffside, he ordered his wife, 'Touch.' Silently, only vaguely understanding, Yasi bent low despite her menstruation. Then the great warrior demanded, 'Kai.' Mute, Yasi gathered talo and waited for the moment her husband's massive crown of fuzzy locks wavered from the ocean.

The veins on Tu'utaki's neck, which held his own bloodline, pulsated as he spoke, 'Drink.' Yasi returned with a young coconut full of juice. Snapping his trunk-like fingers, Tu'utaki cracked the husky shell. As his crown of curls fell once more, Yasi leapt upon him, her thick thighs curling around his throat. Tu'utaki's pulsating veins constricted against the pressure between the legs of a stolen woman.

But the fall of a great warrior was not without sacrifice. As Tu'utaki's shadow plummeted off the cliff, so too did Yasi. Her mahana hair rose above her and fluttered feather-like as she sank to the bottom of the moana. Blood meeting water. Sandalwood meeting sand.

However, the moana did not claim Tu'utaki. Instead, the great warrior plummeted like a stone until he was impaled, upright, on the top of a palm tree. When the sailing army of men from Fiji came, Tu'utaki's shadow loomed over them still.

16.

*C*oconut. That's how big baby was in Mumma's womb by the time my mother-aunt got married. A mix of fibro, brick and muddy grass blurred along the back-seat windows of our dinged Tarago as we rumbled down Carlisle Avenue. Looking over my shoulder, I saw Jared, Corey and Nettie in the second row of back seats playing Spotto – a game where we punched each other in the ribs if we spotted a yellow car. The loose sleeves on Jared's suit jacket were wrapped across a blue tie hanging from Corey's manioke neck. Like a potato bouncing, Corey thrashed in the headlock as a series of milk-coloured blows went into his starchy sides. Those punches were delivered by my sister, Nettie. Thwip. 'Heheh.' Thwip. 'Heheh.' Nettie giggled through the chiffon trimmings of her pearlescent flower girl dress.

'Wutta. Spit. Dummy,' Jared teased with shallow breaths as he struggled to keep Corey down.

'Puck you,' Corey aggro-cried, jerking and shoving both our siblings into the sides of the van.

'Oh, don't headbutt me,' Nettie wailed.

Curving sharply around a roundabout, Dad hollered from the driver's seat, 'Oi. Watch it. If youse wreck your clothes I'll wreck youse.' His voice made me turn away from my siblings to face the front of the car. My father's earthy eyeballs were bursting out of his skull – the top button of his button-down fastened tightly over his Adam's apple.

'Watch yourselves,' Mumma repeated, glaring through the rear-view mirror. Her satin red maternity dress looked like a clot of blood. 'Brothers can't play dirty with their sisters like that anyway.'

As the only kid slim enough to squish in the middle of two bulky baby seats, I sat in the first row of back seats. On my left, closest to the sliding door, was Little Lani, dressed in layers of pink tulle and white stocking. On her feet were enormous red boots; the heel wobbling up and down whenever Lani kicked the back of Mumma's seat. On my right, with a patch of drool on her satin-covered waist, was Little-little Lav. 'I itch itchy,' she dribbled, now old enough to string full sentences, but still young enough that her words came out in spillages of spit.

'Dee-nah-dah. Swipey da scratchy like do me like big girl,' Lani replied, making a show of slowly slapping at her stockings while she kicked, kicked, kicked.

As the Tarago bumped over a speed hump, I steadied my sisters. Their wobbly baby seats were really just an illusion of safety, in case any coppers pulled us over. No matter how tight Dad forced the belts the baby seats jostled – a consequence of buying second-hand goods at Flemington Markets.

Yeah, we were povo, but today was different because our wedding attire was for real new. The layers of white tulle and satin that made up my flower girl dress stunk of chemicals, which meant no one had worn the garment until me. In fact, I knew the dress was made *specifically* for me. In the weeks leading up to Lahi's wedding, and as Mumma's belly grew, Nana routinely dropped off plastic bags full of fabric. 'Chinaman. Jussupah load,' she declared. 'Making for best us cheep, very cheep.'

Mumma sighed in strained tones. 'Mālō, Mam.' Her 'mum' sounded like 'ma'am', bough forearms burdened with loads of embroidered lace and plastic-looking satin. After these visits, Mumma handed Nana wads of fifty dollar bills.

The mystery about Fobs was that we were always broke until it came to three things: weddings, funerals and church. Then all of a sudden we were walking ATMs.

I never understood how Mumma gathered the money, but Nana never questioned it; just took the cash in her melon fingers and counted each corner of every note. While she did this, my dad's mother repeated with an air of fuss, 'No needing, Kamill. Doing flee an'fing for *my kids* aye.' Over the weeks, I started to realise Nana never spoke full Tongan with Mumma. Instead, she opted for the broken English reserved for her grandchildren. All that baby-talk made Mumma's maroon-coloured eyelids twitch as if her bark-skin was full of termites. After all, the one thing Nana and Mumma truly had in common was that they were both born in Tonga . . . it was all kinds of awkies.

As we pulled up to the House of Fe'ofa'aki, I tried to catch a snippet of what my parents were murmuring about. Hidden staples in the stitching of my dress poked into my sides as I bent forward, pretending to do up the buckle of my shiny pleather shoes.

Mumma rustled, 'Do you think Lahi would be tickled pink if she could adopt some of my kids? I saw on the news that the gays were doing it. Against the law, mind you.' Mumma's plum-sized knuckles were warped in the reflection on my shiny shoe straps. She had gained a massive amount of weight, even for a pregnant woman. *So much for the Slim&Trim!*

Jerking up the handbrake, Dad chuckled. 'Youse know what they say, marriage then carriage.' Milky scalp gleaming in my shoes, I wondered what would happen if I actually touched my father's head. Would he fall down a cliff and onto a palm tree like the great warrior? Or would nothing happen, proving my father was mortal? The veins in my knuckles twitched, as my thoughts felt blasphemous. Back then, I only ever imagined reaching for my father; could not yet move beyond him.

'Well, youse agree, was carriage then marriage for us,' Dad went on, his tone deepening by several octaves.

'Hmph,' Mumma retorted. 'Your picnic basket sister is acting like she owns these kids. I'm telling you now, Jared, she's on thin ice.'

Women falling into other women. Bearing children before the exchange of vows. I knew then, without really having the words to express it, that Mumma's out-of-wedlock births were no different to Lahi liking women.

Whatever else my parents discussed was drowned by my five siblings trying to shove their way out of the Tarago. My long fingers twisted in moist and tiny hands as I unbuckled Lav from her booster. All the while the bub of the family dribbled and fidgeted, 'Do-Dora.' The sequins on her dress caught under my nails. Trying to break free, Lav kicked my forearm, and the sharp plastic cut the skin of my pinky.

I cried out in pain, then screamed in my little sister's face: 'Sit still or I'll mama your brains in!' I tugged Lav's buckle for good measure. She spat raspberries in response. Like a baby myself, I sucked on my finger and pouted.

At the back-back seats, Corey was thwacking on the windshield of the boot and wailing, 'Heckin' help, got kidnapped.' The baby seats meant that anyone sitting in the back-back was imprisoned; forced to wait for the boot to be opened so they could escape.

'Shut it,' Dad retorted as he got out of the Tarago. 'Who'd wanna steal youse anyway?'

17.

*B*lossomed blush. Matted mascara. Layered lipstick. My mum-aunt, who wore bulky suits to work and extra-extra-extra-extra-large boxer shorts to bed, was covered in make-up. The upstairs living room, where Lahi was getting ready, was doused in sticky hairspray and stinging acetone. A rush of reggae rhythms blasted through large foam speakers, out the balcony double doors and rasta'd across the rest of Mount Druitt.

The House of Fe'ofa'aki felt like eggs scrambled in a pan. A hair straightener, two hair dryers and a single curler – all eliciting slivers of steam; each protruded from the only power socket in the upstairs living room by the frayed blue couch. Thick pink wax strips with carpets of follicles littered the floor. A black plastic bag was filled with empty Cruisers, ant-covered Macca's cups and squished ciggie butts. My aunts were a collection of mahana curls and powdered freckles.

Their multigrain rolls of skin stuffed into tan-white spanx. As they got ready, my four younger and less-favourite aunts squawked over bongo beats like a flock of hornbills. At the stairs, I peeped at them: Aunty Jasmine, in a half-open nightgown, sucked on a lit cigarette. Aunty Heilala patched the dark holes of her face with carefully cut Band-Aid strips. Aunty Swa rubbed coconut oil to the ends of her Woolies-dyed curls. Aunty Daisy snapped at the elastic of her spanx, slapping the rubber aginst her soft-tissued hips.

'Chicken-scratch, got enough gorilla glue?' Daisy grumbled, half of her wiry strands standing statically as she waited for the hair curler.

'Bubba kush it, tiger-limbs,' Aunty Swa blurted, burning the ends of her blonde-red fringe.

'Sucker,' Chubba teased as she emerged from Swa's shag carpet bedroom. Chubba was the only non-aunt of the bridesmaid line-up. She was the daughter of the lead faifekau in our church. Despite her holy status, I called her Chubba-Chup because she had a big head and stick-thin neck, not to mention the bubble-gum mole hanging from her left earlobe. I knew Chubba only a little bit: on the rare occasions she visited the Home of Fe'ofa'aki, she stayed in Swa's room until the whole upstairs smelt of fried manure.

Twirling into the centre of the lounge room, Big Sesi shushed the other bridesmaids in a holier-than-thou tone. Over Big Sesi's apple belly was soft hot-pink fabric, over her large and freckly face was delicate white-netted trimming connected to a fuchsia headband – making her look like

Mother Mary. Placing another lit cigarette under her netting, Big Sesi mumbled, 'As Maid of Honour, I say ya'll way past the beauty sleep thing. Trust me.' All my aunts bellowed and clucked.

Comforted by the familiar sound, I climbed to the top of the steps and Lahi appeared before me. The woman I was named after was fidgeting at the Fanta-stained computer desk on a wonky wheelie chair. Aunty Heilala shuffled between an array of colourful plastic zipper bags. The computer had been turned into a makeshift make-up station, which over-flowed with used Revlon sticks and Maybelline compacts. I knew, without having to look closer, that those powders and waxes were slowly being covered by the ant infestation leftover from our weekend Macca's binges.

Lahi's full frosted face popped out of a silken robe with the word 'bride' embroidered in pink cursive atop her left breast. My namesake had become a decorated couch cushion.

Huffing through a mouthful of bobby pins, Aunty Heilala muttered, 'Meadow Lahi. Stay still, will ya? I'm poking a woman out of you.' Heilala puffed powder over her eldest sister's freckles and kept adding more and more dust until Lahi's beauty spots were completely covered. This new girly-girl appearance made Lahi look exactly like The Matchmaker in *Mulan*. Thinking of the plump, caked-up Chinese woman who looked like a clown made me cringe. *Far, whatever happened to Miss Man? Wutta disgrace.*

'Meadow Si'i, you pricked pore,' Heilala spat my way, bobby pins flying. She'd caught me scratching my scalp.

I was itching because I was trying to piece together the stranger who'd replaced my mother-aunt. Pursing my lips, I continued to scrape the kutus in my follicles as I plopped myself at the head of the stairs. The lice were extra irritated today because of the styling gel Mumma had gooped onto my misshaped braids.

'I'd say you looked blue if you weren't so brownish-gold, Si'i,' Lahi beamed at me. She widened her kimono-like sleeves for a hug, and I crawled into her sizeable sides like a limp little lizard. Unsure of what to say, I whined as Aunty Heilala tugged at my crooked plaits until they were undone.

'Hipa and rammed with critters,' Heilala exclaimed, her elongated nails clawing against my scalp. She spoke through a glob of saliva as she pried open a bobby pin with her teeth. 'That Camellia. You'd think she'd stop popping out babies long enough to clean up the ones she already got – so ungrateful. If I could have kids, it'd be a different story.'

Lahi smoothed a sweaty palm over my forehead, knocking Heilala's claws off me. 'If we could have kids?' Lahi scoffed, bringing me closer into her folds. 'These *are* our kids.'

Hiding my face in the folds of Lahi's upper arm, I rested my cheek against the elastic strap of her bra. Salty sweat. Ocean Breeze Rexona. Whiff of Calvin Klein. Lahi's familiar scent settled me. She wasn't all gone. Her muchness was just hidden underneath. But her muchness was changing: she was not just my Lahi anymore, soon she would be the wife of Lotemi from Popua.

Will you change with me too? I felt like we were going to a funeral rather than a wedding – eleven-and-a-half years old and already burying my second mother.

As the morning wore on, my mahana tendrils were re-done into a bun the size of a bouquet. Aunty Heilala stuck me with so many bobby pins I felt like a walking pin cushion. The new style didn't help; the kutus twitched their thousand legs across my gel-coated follicles, desperate to escape.

Gathering up her dressing gown, Lahi went into her bedroom to get stuffed into a wedding dress. My aunts followed, now completely dolled up in matching purple taffeta like a line of rotund geishas. Even Aunty Heilala found time between fixing my do and caking up the bride to squeeze into her own copycat dress.

My aunts, plus Chubba, spent all morning fumbling and yelling over each other for missing earrings, for extra bobby pins, for a smoko and for a turn with the curler. But as soon as they were wedding-ready, the hems of their skirts made short tails at the back of their mauve high heels. Instead of bridesmaids, they all looked like Barney the Dinosaur.

The Islanders must've thought otherwise because all of them fawned in front of an over-the-shoulder camera, held by a stout Tongan man with a bushy beard. I recognised him from Fakamē, the annual church day in which Tongan children dressed in all white and performed verses, sang hymns and re-enacted Biblical scenes.

'Ihu nofo ki lalo. You ruined my good side,' Aunty Jasmine screeched with a stomp. Her swollen yet manicured toes poked from her heels, shining rose-tinted shades of Pink Lady apples.

My aunts, plus Chubba-Chup, only dispersed from the camera's lens when Lahi yelled from her bedroom for assistance. 'Let's keep it moving, heifers!'

As ever-dutiful sisters, Aunty Jasmine, Aunty Daisy, Aunty Swa and Aunty Heilala bounced on each other, gasping and squealing at what they saw. Shuffling my feet, I reluctantly followed. Beyond the wonky heart-shape I once graffitied with Lahi's Ocean Breeze Rexona can was a primped and polished woman glittering in princess-puff white.

'Tiny waist makes an instant virgin,' Big Sesi crooned from behind her eldest sister, pulling tighter at Aunt Meadow's laced straps.

'I – I – I . . .' Lahi stammered as her sloppy sides got stuffed. 'Didn't mean – to – go – this far.'

No one heard. No one but me. My face started to melt and my nose started to run. I hated this. I hated that Lahi was getting married. Getting married in make-up, which she never used. Getting married in a dress, which she never wore. Getting married to a man, which she never desired. Ever since www.wetpussycats.com I knew. I knew Lahi was (and I did not shy away from the word now) a *lesbian*.

Sniffing snot back up my nose, I slumped my shoulders in defeat. What could I have done back then? I was just a kid, unable to fully comprehend the sacrifices women like Lahi had to make for family and culture.

As my mother-aunt struggled to breathe, her sisters fixed her gown. Heilala hollered in a gooey voice, 'Lotemi is lucky to have picked you before you glammed up. All these Freshies be goin' war over you.'

Squatting, Aunty Daisy and Swa shoved Lahi's flattened feet into wedged, eggshell-coloured high heels. 'Cut it out,' Daisy yelled in frustration. 'Hold it, hold it,' Swa bubbled, sucking in the air around her. Once they finished fixing Lahi's heels, both ladies stood up and declared in unison, 'Even you can't blow this, sis.'

'You blow *after* the nuptials,' Big Sesi jeered under her fascinator.

Once the final touches were made, my aunts, and the loitering lollipop, stepped back and cooed. Slowly, Aunty Meadow blinked her elongated lashes through her sisters – right at me. 'Wudd'ya reckon, Si'i?'

I swallowed, a lump of kapa pulu caught in my throat. How could I tell her the truth? I wanted to shred sateen lacing, tear at soft netting, rip into the intricately embroidered sequins – wreck it all until I found Lahi again. Lahi with her baggy basketball tees and boy boxer shorts. But all that came out of my trembling mouth was: 'Who's that girl I see?'

Smoothing the bodice of her gown with stubby fingers, Aunty Meadow stared down at herself; a big Brown woman sashayed and glittered in gossamer. Only Lahi's nails were familiar. No polish. No acrylic. No nothing. Just plain keratin chewed down to the bud. 'Who's this girl?' Meadow Senior said out loud, looking back at me. 'She's one that brings honour to our family.'

18.

*E*longated and glistening like an Uncle Toby's fruit roll-up, a limousine turned into Avery Street on eight fully silver rimmed wheels. I finally understood the meaning of rich: crazy stretch metal. Pouncing from the shiny hood, between the headlights, was a chrome cat leaping in mid-air. The ornament looked exactly like Scar, right before Simba kicked him off Pride Rock and into a den of double-crossed, double-hungry hyenas.

All five bridesmaids, with their Zazu-like screeches and dinosaur-inspired dress tails, flocked to the flash car. 'Pakololo girls, we ridin' and pimpin',' Swa hollered, her Quarter Pounder face half-hidden in thick sunnies.

'I'm the pimp, you the skanks,' Big Sesi quipped under her fascinator. She was referencing Xzibit — an African-American rapper who had a show called *Pimp My Ride*. Every episode he'd find some poor loser with a run-down poo-box, and completely upgrade his car into a shiny new toy straight from a *Fast and Furious* movie. But there was no gangsta rapper coming to save this poor family from our run-down Tarago.

Instead, a tall pālangi man stepped out from the driver's seat of the limo. He wore thick white gloves and a cardboard-stiff grey three-piece suit. *Bugs Bunny!*

Adjusting the shiny black paddy cap that matched his leather dress shoes, the driver stepped cautiously over the muddied gutter of our front yard. He bellowed, 'Mud spelt backwards is dum – let's step on it.'

Leering inside the vehicle, I discovered white leather-lined seats, rainbow-hued lights, a mirror separating the driver from the passengers, silver buckets of ice crammed with champagne and flute glasses that sung 'Be Our Guest'.

'Bleeding for the back seat,' Aunty Daisy proclaimed, a whir of taffeta. 'Puff, puff, pass,' Swa squealed. 'Suck it,' Big Sesi and Chubba yelled. Heilala was the only one who remained silent, soaking in her surroundings. Bongo beats played to the tune of long-long-di-long-long pop! Within seconds, my classless aunts had turned this limo into any other doof-doof wagon speeding down Carlisle Avenue.

'Squish in the back, kernels,' came Lahi's blanket-soft voice from behind me, my sister Nettie and my brother Jared. Shuffling all three of us into the limo, my mother-aunt was shimmering like a watery mirage under the made-up make-up.

'One day, Aunty, I'll get married in a pretty dress too. Then after have babies?' Nettie chimed, twirling in her own white dress, as she sat down.

Squishing himself right next to Lahi, Jared pinched the sides of our aunt's stuffed waist with a big soda-stained grin. 'So I come up after Net and Mead and give the ring to Uncle?' Jared questioned every step as if he was preparing for a grand final. Then he chuckled to himself. 'What if I don't give it? You can't get married.' The only person as close to Lahi as me was my brother. When Mummy Le'o died, Lahi made a promise to attend every one of his footy games. Each try he scored she'd buy him a McChicken. At Jared's last match against the Minchinbury Jets, he nabbed himself six burgers.

Patting Jared on his fuzzy head, Lahi twitched her puffy and powdered cheek to try to force a smile. Sighing, I climbed over my siblings to sit near Aunt Daisy, who was skulling down a flute of bubbly.

The limo smelt like gum leaves dipped in Dettol. Staring through the small opening in the glass partition, I watched as Bugs Bunny hopped into the driver's seat, adjusting his paddy cap.

Pop, bubble, crackle went another champagne bottle. 'Roof off,' my aunts Daisy, Swa, Heilala, Jasmine and even Chubba-Chup yelled as we pulled away from Avery Street. The limo took the extended route back onto the main road as it was too long to do a U-ey.

Throughout the drive, I kept leaning heavily into Nettie, who'd started nibbling on her wedding-ring nail.

Mount Druitt was falling behind us, unable to stick to such luxury. Fibro houses turned to stacked brick apartments to concrete fields of warehouses until we were going one hundred kilometres per hour on the M4. Jared picked his nose and yabbered on about riding rich. Nettie nestled between us, comfortable in her middle-child middle-seat, sucking on her wedding ring knuckle. Kutus burnt under my fingernails.

Pop whoop went Chamillionaire's 'Ridin' Dirty'. My aunts and Chubba were partying like it was the hens night all over again.

'Oh, move. You're going to squish all the blood from me,' Nettie grumbled. In a huff, I kept pulling at the nits in my scalp. To kill a kutu, all I needed to do was balance the nit on the cuticle of my thumbnail and, with my opposite thumb, press down on the parasite like a jaffle-maker until it fully exploded into an orange blot of blood and guts. Not that time in the limo though. I kept the creature alive; little brown specks embedding into the leather seat, desperately searching for a vein.

We glided off the M4 via Woodville Road and the kutus just kept coming. Every time my fingertips foraged through my follicles, I found one, two, sometimes three little lice writhing.

Lyrics about rollin', patrollin' and grindin' blasted as we pulled up into the kerb at The Trongate, Granville.

In front of my family's church – the church that held my mother's funeral and now my mother-aunt's wedding – I flicked my head back and began laughing. The nits had come to pray.

19.

*E*ncrusted in mother-of-pearl, Nana was decked out in a handmade puletaha the colour of lavender and pointed satin heels the shade of blueberries. Her hips were thickened with layers of feather-weaved ta'ovala. The kafa that bounded her puffy waist held a collection of oyster shells painted in silver. Upon her freckly neck lay a shiny garland of pearls, each the size of a pebble. All of this made Nana rainbow-radiate in the sunlight.

'Stealah, stealah. My daughta be stealah,' Nana wailed as Aunt Meadow stepped onto the large ngatu that covered the entire front of Tokaikolo Church. Slowly, I skipped on the edges of bark, unsure if it was a threshold I was willing to cross. My brows pinched when the girly-girl version of Lahi grabbed onto her mother; the beads of her wedding gown intertwining with the husk-like strands of Nana's kafa. My grandmother pressed her withered lipstick into her eldest daughter's powdered cheeks. The black liquid that coated their lashes held steady as both women cried.

Scraping my dress shoes across the ngatu, I wondered what their tears meant: was Lahi crying because she was in love, or because she *wasn't*? Was Nana crying because she was proud, or because she was *relieved*?

'Oi, you mut, stop itching,' Big Sesi snapped as she tapped the butt of her freshly lit ciggie on my forehead. Rubbing my temple, I whinged, 'Far, you nearly burnt me!' Big Sesi didn't care, shoving me along the ngatu ahead of my aunties and grandmother. 'Don't tempt me,' Sesi grumbled, the blush on her cheeks clumped like cellulite. 'Be grateful them cooties not in ya pipi.'

I could feel Nettie and Jared's heavy breathing as they trailed Big Sesi, their new footwear clapping quickly against the ngatu.

Adjusting her fascinator, Big Sesi shoved Hot Dollar plastic baskets into mine and Nettie's hands – cheap imitations of the woven fibres Tongans used to make a binga basket. Jared held a pillow so small it looked like it came from Barbie's Dreamhouse. While we lined up, the Tongans of the westside filed into Tokaikolo decked out in bright puletahas and ta'ovalas. Among them were my step-grandfathers, my uncles, my cousins, my second-cousins and my third-cousins.

I also spotted the familiar outlines of my family: Dad with his mountain-range shoulders; my little sisters nestled in each of his muscular arms; pregnant Mumma, like a walking tree with a nest in its branches; and Corey following close behind, making popping noises with his finger and cheek.

It became clear to me that my grandmother was making the distinction between her blood-related grandchildren and her step-grandchild. I reckoned she even considered Lani and Lav to be her step-grandchildren because they looked too much like Mumma for her to fully love. I remembered my father's words to Nana the day he collected us from the Home of Fe'ofa'aki: *Nufing, Mum. Just youse, ours, same. Just together.* But in that moment at the steps of Tokaikolo, I simply gripped my basket full of petals and puffed my chest with pride. The separation made me feel important, like one of the main characters in my favourite stories: Lilo, Mulan, Ariel, Lucy, Belle, Alice, Violet and now, Meadow Reed.

We waited patiently as all the guests were seated. Tokaikolo, which my grandmother helped to establish in the mid nineties, was a wonky wooden structure of tacky timber and peeling paint. It stood on flood poles ridden with mites and its ceiling was pointy like a pyramid. The windows on Tokaikolo's walls were empty squares with no flyscreens. The only thing that protected us from the sharp sun or rushes of rain were boards made of resin and wooden particles. If Tokaikolo could hold us Tongans together, then maybe there was a God . . .

Met by a red carpet aisle, at the very end of the church, Nettie and I suddenly found ourselves standing before our newest uncle. Skin slick and shiny as olive oil. Busted brown head as flat as a saucepan. Stance as long as a chopstick. Gait as wonky as a whisk. These were the features that made up Lotemi, Lahi's soon-to-be husband. When he looked down at me, his eyes were tea-saucer large. 'Meadow Si'i,' Lotemi said in recognition, his voice as thick as batter. Then he bent down low so we were eye level. His lashes were as long as ī, a type of Tongan fan. 'No liking me, huni?'

Shoving my flower basket between us, I poked out my tongue.

Lotemi chuckled. It was a tender and filling sound and I felt myself melting a bit. 'I knowing why you no like me. I'm steal you mum. But promise, she no leaving you.'

Before he could say another word, Lotemi was ushered to the sanctuary by a man who looked like Andrew Fifita. He had long lashes too but a crooked back; dressed in a black suit as well, but a frangipani pinned to the welt pocket. This was my uncle's best man.

My chest began to tighten as my aunties lined themselves beneath the entrance like sardines. Nana was heckling at us from the back of the bridal line: useless vowels and the sharp sting of Chanel perfume.

Our cue came when the hymns finally dimmed. I turned to my aunt Daisy, who was first in the bridesmaid's line. She nudged me and Nettie to start the procession. Facing forward, we started to walk down the aisle, dyed purple petals twirling from our fingertips. Even though we were sisters from the same mother, we skipped out of sync. With every half-step, I tugged on Nettie's elbow to bring her forward with me, but this only made her stumble.

'Oh, you klutz,' Nettie seethed as rose petals burst from her fist like confetti. 'I'm practising for my big day, don't ruin it.'

We continued to wonkelate towards the altar at the sanctuary where Lotemi waited. Only then did I realise there was just one man behind him: the best man. Even a hafekasi like me understood that was weird. *Where the rest of his family?*

At the centre of the altar was a faifekau, a pastor, who was as round as a bowling ball. All around me were familiar bloated faces, lining either side of the aisle on wooden rows. The pew-packed Tongans wringed their neck rolls to watch us.

Canned beef in my throat, this was all starting to feel too intimate. Somewhere in my head, lyrics about a dying spot of land in the middle of the ocean and images of a dead Mummy Le'o played on repeat.

At the altar, my sister and I waited. A single harmonica hummed an upbeat tune. Then our brother marched down the strewn-petal aisle holding up the silk pillow. Jared's spotlight-bright face beamed from side-to-side as he soaked up the attention. He handed the rings to Lotemi, who ruffled his hair. Jared took his position alongside our sister and me. In pālangi ways, the procession was mucked up. But in my nana's way, it was just right.

The harmonica started again as each of my aunts walked down the aisle. Daisy, with her squished toes tapping one-step-two-step-together. Swa, with her bulky sunglasses removed, wobbling on her heels, broad black rings for pupils. Chubba-Chup quickly followed suit with a sticky smile beneath her syrup-flat nose. I couldn't help but think: *Wutta suck-up.* Aunty Heilala's dark feet oozed like mud between her flats; the band-aids across her face hidden by a fresh layer of foundation. Then Aunty Jasmine, with her bright pink fascinator, as if she was from the Big Apple rather than the bum-end of Sydney, started to walk down the aisle just as the harmonica reached its highest pitch.

At last, the mouth organ whistled to a hihooom close, and up from the church speakers came the pre-recorded piano tune of the bridal chorus. Together, one hundred and twenty-seven Tongans rose. The majority were my extended family, the village of Afeni; which was my grandmother's maiden name. I'd seen their familiar faces fill these termite-ridden walls every year for Fakamē. There were also some darker-skinned Tongans, who carried Tata's familiar wide nose and preggo tummy. And lastly, in the far left corner of Tokaikolo, there was a small group of Tongans I'd never seen before. I guessed these were Lotemi's relatives; a small handful of Fobs he'd shipped over for the ceremony. As all these Tongans stood, the wooden pews whined in relief.

A swirl of purple and white like a budded dawn emerged at the church doors. Aunt Meadow, whose folds of freckles were covered in a veil, shone like a blanket of snow: shimmer of sequins, shiny satin and lacquered-look of lace. Where Meadow Senior appeared as a hazy frost, Nana and her stormy afro were starkly defined. Rainbow oyster shells on her droopy waist. Galaxy-like puletaha. Tears clung to the ngatu marks on her face and into her pearl necklace.

As my grandmother and my aunt strolled towards us, towards the altar, my chest pounded with each of their one-step-two-step-together steps. The heart I once tagged on Lahi's bedroom door with a deodorant can – *my* heart – crept up my oesophagus. Without looking at me, Aunty Meadow arrived at the altar and kissed her mother on the cheek. Then she fully turned her wide back on us in order to face her almost-husband. And my heart screamed: *Please. Please promise after this you'll take me back.*

As the faifekau droned on about the unions of man and woman, which he declared sacred, my eyes fell open and shut in lashy waves: *Tongan men made from worms, hehe.*

Holding back a bubble of laughter, I began swaying on the spot. The scent of roses and saltwater filled my nose. The freckles on Lahi's blanket-back; half-hidden under a blur of lace, wriggled like maggots in cooled lard. In front of me, flecks of gold peeked from skin so dark it was night. Once again, I poked my tongue out at my new uncle, who was smirking at me. Maybe he thought we were playing a game because he quickly poked his tongue back my way. I shoved my knuckles into my mouth to stop myself from sobbing.

'Oh, don't chuck a fit now. I'm learning my lines,' Nettie hissed, her breath like melted plastic against my ear.

When the faifekau started mumbling about 'tauhi 'ofa', which meant 'cherish', 'faka'apa'apa', which meant 'honour', and 'mahamahaki', which meant 'sickness', I stumbled backwards and landed into the forearm of my aunt Daisy. Without a word she cradled me, the thin silver slivers on her wrist cold as a knife; her hands as warm as the flame of a matchstick. As the faifekau kept preaching, I closed my eyes and tried to think happy thoughts: *Dead mum. Pregnant mum. Married mum. Infested house. Infested head. Infested Tongans.*

'Psst.' I turned towards the sound. On the pew adjacent to us was my grandmother. Sweat exuded from her hairy upper lip while the cluster of beauty and sunspots on her face, which marked my family, flushed red. When I finally saw what she was doing, I tried my best not to hyena-heckle: My grandmother was using her thick forefingers and thumbs to widen the endless creases in her eyelids. 'Psssssst,' she spat again. Translation: 'Stay awake, feral.'

Biting the inside of my cheeks I turned back towards the altar as Aunty Meadow and Uncle Lotemi said 'I do' before the faifekau – making their union official.

How many times had Nana yelled at me to 'alu mohe – go to sleep – when she caught me watching a re-run of *The Lion King*? Now, for Aunt Meadow's wedding, she demanded I keep my eyes open! Keep my eyes open to a language I didn't understand to care. Keep my eyes open as Lahi married a man I didn't care to understand. My aunt and uncle pecked on the lips, and one hundred and twenty-seven Islanders cheered, 'Cheehoo!', and my grandmother finally wiped that oozing sweat off her lip. *What did Nana know? What did any of us know?*

20.

*B*efore us, the bright blinding lights of Grand Paradiso, Fairfield. The air was thick with kebab smoke. Next door, in the tinted windows of an Indian sweet shop, I saw my reflection: the twisted twirls of my tendrils loosening from my many bobby pins. I scratched at a patch of sweat forming on the satin in the middle of my chest. In my baby days, Lahi would change in front of me and complain about boob swamp: the summer heat caused rashes under her sloped nipples. 'Sweating from my head, bleeding from my legs. To be a tomboy.' I couldn't help but think of Lahi right now; sweating buckets under her girly wedding gown.

'Wake up, sleeping ugly,' Big Sesi puffed in a plume of smoke. She swiped at my hair, but I ducked as soon as I spotted her pink-frosted flabs in the window reflection. In a huff I whipped back, 'Drag show on the road much?'

'Oh, what a dark and mean girl. Get some manners, thank you very much,' Nettie gasped. She sounded older than her age. Older than me. My sister's milk-skin and golden thread of hair was still perfect. No bobby pins bursting free. No mahana tangles. No sweat patches on her dress. Flashing her gums at me she wrapped herself in Sesi's freckled arms, all white and well-kept.

'Aw, knocked ya on, but,' Jared tittered, his oval-shaped head bouncing up and down. My brother's tie was loose and his tux jacket ruffled.

Big Sesi jostled her fascinator back into place while she sucked on the butt of her ciggie, salvaging every last fleck of tobacco – she'd spent all her money on the wedding. 'Honey, I heard worse.' Then she pushed Nettie into me, and I got thrust into Jared, and we got shoved through the glass double doors of Grand Paradiso.

In the glow of the reception hall, diamond teardrops dangled from the golden branches of chandeliers. The precious stones radiated rainbows when the fluorescent lights hit each shiny curve. Chandeliers hung from a sunset-painted ceiling – portals to heaven. Neon spotlights lit up all four walls of the hall, casting pillars of purple. Hundreds of round tables were clothed in cloud-thick white fabric, decorated with bouquets of red roses bursting from crystal vases. Each table had high-backed padded chairs that looked like mini thrones. My brother and sister bolted off while I swivelled my neck and murmured, 'Far, posh as.'

Every Tongan in The Area was there; seated, standing or sashaying in clacking kiekies. I couldn't pick out any individual because when Islanders got together, we blended like a mountain of clay. Over an ear-thrashing bass speaker blasting ukulele, I discovered that I hardly knew anyone but everyone seemed to know me:

"Oiauē, Musie Si'i,' came a tinkling call from a tall lady decked out in silver diamantes. Her pancake-like flabs were fastened into her dress, which was so shiny she looked like a melted disco ball. I pivoted on my heels and began walking in the opposite direction before she could trap me with a sticky 'uma. Back then, I'd have rather eaten dirt than have strangers press their lips on my face.

'Weh, weh, Malapo.' A gruff chuckle interrupted my escape. I recognised the wood-chipped voice as my step-mum's dad. Grandpa Misi, or simply, Pa. I liked him because he called me by my nana's village name, Malapo, instead of trying to wrap me up in his own side of Tonga, known as Kolonga. Even back then, I understood that Pa had no problem with me being his step-grandchild; he saw every kid that made up the next generation of our people as a grandchild.

Pa was much thinner than my other grandfather, Tata. And, where Tata stood tall, Pa was hunched from years of physical labour. But both my grandpas kept a full head of thick and wavy grey hair.

I tiptoed over to Pa and he gave me a whiskery peck on my forehead. Grandpa Misi was wearing a generic Hawaiian-print button-down, loose dress pants and leather sandals – no ta'ovala because, for reasons I will never know, he was just a weirdo like that.

'Where issa you mum, aye Malapo?' He was referring to his daughter, Camellia, who had the same bark-like skin as him. 'Wunna make your Pa cuppatee?' He laughed like his heart was in his nose and he buried his whiskery upper lip against my forehead again. Pa smelt of sandalwood and wine. Even though I considered him my actual grandparent (I knew him more than Liam, the pālangi grandfather I never met), I avoided his makeshift shack in Blacktown. Pa lived in a cramped houso stacked with decades-old building materials in the front yard and red flags with the crest of Tonga shoved into the slats of street-facing windows. *Mad shame.*

'Dunno, where's Ma?' I shot back, knowing Grandmumma Sela, my step-mum's mum, was probably lost in the crowd. Dementia riddled Ma's brain, so I always needed to remind her who I was: 'Camellia's daughter, but I came out of another woman.'

Pa called out for wine as I snuck off to find a bathroom to hide in. I wasn't even a few steps away before a grainy old voice called out, "Uma, 'uma. Ha'u 'uma, Mafile'o." An incredibly wrinkly lady leant against Big Sesi's enormous love-handles to keep upright.

'Si'i,' Big Sesi demanded from under her fascinator. 'Come here, I want you to meet someone.'

My mouth folded in on itself like I was sucking a Zombie Chew. I could now see the girls' toilet behind the DJ booth, but I knew I couldn't duck Aunt Jasmine.

Reeking of several dizzying perfumes, a hairy mole jiggled on the ancient woman's chest as she bent down to smack her feathery mouth into my cheeks. Wrinkled knuckles locked on my lips, twisting my chin from side to side – her dark, dark pupils prancing as she assessed me. I fidgeted all the while, ready to kettle-burst.

'Listen up,' Big Sesi puffed. 'This is your mum's mum's auntie, so show respect.'

The ancient woman finished looking me over. She laughed toothily, spraying flecks of spit and Juicy Fruit, the same gum Nana chewed, into my eyelids. As soon as her stiff-fingered grip slackened, I dashed into the ever-filling reception.

The ancient woman called out, 'Mafile'o. Mafile'o, come back.'

But like my real mum, I was long gone.

21.

Guests chewed and gossiped for the next hour and a half. It was like being inside Mounty food court, just browner and sweatier. Everyone screeched through well-fed bellies – 'Bawharharharhiiiiiee.' Their laughter reverberated against the grand walls of Paradiso. Every now and then, I caught the smoko-cough of Aunt Sesi as she yelled whenever we ran past, 'Aye. Siddown, muts.' We ignored her, ducking through thickly draped guest tables. I was with Nettie, Jared and Corey; and we were with our cousins, Giselle and Curtis.

Our cousins were the kids of my uncle, Talasi, who was Tata's eldest and only son.

But here's the thing, in Tongan, just like there is no word for aunt, there is also no word for cousin. The children of my parents' siblings were all my brothers and sisters too – that's why I was always so disgusted when my Lebanese friend Sarah would mention that her parents were cousins: for her people, cousin was community; for my people, cousin was incest.

'We girls, you girls, our girls,' Giselle crooned towards me. Even though we were both in Year 6, she looked closer to someone in Year 12 because she was tall, chubby and her bust busted from the straps of her maxi dress. Giselle's earthy skin was riddled with patches of eczema. She kept scratching at her rashes between belting out lyrics from her namesake, Beyoncé Giselle Knowles. I felt as if I were a pile of bones next to her.

We were hiding under the thickly draped white cloths of Table 27, which was the designated kids' area. With boys on one side of the table leg and girls on the other, we played rounds of Slime Yuck: a hand game in which a series of co-ordinated and criss-crossed hand claps climbed up in number until someone lost count and fumbled. Under the table we could hide from all the lipstick-slobber aunts and uncles who demanded 'umas. Above us, bongos blended into the haughty hum of ceaseless vowels; the air thick with sticky perfume and sweat.

'Oh, gosh. Who can count and clap with boys and babies on the brain?' Nettie lamented in our little under-table world, fumbling on the tenth slime-yuck.

'Ask for God to make you preggers,' I teased as my sister glared at me. *Wutta virgin birth weirdo, liking babies that much.*

Giselle hummed in victory, body jiggling as a bulbous beauty spot bounced on the corner of her flaky maroon lips. If Nettie and I were flower girls, Giselle was a tumbleweed.

'Say again, say again,' Giselle sang, her thick fingers intertwined with Nettie's thin ones.

Across from us Jared and Corey, and our boy cousin, Curtis, were a collection of stiff tuxedos and tight ties, huddled together in a scrum.

'Try. Just try, bro,' Jared heaved, smacking the backs of Corey's spasming hands.

'You betted a dollar but you won't get it out of me,' Curtis snickered through the gaps in his crooked teeth.

Corey hissed, 'F-yuck. F-yuck.' Sweat beaded between his brows while the little freckles under his eyes blazed.

It was extremely difficult for my step-brother to express himself. Either he would bottle everything up or explode everything out. As Corey fumbled his counting, I could see how much he was trying to hold himself together. *Looks painful as.*

Buffing her thumbnail, Nettie giggled to herself. 'Oh, know what I heard was yuck? Two girls marrying. Mumma told it was on the news.'

Furry flaps, freckled folds, skin-on-skin and an alleyway hug. That's what I saw. And it wasn't yuck. I bit my lip and snorted at Nettie, 'What do you know about grown lady stuff anyways?'

Knuckles squeezing, Nettie continued with a glint in her flashlight eyes. 'Oh, but we are big girls. We need to know that two girls can't make babies.'

Giselle warbled in agreeance; itching at a dry patch on her forearm. 'Us girls are scrubs like that. Look at all the messed-up stuff we did in the Bible: Eve ate the apple, Delilah cut Samson's hair, Bathsheba seduced King David.' I was too confused to reply, but I remember thinking to myself: *Wutta idiot.*

Humming in thought, Giselle shifted the straps on her chest, covering her pre-mature cleavage. 'God made women lesser to men. So we need to serve them, not destroy them.' Then Giselle raised her flaky mole as she smiled. 'Best way to cater to a man? Feed him, run his bath, give him a foot rub and then supply all his desires.'

Scooting her way between me and Giselle, Nettie asserted herself. 'Oh, yes. That's why women were made.'

Idiots. Both of dem.

22.

'Fēfē? Fēfē' A deep voice reverberated into the microphone. Curiouser and curiouser, I flung my head from underneath the table; standing up and looking on. A rustle behind me meant my siblings and cousins were doing the same. Paradiso was a sea of glittering sausage-stuffed dresses and a tide of woven straw – the guests of Meadow and Lotemi's wedding. The man on the microphone looked like Tweedledee and Dum stuck together; one very huge egg. Tweedledeedum continued in gibberish until he broke out in broken English, 'Off kose, sum pālangi hea wif us at da beaudy Paladisko. Solly my Englan' eh.' The guests laughed in a chorus, 'Ouuuuaaaa.' With a yolk-like chuckle, the MC continued. 'Onli say Donga soon aye. But we welcome, welcome. Welcome wif da plidal laties and glooming man.'

Speakers rolled out a series of strums before a mixture of doof-doof bass and distorted hip-hop beats. The glass double doors of Grand Paradiso swung open and my bridesmaid-aunts made their way between the tightly placed tables towards the dancefloor.

My youngest aunt, Daisy, was first in line; twinkling silver scars across her forearms, waving a pink bouquet above her mahana head, double-stepping to the Michael Jackson beat.

Record scratched. Whitney Houston. Swa and Heilala sprung together like two bobbing coconuts.

Record scratched again. 50 Cent. Up came Chubba-Chup, her bubbly mole pulsating as she stumbled over her feet. The Islanders heckled, 'Eiiiahhh.'

Record scratched again. Disco ditty about a man after midnight kicked in. Aunty Jasmine in all her Pink Lady glory; rolled her belly against the stiff stature of the best man.

Finally, the music stopped and the MC spoke two eternal words: 'Losē Afeni!'

My grandmother stepped out, dressed in an entirely new outfit – a shimmery silver puletaha with gold embroidery. Holey ta'ovala around her waist. Ta'ovala was funny like that; the poorer it looked the richer it was, because it meant the garment had been passed down for generations. And that's exactly what my grandmother had done: married a pālangi in order to secure our place in Mounty County for generations to come.

More and more guests rose to their feet as Nana waded past. I craned my neck and jumped on my tiptoes. Up close, my grandmother's skin was flushed pink and glowed rose gold.

Tears sparkled on Nana's sun-spotted face, creating a rockpool on the blotch under her left eye, which she once taught me was the mark of my father. I slammed my palm into my own bony breastbone, my heart ready to burst. The only woman who was able to bring a tide of Tongans to their feet was my grandmother.

At the centre of the dancefloor, Nana's daughters fell to their knees and cried out to her – it was rude to stand above the head of your elders. My aunts grovelled on their gowns, 'Tulou, tulou!' – 'Excuse us, excuse us!' My grandmother lowered her melon hands and lifted her daughters up one-by-one.

"Oua lau e kafo kae lau e lava,' Heilala exclaimed, wiping at her pinpricked cheeks. This meant, 'Stay positive and count your blessings.'

'Holo pē e tu'u he ko e ngalu e fasi,' Daisy and Swa gasped in unison, which translated to, 'Stand firm and the waves will break.'

'Ko e koloa 'a Tonga ko e fakamālō,' Big Sesi exhaled. 'An expression of gratitude is the treasure of Tonga.'

Then, embraced by her four unmarried daughters, my grandmother took the mic from Tweedledeedum – impromptu speeches were a key staple at Tongan gatherings. Wiping sweat off her brow, Nana exhaled. The crowd called out her name in irregular intervals: 'Los-Losē-sē-Losē-Losē.'

Nana took in a deep breath, and then in fluent English she declared: 'The villages of Malapo and Popua are connected, as we all are, by the fonua. The dirt of Tonga.' The Islanders erupted in cheers; for Nana had transformed us into the House of Roses.

Together, we held our gasps and waited. I could hear the vibration of our vocal cords under the hum of whirling air cons and the vigorous sways of woven fans – ī. The lights from the chandeliers dimmed. Tweedledeedum cracked out, 'Mistah an' Missus Fehoko!'

Me, Nettie, Giselle, Curtis, Jared and Corey – we all jumped up on the cotton-draped dining chairs. Hundreds of Tongans stretched to the tops of their toenails and leant in with chunky chests as they cramped up to catch a glimpse.

And then I saw her: Standing right next to my father, under the arch of the fire escape, was the red-headed pālangi from my mother-aunt's hens night. Kate's pallid face was streaked with watery mascara; her freckly décolletage rising and falling.

Sparks erupted at the grand set of doors, diverting my attention. 'Che. Che. Che,' Tongans cheered. Lauryn Hill wailed from the reception speakers: Singing about strumming pains and a stranger to her eyes.

In a cream kimono-style dress, Aunty Meadow emerged, beside an oversized black suit, to a rip of applause. Her arms were entwined with her husband's jacket sleeves. I knew then that my namesake was gone for good.

My shoulders slumped, my face hardened and I fell back on my heels as I watched on in tears.

My new uncle's doughy mouth was opened wide, revealing a set of straight teeth stained by bits of melted gold. Lotemi's thick black hair was slicked back with oil so his curls stayed still as he bounced up and down in his enormous dress loafers.

'Cheehoo, cheehoo, cheehoo,' went the crowd. Pfffzzt; went the fountain sparklers.

Lauryn Hill wailed and mourned as the newlyweds made their way to the dancefloor, where their family waited.

'Paspasi Mistah an' Missus Fehoko,' Tweedledeedum bellowed over the music. *Mr and Mrs Fehoko.* My heart caved. My soul roared. My tiny brown body twitched and spasmed.

And that's when it happened: Lotemi caught sight of me, just for a split second, and he winked. And then as quickly as he appeared, he was engulfed by the crowd once again, and I was alone.

23.

*L*ast Supper. Only in this version, there were four brides-maid Fobs, and one groomsman Fob. In the middle, a Fob wife and a Fob husband. Aunt Meadow was wiping mascara off with the back of her hammy fist and to my surprise, Uncle Lotemi was helping her, swiping the runs that escaped down her cheeks. Maybe, hopefully, he liked Aunt Meadow as she was: boyish and plain. *But would she ever be that way again?*

Bass boomed from the enormous speakers, pounding my ears like a belt. Below the bridal party was a longer table full of faifekaus that picked at puaka and tore into taro. Faifekaus always got front and centre stage at every Fobbo function. That way, they were the first to be served, the first to give prayer, the first to grab money for the church.

Hopping pigeon-toed, a trio of ta'ahines decked in red feathers stood in unison. Meadow and Lotemi looked down at them. My new uncle called out, 'Pick up, hunis.' The groom and groomsman heckled as Aunt Meadow slapped the side of Lotemi's head. This told me that the first dance item, which was technically a wedding gift, was from my new uncle's side. Red feathers plumed from the ta'ahine's mahana buns while their deep dirt skin shone with lolo. Before every dance, tau'olunga girls were rubbed down with coconut oil (sometimes baby oil) so the money people threw would stick to their moving limbs. Nana once explained that the shinier the girl, the purer.

All three tau'olunga girls stood firm, waiting in anticipation for their song to play. The bare bulky feet of each dancer were pressed firmly and tightly together; also strapped in red feathers. Stocky knees bent, rounded elbows up and out, heavy hands folded onto each other and tight bright-white teeth spread from ear-to-ear.

The faifekaus continued to cut their gums on crackling until, finally, a ukulele strummed and wooden drums tapped and all at once the red-feathered girls moved in unison. Tweedledeedum boomed more vowels.

To dance tau'olunga: Fingers must stay together. Arms must be bent like wings. Ankles must lift and shift while toes remain firmly on the ground. A little head wobble, known as teki, must accompany every dip and half-turn. The tau'olunga weaved Tongan hands into a story, but I could never work out the beginning, middle and end. If only my Gifted & Talented teacher was there . . .

All too soon came pink, blue, red, yellow and green. Money slapped this way and that as Lotemi's fresh-off-the-boat guests, made of just twenty-ish people, stood up to honour their gift; the union of our families and, above all, God. Hundreds of dollars rained as they slapped notes onto the girls' oiled limbs, letting the cash twirl downwards to the dancefloor. One man, with a Moai-looking tattoo on his right bicep, flopped on his stomach and smacked the ground. Even the gorging faifekaus, eternally feasting, were fisted with fifties. Meanwhile, a conga line of oldies in multicoloured puletahas swept in like lorikeets, holding satin-lined hampers filled with bottles of fancy perfume, mangoes, chocolates, and hundred-dollar bills.

Two to a stack, the men in my family carried over kafus, ngatus and finely woven mats entwined with coloured wool. The gifts, which were meant for the bride and groom, were laid at the feet of the faifekaus – the representatives of God.

As the night wore on, so too did the rain of money and the hail of hampers and the clouds of kafus. Tables, half-empty as more and more Tongans joined the dancefloor, contained the remains of puaka and taro, white-sauced chicken breast and untouched steamed broccoli. Eventually, I spotted Dad with Uncle Talasi and Grandpa Misi and so many other meandering men at the bar chugging back bevvies.

I ran towards my father's bald head and embedded myself into his side. Tearily, I murmured, 'Why did we give Lahi away? I already lost one mum. Why do they keep leaving me?'

Smiling tenderly at me, Dad went down on one knee and crooned in my ear, 'Youse look like your mum in your flower dress. She sees you reading and growing – so proud of you.' Dad's Long Beach Blues breath was mixed with fizzy Cola and yeasty sugarcane. I didn't know which mum he meant – Lahi, Camellia, or Mummy Le'o – but his words brought me comfort.

'Weh, weh, Malapo. Gotts mah cuppatea all after,' Pa whistled at me, dunking his whiskers into a large glass of red wine. The top three buttons of his Hawaiian shirt were undone, revealing his sagged and wrinkled shoulders.

Uncle Talasi, with dried flecks of skin around his pouty mouth, ruffled my hair. 'Shouldn't be here, Si'i. Should be singing with your cuzzies. Where's Gizzy?' That was his nickname for Giselle, but I didn't know why he was asking; he was usually too drunk to take notice of her.

Blundering through the men in my family was a tubby and balding Fijian-Indian in a blue suit and rainbow tie. Lahi's best friend, who she met on Oxford Street.

Uncle Tomasi's eyes shone like streetlights when he saw me. 'Oh, honey,' he giggled, swirling a cocktail in his chubby hands. 'Little Meadow, how silly is Big Meadow being? I told her, "Your family will forgive," because I've been there. She wouldn't hear it though. Something about Tongan being different from Curry Islanders.' Once again, Tomasi swirled his cherry-coloured concoction. Then he reached out and affectionately squeezed my nostrils together with his coarse fingertips. 'This is some real queer mess, honey.'

Before I could respond, Dad lifted me up into a hug. My father's goatee twisted as he rumbled over a soft new melody: 'When I danced with youse mummy, I was dancing with youse too.'

High in Dad's arms, I could see the entire crowd of wedding guests clearing away from the dancefloor.

Slowly, Aunt Meadow carried down the hem of her cream kimono-style gown while Uncle Lotemi shuffled his suit jacket back into place.

The newlyweds quavered foot-to-foot, Meadow's unfurled hair tucked under Lotemi's mixing-bowl chin, her long satin sleeves shimmering as she twirled. Big as they were, the pair swayed in the spotlight like angels.

Every now and then, Meadow and Lotemi faced the crowd and bowed, earning cheers of admiration. I could clearly see Lahi's gold tooth glimmer with each flash of a camera. *Meadow Fehoko. Meadow Fehoko.* Again, my breath blocked my tonsils and I squirmed to be released from my father's stronghold. I was struggling so much that Dad's glass of fizzy fell down his suit and splashed my dress. He dropped me to the floor and then bellowed, 'Oi, youse watch it.' The sweetness in his breath gone.

Without a word, I pushed past Dad, Uncle Talasi, Uncle Tomasi and Papa; my flower girl dress stained in Coke. The lateness of the hour blurred the crowd of Fobs into the neon purple lights and the dangling chandeliers. Lost in Wonderland. *Where oh where oh where is Meadow?*

Running like a headless chicken, I finally found myself near the fire escape at the back end of Paradiso, crashing into a wall of orange. Red hair. Blue eyes. I blinked up at the puffy, freckled face of Kate. Beaten-up blush. Mucked mascara. Licked lipstick. A short glass of petrol-smelling water in her dainty fingers; her nails cut-down short.

'Little Meadow,' Kate hiccupped. She slurred her words. Then she hiccupped again.

The red-headed pālangi widened her freckly jaw until she was full showing me the inside of her throat. She yelled open-mouthed, 'Does my heart look infected to you?'

Pālangis like Shazza hated our culture, while pālangis like Kate wanted to be part of it. All the while, us Islanders wanted to be pālangi. *Why?*

Burning from the inside out, I shoved my shaking fist between me and Kate. 'Saw you push my lahi. I'll punch you in the face.'

Chuckling, Kate crouched down to my eye level and pressed her pointy nose into mine, like she was giving me a Māori kiss. 'You're just like *her.*'

I stared at a small speck of mascara that was trapped inside a single tear dangling on Kate's left eyelash. In that smudge, I saw my lahi. Her hair, peppered with grey strands, cropped short like a boy; pillowy cheeks free from any make-up. Lahi wore a lacy bubble-gum pink puletaha; the three distinct folds of her waist wrapped softly in a frail ta'ovala. In this vision, I stood beside Lahi as we stepped on a ngatu; the very ngatu I once painted with my grandmother in front of our neighbour, Shazza. Hanging from my neck was a string of shined oyster shells and a pearl necklace. As an arch of flowers came into view, there stood Kate, holding a plastic bouquet made of violets and lavender. She smiled brightly in an off-the-shoulder mermaid-tailed white wedding dress, a flower crown of white roses over her fringe. Kate was waiting at an altar, waiting for her wife.

The portal peeled away as Kate's tear rolled off her chin. Suddenly, everything in Grand Paradiso began to flake, like the gold foil on the grey plastic handles of Nana's special cabinets. We may have dressed up, glammed up, borrowed up from the bank and rolled up in stretch limos but underneath it all we were still just dirt poor coconuts.

Lowering and unclenching my fists, I started to cry too.

'Fe'ofa'aki,' I told the red-headed pālangi, pressing our pointy noses together again. 'Love is love.'

BLOOD

Sacred root sprung from death. On a desolate island, there lived Fevanga and Fefafa and their only child Kava kilia mai Faa'imata. The three dwelt on barren fonua with only the fā to eat. As Kava grew over the years, so too did her insides, until blood trickled between her thighs.

On a single windswept day, the moana pulled a fleet of vakas to their sterile shores. The boats carried Tu'i Tonga – king of kingdoms. Crawling upright on their knees, Fevanga and Fefafa greeted the royalty that ruled over them; for he was a descendant of Tangaloa.

As empty as the fonua was, the couple still offered a feast in celebration of such an honourable visit. 'A gift,' Fevanga declared to the dirt, in a croaky salt-crusted voice. The lower their height, the lower their gaze, the higher their humility. The pair was dismissed with a pounding of belly and a smack of wood against their knees.

Out of sight from their ruler, Fevanga and Fefafa began walking on their feet once more. 'Not even fā to throw,' Fefafa whispered in a sharp click as she rubbed at her beaten flesh. Her skin was drying to scale. Fevanga snapped back from his beak-pouted lips and pulled at his hair; thick and curly as toa roots. 'Still sacrifice.'

Ashamed of their desolation, the couple crept through the trees, drifting and hiding as if in a shell. If they could feed the Tu'i Tonga something, anything, they would never starve again — such was the miracle of feeding a god.

Since she was menstruating, Kava kilia mai Faa'imata could not meet the king. She stayed hidden in the deepest parts of the toa, awaiting the return of her parents. She hungered to lead them through their fruitless land. Only Kava could find fā, even when the soil was soaked with salt or splintered like wood. Their land was barren . . . unlike herself.

'Gift,' Fevanga quaked, wading through the trees. 'My gift of a daughter.' With a hiss, Fefafa drew back. Only a mother could understand what fate loomed over her child. Scutes formed all along Fefafa's dried skin as she wailed in pain.

When Kava saw the familiar toa curls of her father, she sprung to her feet. In an unfurling voice she replied, 'Fā.' Thinking that her mother was screaming from starvation, Kava turned her back, closed her eyes, and let the blood pooling between her legs pull them towards fruitfulness. The king was to be fed.

Before Kava could lead, air swept from her throat while her leafy limbs flailed. As her flow congealed, the call of fruit pounded in her womb until it ceased to exist. The flipper-like hands of

Fevanga, her father, were clasped around her neck. By night-fall, Fevanga tugged his gift back to the king as a month of time streaked red across the fonua.

When the king of kingdoms saw the bloomed and cut Kava kilia mai Faa'imata, he tumbled to his thickened knees and wept; stomach empty. 'Too much love you have given. Too much love is to be buried.'

Fefafa hunched her back like a turtle's shell and wailed to māhina, the moon.

The very night Kava was shoved into the dirt, small shoots rose from where she lay – kava and tō. The fruit of her menstruation was a gift.

When the king consumed these plants to his fill, surrounded by a circle of men, the king of kingdoms uttered a single word: Fakataha. Together.

24.

My sister was having our period. Mumma told me this as she took off Nettie's pink mahis. 'Our period is lady business,' she whistled that morning. The night before, Nettie asked to sleep next to me in the bottom bunk because her belly was sore. We squished on the single mattress underneath my knock-off Pokémon bedspread like Exeggcute. With a gurgle of pain, Nettie clutched onto me like a hot water bottle all night long.

By morning, she elbowed me in the eye as she pulled off our duvet. 'Shug,' I snapped sleepily, fully ready to push her off the bed. But I slowed down when I saw Nettie's headlight eyes all high beamed. At the same time, we gazed downwards at a series of red marks streaked across our grey trackies. The tip of my nose cramped at the splotches of maroon, thick as cordial concentrate, which were drenched into the fabric of the blanket. Shakily, I poked the wetness that covered both of us; the blood dried to a brown stickiness on my fingers.

I screamed while Nettie cried. 'Oh, is that what it actually means to have babies? Oh, no!' The blood we shared inside us as sisters had found its way outside.

Now in the bathroom, Mumma pulled Nettie's undies tight. The blood looked like a puddled pothole in the Mount Druitt Westfields carpark. With a sigh, Mumma scrunched the mahi in her stumpy hands and held the soiled cloth to her big baby bump, the size of a pineapple, which meant she had been pregnant for eight months. Mumma's fingers were swollen with all the weight she continuously put on. A birthmark, the shape of New Zealand, peeked out from the stretched skin of her stomach.

I tried to imagine how my crown could be birthed from that birthmark – struggling to remember my birth mother, Mummy Le'o, or even the freckly folds of Lahi. And so Camellia, who stood in front of me fully pregnant, was simply Mum. 'We are kith and kin – blended not just by blood but by skin and soil too.'

From the living room, which was just past the bathroom, my siblings' voices echoed. Our bulldog, Povo, whined in the washhouse, begging for scraps. Crumbed oil coated in secret herbs and spices saturated the air as they started to eat KFC. Jared gloated loudly from the lounge room, 'Forward-pass that drumstick.' Corey shouted back, 'Bruuuhahk.' Lani and Lav crooned, 'Aiaiai.'

Back in the bathroom, Nettie sobbed and sucked snot up her nose. 'Oh, if it hurts now, what about giving birth?'

Thanks to her, I now knew exactly what it was like to have blood flowing between our legs. My brows furrowed. *But I'm older. Are my insides broken?*

Mumma chuckled. 'It will be the worst pain of your life.'

Nettie squatted on the family toilet and tucked her knees under her chin; scrunched her toes so tightly on the porcelain rim that her joints turned pink. Curled up like this, my sister looked like an egg. Knocking Nettie's knees apart, Mumma commanded, 'Spread the word.'

A blaze crept up my spine and I knew Dad was standing behind me. I turned. He was in the doorway like a statue. One of Dad's black bushy brows rose up with The Rock's signature expression after winning a wrestling match. My dad was looking more and more like Dwayne Johnson: bald, brown and brawny. I'd only find out later in life that my father actually saw a better version of himself in The Rock – a life he could be living if he hadn't settled down twice and ended up with six kids all before he turned thirty.

Dad stood next to the bathtub, blocking me from Nettie, who was still sobbing on the toilet. This was how I knew my sister was seriously durr in the head; she was always unresponsive to the magnitude of our father's presence.

Inside the bathtub were white t-shirts soaking in water because the second-hand washing machine was broken again. The stench of bleach stung my lashes as I shifted foot-to-foot, watching Dad groan as he lowered himself onto the edge of the tub. All the while, Mumma was using a warm wet cloth to wipe down Nettie's inner thighs, which were the colour of strawberry milk.

Thck. Thck. Thck. Dad tapped his shale palms upon his knees. The sound took me back to a night at a carpark in St Marys. Me and Mumma went to drop off some KFC for Dad's dinner, which we sometimes did when he worked overnight shifts as a security guard. It was an excuse for us to see him since we so rarely could. In our dinged-up Tarago, we pulled over in front of Astley Pharmacy, right next to a neon sign that was blazing in purple: Saint Mary's Pleasure. We parked just in time to see Dad pushing a scrawny dude in a flannel shirt against the side of a rusty red ute. Pinning the stranger with one fist, Dad raised his granite knuckles. Thck. Thck. Thck. He was punching right into Derro's concaved stomach. Groaning, Derro spat out in pain as my father kept hitting him.

Swearing up a storm, Mum stopped the Tarago crookedly and flew towards the men until she was in-between them. Taking his chance, Derro stumbled on bitumen as he ran away. Dad was ready to chase but Mumma placed her branchy limbs in front of her husband and screamed, 'Screw your head on. As if you're going to jail for that mohe 'uli and leaving me with all these kids.'

Once Derro was gone, I wound down the window; my heart hammering in my breastbone.

Dad shouted, 'Stuck it in but didn't pay 'cause she was on her rags. Youse believe that?' With a grumble, Dad bashed his two palms into the rusty red ute.

My father was a man crafted from the earth's mantle. That moment taught me the strength of his capacity to love: If he was willing to protect any woman, then he was ready to die for the women that were his own.

Now, with a tobacco-scented sigh, Dad sat me on his stony lap. I trembled as he combed his heavy hands through my hair. Eventually, my father's knuckles got caught in one of my many knots. Tugging at my roots, he untangled his rocky fingers and placed an 'uma on my forehead.

With a shaky breath, Dad asked, 'Puke māhina? Are youse bleeding too?' From the years I spent listening to Nana, I knew puke meant 'sick' and māhina meant either 'month' or 'moon'. However, since Dad and I were both half-pālangi, Tongan was muddled on our tongues and in our heads. *What did the moon have to do with being sick?*

Unsure, I shook my head. Spit foamed on the sides of Dad's thin pink mouth and yellow flecked in the corners of his earthy eyes – exhausted from all the nights he spent guarding brothels.

Every now and then, one of my aunties reminded me that I had my father's eyes. Looking into them now, I saw rain, sprinkling over every inch of Mounty County, transforming the soil beneath our feet to mud.

I shared so much of myself with my family: my bed, my period, my eyes. Who was I without them? I couldn't even be a real woman without my younger sister doing it for me. Before I could say anything, Dad whispered in my ear, 'Youse can't be first every time but youse will always be my firstborn.'

As Dad patted my crown and left the bathroom, I still didn't understand if bleeding between my legs, when it did happen, would be a good or bad thing.

Without looking back at his two oldest daughters, our father yelled down the rabbit-hole hallway in a rumbling voice, 'Oi, stop chucking a sook and eat youse food.' This was what us Fobs did, we crossed the ocean, moved into Mount Druitt and shouted at each other over fried chicken.

When I turned back, Nettie was naked. Her thin and fair arms were crossed over her blossoming chest. I could tell my sister was holding her breath because her ribs stuck out like twigs. Mine did that without even trying. Voice rustling, Mumma asked me to bring Nettie a dry washcloth. Immediately, I grabbed one that was folded on the windowsill next to a pile of clothes for Nettie to change into. Mumma smiled big and explained that, now Dad was gone, she could show us what to do.

Together, Mumma was golden like dust and Nettie was white like powder. My sister's complexion was all that remained of Nana's first marriage to Liam, a man we never met, a man who left before my dad could even remember him, but a man whose memory was reflected in my sister's flesh.

Slowly, Mumma wiped my sister dry. Shakily, Nettie traced the New Zealand-shaped birthmark on Mumma's big belly. Giggling, Mumma explained how she came into this world. 'Pulled her weight, your nana did! Grandmumma Sela squatted and pushed me out in the middle of a sugarcane field. No nurses, nothing. I was born in the thick and kaka and sweetness of it all.'

Nettie kept her rosy mouth pressed on our mother's birthmark as Mumma reached for clean clothes from the windowsill. 'There are rules for when you are on your period,' Mum explained. 'Have your ears open.' She tied Nettie's straw strands into a high bun. 'Comb your knots and don't wash for three days. All ears?' Then Mumma put on a new pair of underwear with a ginormous white Band-Aid. Mumma explained it was actually called a pad. The pad made me wonder if Nettie's pipi was going to be a huge sore forever. 'Close your legs and don't let boys see. Pricked ya ears?' Gently, Mumma moved Nettie's pale legs into a pair of thick grey tights. 'Keep warm. Never play that last one by ear.' Finally, Mumma put Nettie in a jumper and thick woollen socks. My sister laughed and it sounded like the wings of a butterfly unfurling from their cocoon – forever transformed into adulthood.

My head grew heavier than a dumbbell and my cheeks flared up with jealousy. For some reason, Nettie and Mumma had no problems acting like a real mum and bub.

Rubbing her rounded stomach and patting Nettie on her milky crown, Mumma continued. 'Your period comes from me, Nana Losē, Grandmumma Sela, Aunty Meadow, Aunty Jasmine, Aunty Daisy, Aunty Heilala, Aunty Lily and, especially, your mummy Le'o – all the women from Malapo, Kolonga and Kolomotu'a that make you.'

For a moment, in the corner of my eye, I saw a swish of black hair, a swan-like neck and a sharp wing-shaped elbow. Mummy Le'o had joined us in the bathroom. 'Ofa atu. 'Ofa atu.

25.

Trouble. Trouble for letting babies sit in soiled nappies until they got bum rub. Trouble for leaving stacks of dirty dishes after going to bed. Trouble for not doing homework and getting detention. Trouble for trying to do homework and letting wet washing pile up in mouldy hampers. Mumma and Nettie were bed-ridden; Nettie from having her period and Mumma from not having her period.

Still sweaty in my school uniform, I was engulfed by my baby sisters as soon as I shut the front door of Sugar Drive. I balanced both babies in the crooks of my elbows; Lani tugging on my right earlobe and screaming at me through her *Dora the Explorer* bowl cut: 'Can do-do-do-do like Dora.' Lav raspberried in my left ear. Her own Dora cut was so thick and overgrown she looked more like Cousin Itt.

'Sisisisi, happy si you sissy!' I fumbled under their weight, as well as the weight of my school pack, which was filled with homework and the twelfth book in *A Series of Unfortunate*

Events. I was systematically going through the collection ever since Lahi gifted me with the box set for my last birthday. She had crept into my room while I was still asleep and left the box on my pillow. When I woke up, the lanky and sullen illustrations of Violet, Klaus and Sunny greeted me. Only Lahi, my mum-aunt, my encyclopedia, could know that the miserable story of the Baudelaire orphans would be the strongest way to remind me of how fortunate I was in my life, even with my own misfortunes.

I held onto my baby sisters, but I was desperate to be relieved from the burden of their heavy little bones. I needed to spend the rest of the afternoon finishing my short story about a ngatu and an angry neighbour. Ms Indigo from Gifted & Talented was *still* upset with me for attacking the only pālangi in our class, but she promised to finally move on if I completed the task she had set. She told me this would provide all of us with 'closure'.

From the ajar bedroom door, I could see Mumma's large frame on the mattress and Nettie nestled up next to her. Mumma's breezy voice groaned: 'Me and your sister still sick. You got the babies all night long. Milk is in the fridge and cordial is in the cupboard. Bread is in the freezer. Don't be throwing out baby with the bathwater, okay? Thanks heaps, my girl.'

Grunting, I carried my toddler sisters along the tiles of our hallway like shopping bags. They screeched and spat. My brain, like our house, was filled with Lego, pee-soaked nappies and saliva-covered sippy cups.

In the living room, Lani kicked her too-big-for-boots feet into my rib cage. 'Cross the potty. Cross the potty.' She was all rojo in the face; unable to conquer the act of going big toilet by herself. Jared squeezed himself past me and Lav's dribbling head. He knocked us with the side of his football and yelled back before gapping it to the backyard, 'Break it up for training.'

Lav's dribbles turned into snot as she cried out; football nicking her eye. I set my baby sisters down on our couch and scolded Jared with my glare: He got to do his hobby no worries, but when I wanted to do mine, babysitting took priority. 'Quiet,' I seethed at my sisters as I pulled out *The Penultimate Peril* from my bag. 'Don't make this harder and more annoying than it already is.'

Steaming in his school uniform, Corey bashed his backpack this way and that between the walls of our rabbit-hole hallway, slumping towards the washhouse. Mumma was only a short time away from giving birth and we were trying our best to make space for our upcoming sibling. The half-dismantled nursery in the indoor garage had been set up again. My toddler sisters' bedroom was fully furnished with a scraped-up rocking chair, a chipped wooden crib topped with a handcrafted baby mobile, and a rickety white dresser that matched the flaky paint on the crib. Lani and Lav had been moved into Corey's bedroom – sharing his queen-sized bed, and Corey was finally shafted into Jared's room.

But the biggest change happened last week when we arrived home from school. Like usual, Corey started whistling for

Povo. When our dog didn't respond, Corey rushed to the washhouse looking for her. He began screaming, 'Where is she? Where is she?' Over and over.

'Son,' Mumma said slowly and sadly. 'From the bottom of my heart, I'm really sorry. There just wasn't enough room. You can still visit her at Pa's house. I can take you now if you want.'

In response, Corey thrashed the fur-ridden clothes in the washhouse looking for our whiny bulldog. When he really couldn't find her, he screamed for ages, punching the walls and busting his knuckles. We watched on as Mumma held him on her planet-sized stomach, crying that she should have known to prepare him better. She had just been so distracted working extra shifts to save money for the baby. 'Take heart,' she finally said when Corey's fit simmered down to a whimper.

Ever since then, Corey had spent the hours between after-school and bedtime in the laundry, just sitting there and staring at the broken washing machine. That afternoon was no different. From the lounge room I saw him reach the end of the hallway and turn right into the washhouse.

Lani had begun slamming drawers in the kitchen while Lav clung onto me, her sticky dribble splattering all over the Helquist cover-art.

After an hour of trying to put a nappy back on Lani and wiping up Lav's mouth every few seconds with the hem of my school shirt, I was still unable to read a sentence. Right on that moment when I began to hyperventilate, Jared popped in from the backyard, having finished his training. 'When we kicking off dinner?'

All at once the sippy cups, nappies and pieces of Lego around the house exploded through my mouth. 'Get your own dinner, you gronk!'

My outburst made my toddler siblings screech with laughter on the couch while Jared mumbled back at me, 'Aw, red card. I was just asking. You didn't even signal for an assist.'

Jared looked genuinely remorseful, his eyes wide open and glassy, but I was too upset to let him off the hook.

'Why do I even have to ask, you should just do it,' I spat.

'Why ask? I play footy not read minds,' Jared retorted.

'Up, up, up,' Lav hollered.

Corey entered the kitchen and slammed his fists on the kitchen bench. 'Fuhhup,' he exploded.

For a long time, I thought Corey cared about animals more than Fobs. But since Povo left, I formed a newfound affection for him. He could have ditched our family at any point to live with his wealthy eastern suburbs pālangi father, but instead, Corey chose to stay here in Mount Druitt with *us*. Whenever he needed some love, Mumma was there to cuddle him, and whenever he needed to vent, I was there to fight him.

'I said to friggen fuhhup,' Corey repeated. 'My head fully full.'

I pressed my lips down and gripped toddler flesh so hard that Lani and Lav sqawked out in pain. 'Why hurting?' Lani cried. 'Not us fault.'

It wasn't their fault. It wasn't their fault *I* was hurting.
Dad had called Nettie a woman, even before my younger
sister got her period, and it was true. Nettie could care for
babies, clean the house and boil buckets of noodles for dinner
when Mum and Dad were too tired to cook. And when her
grades came back all D's and teachers reported that she was
falling asleep in class, my parents stayed silent – unwilling
to admit that they needed at least one of their children to
give up on their education in order to have a semi-functional
household. My sister was made of mothers, which is why
she bled so soon. And I was made of steam, which is why all
I could do was yell.

'What good have you been?' I rounded on Corey, letting go
of my baby-lings. 'Just sitting there in the dirty-as washhouse
like some coma patient. Why are you even here? There's no
space for that. Go get lost to your dad's.'

Slamming his fists against the bench for the third time,
Corey's eyes drooped into semi-circles. 'I'm not walking
'round with my nose in bum-fook books acting better than
us. If you wanna be pālangi so friggen bad, why don't *you*
piss off to my dad's?'

Lani wrapped her unco arms around Lav's drooling
head, shielding her little sister even though she was still
little herself. Meanwhile, Jared pounced between me and
Corey. He puffed up his chest and said, 'What the heck,
sis? That was totally offside.'

It suddenly felt like my full brother and half sisters were
dogging me for a stranger.

Locking my eyes on Corey, I replied, 'Maybe I will then! Better a pālangi than some dumb dirty spazz.' Before anyone could respond, I barged past my brothers, sprinting through the rabbit-hole hallway and into my room, where I hid under the dark, dark gloom of a cheap dingy bunk bed.

That evening, on the floor of my bedroom, I packed my threadbare and brandless bag for the next day of school. From the living room, I heard the burning tyres of *The Fast and the Furious*. My siblings had gathered in the lounge to watch Paul Walker and Vin Diesel pretend not to be super-gay for each other.

As I packed, shaky sentences from my short story fell from my notebook – I had torn it to shreds: *What's the point?*

Even through the echo of surround-sound street racing, I felt Dad's steel-capped boots beating down the hallway. My back burnt immediately and my throat shrivelled to a cocoon. I knew I was going to get in trouble for fighting with Corey. In our house, we were forbidden to make anyone feel less like a family member than anyone else. Our parents had worked too hard blending us together.

I could already see what was coming: Dad would arrive in my doorway with shiny silver lettering spelling out 'Guard'. Already crying, my vision would be filled with fluttering light auras as I cowered back under my bunk bed; terrified of his fists flying through plastered walls. His thick brows would brood and his large chest would heave and each word would come out in a sharp avalanche of spit. Then he'd yell and punch, punch and yell until I was snivelling at his steel-capped boots. He'd call out before leaving my room, 'Why youse crying for?'

Thck. Thck. Thck.

When Dad arrived in my doorway, his shoulders were slumped, his lids were heavy and red from exhaustion and his mouth was cracked. Clicking his tongue, tck tck tck, he slowly sat on my bed. My bunk whined under his weight. Shaking on the floor, I stayed silent. Flatly my father said, 'Youse called your brother stupid. Meadow, youse need to explain.' I shook my head, still unable to say a single word.

Then, thck! My father's marble fist collided into my bedroom wall, knocking down my copy of *The Penultimate Peril*, which I'd left on the edge of my small bookshelf. Dad's boulder-like knuckles pulled out shreds of plaster, leaving a dark, dark hole for a dark, dark girl. Snot gushed down my top lip, tears melting my face. How I wished for the dad who once towered in front of a suburban sunset and single-handedly stopped an out-of-control Tarago in order to save his children. I wanted the dad who held me as I cried for my mummy Le'o. I was too terrified to look at this father, lest a mountain crumble.

'Do youse have an explanation?'

Slowly, I looked up at my father. He wasn't made of granite. I was facing the statue of a very exhausted man, plaster dust on his hairy knuckles. Reminding me of the beautiful brown bodies toiling the ancient soil of Tonga, I found my breath; unafraid.

'Just because I'm the oldest, doesn't mean I wanna waste my life looking after babies. Am I not your baby too? Whose baby am I? Mummy Le'o died before I could know her. Lahi's married now and forgotten all about me. And what about school? I wanna learn. I wanna read. I wanna write. You all so mad at me for punching that White girl, but she gets to be smart and all I get to be is Tongan . . .'

My heart heaved and my tears swooned and Dad slid to the floor. He wrapped his biceps around me, soft and familiar as kafu. 'My baby,' he crooned, clicking his tongue, tck tck tck. 'I don't want youse to hate youseself, I want youse to love youseself.' Taking in a sad solemn breath, he went on, 'Us hafekasi always feel like that when we young. It's time for youse to know what being Tongan truly means.'

26.

*P*iled into our dinged-up Tarago. I was nothing but a groggy-eyed gronk. The stars above 8 Sugar Drive were winking at me, as if they knew my future. Silently, my parents stuffed brown-taped Styrofoam boxes into the bent-down back-back seats like they were playing a squeaky round of *Tetris*. The foam made my teeth grind and my ear canals boil over. Within the Styrofoam were nappies, tins of baby formula and assorted shoes and handbags with the tags still attached. Gifts from relatives of relatives of relatives to their relatives of relatives. Tongans were too poor to pay for Australia Post shipping, opting to wait for a call down the coconut line about some family travelling to Tonga with excess baggage space. Somewhere in the Styrofoam, my too-old-for-Op-shop-even clothes had also been snuck in. Not to mention a log of black plastic, which had a ngatu wrapped inside. With a sigh, I pulled up my brandless schoolbag, the only luggage I could take to store my own things; one change of clothes, one pair of pyjamas, socks, undies and a toothbrush. Real Fob kids, by which I mean the naughty ones, were sent to the islands until they were all straightened out. As for the mucked-up hafekasi kids, like me, we got flown to Tonga for our aunt's delayed honeymoon.

Rubbing her ready-to-pop belly, Mumma yawned as she waddled into the front passenger seat of our Tarago. Illuminating the night with a red halo of tobacco, my father chugged on a ciggie. The red flame, along with the shadow of his mountainous torso, turned my father into a volcano. He only smoked when he was stressed out to the max – his first-born would soon be in the heart of the Pacific Ocean without him.

As we drove through the Westside, streetlights leading the way, my parents said nothing to me. We pulled out of Plumpton and onto the M4 motorway, destiny unfolding before me.

At Sydney Airport's international terminal, I finally understood the meaning of the songs by Mr Worldwide. Flags from every part of the globe were branded across endless LED-screens, which scrolled phrases like: 'Gate Closing', 'Boarding Now' and 'Delayed'. With wide eyes I tried to decipher words like Dubai, Osaka and Qantas. *What the actuals?* The endless scrolling of endless countries made me realise there was a whole universe outside the confines of

Mount Druitt. I was nothing but a grain of soil inside an endless desert island.

Dad stacked the Styrofoam on flat-bottomed trolleys that needed a two-dollar coin to use. As we walked through the airport, I spun silly, trying to take it all in. Wheelie bin-like luggage rolling over tiles while people of all shades were decked with neck-pillows, layered puffy jackets, headphones, hats and sunnies. Throughout the crowd, a robotic voice repeated over a chime of bells, 'Carry-on must not exceed seven kilos.' The air was stale and tasted of metal.

'Keep still or you'll break your neck,' Mumma commanded, sipping on a wrinkly Mount Franklin's bottle filled with chocolate milk instead of water. Mumma said milkshakes were the only thing that kept her heartburn down. But I reckoned it was just an excuse to be fat *and* pregnant.

Flicking my gaze at my father's stiffened back, I moped. 'Then let me stay in our neck of the woods.'

With a twitch of her purple eye-bags, Mumma growled, 'You're a pain in the neck.'

Squeaks of Styrofoam were silenced by the chaos of the airport. My parents and I strolled heavy-footed all the way to a blue, white and black section. The LED screens on this side of the terminal glowed with the words: 'Air New Zealand'. Yawning, I shifted side-to-side as we lined up in aisles marked out by retractable nylon belts.

In front of me stood a pālangi couple carrying backpacks and long tripods. 'Drink my piss,' a man with shaggy dark hair groaned in an English accent. He was glaring at the

behemoth of bodies in front of him; all waiting to check in
the same sticky-taped foam boxes as ours. The man looked
and sounded exactly like Bear Grylls. A lanky woman stood
next to him, her green eyes widening in a flash. When she
spoke, her accent was as Aussie as mine. 'Should we be
filming this for the doco?' With a scoff, Bear Grylls looked
at me all red in the face, like he'd been caught.

Ducking in-and-out of line, Dad chugged on a Gloria
Jeans coffee, complaining that it cost him a full six bucks.
We waited and my parents mumbled every now and then
between each other, 'Always "Island Time" with Mum.'

The check-in guy was a spikey-haired hafekasi whose smile
was bigger than The Cheshire Cat's. We were still far off
when a familiar afro bobbed between passengers, followed by
the three-set pillowy waist I'd know anywhere. On instinct,
I swooped under the nylon belts and ran towards Lahi, but
stopped short when an unfamiliar shape took form next to
her. Oil-slick black hair and gold grin: Uncle Lotemi.

'Ah, I am whole again,' the woman I was named after
laughed, then she opened her full-freckled forearms for a
hug. She was wearing a plain shirt, cargo shorts and ratty
Converses. *Lahi, Lahi, Lahi!* I stuck to my mother-aunt like
a husk and inhaled her Calvin Klein for Men perfume.

Eventually, I grinned up at Lotemi's grease-soaked strands.
'So you did bring her back.'

My new uncle licked at the shiny metal bits on his teeth.
'Oiya, honi.'

Honey? Pinched brows, I walked back to my parents, who were holding the line. Nana was standing between them, already complaining:

'Wut why say? Where is? I say bring, bring it. 'My son. 'Oiauē. No telinga!'

Already, I could feel the spit sprinkling from Nana's gummy mouth. She was stripped back to her usual trackies, plain purple hoodie and a fabric tupenu wrapped over her thighs.

Ashen-faced, Dad mumbled, 'Youse can't take dead birds, Fa'e.'

Mumma stood back out of the line. Her head cocked and the rings under her eyes went black as she sipped her flavoured milk. Suitcases trundled between us as Nana erupted, stringing vowels together with huffs from her outstretched nostrils. The mark under her left eye, the mark of my father, burned like a freshly lit ciggie.

'Enough,' Lahi declared, stepping through her brother and mother.

Nana just started up louder, 'Siko. Mata'usi. Ta'e.'

Dad's boulder fists rammed through a lid on one of our Styrofoam boxes. 'Youse put skeletons in the bloody box. Youse think I wanna go jail for youse? For what? Youse is taking *our* kid don't forget.'

Here's what my father was going on about: Real ta'ovalas, the mats Tongans wore around their waists, needed to be properly decorated with actual red feathers. Nana believed that rosellas, like the Arnott's biscuit bird, had the best hue for such a cause. So apparently, the red plumages Nana had packed were still attached to the sun-soaked carcasses she picked up from the side of the road. This act of bio-terrorism was my nana's way of bringing 'Made in Australia' quality to those in Tonga that she could not bring to the first world.

Enduring the wrath of his mother for her own safety, Dad pointed at me, Lahi and Lotemi, and said directly to Nana: 'These are the only three carcasses youse taking with youse.'

I could not recall ever seeing my father so squishy and squirmy, as if he were torn in two. One half was a boy who wanted to appease his mother. The other half was a man who wanted to protect his daughter.

Gawking from the left of us, Bear Grylls linked arms with his lanky green-eyed companion as she fumbled her camera. 'Why aren't ya bloomin' filmin'?'

Tonga was so lonely that no direct flights existed. First we'd catch a plane to Auckland, followed by a smaller plane to Tongatapu. Nana rolled up her purple jumper sleeves and wisped her afro. Mimicking the genie in *Aladdin*, Lahi swivelled her full face between Nana and Uncle Lotemi and repeated, 'Poof, whadda-ya need? Poof, whadda-ya need? Poof, whadda-ya need?' The wishes of her mother and husband were drowned out by a PA's last call for late passengers. With a tightened chest, I turned back to my parents. Dad grabbed me and pulled me into a boulder hug. He said softly, 'Fe'ofa'aki means to love one another but it also means to love youseself.'

Winking at me with her purple eyelids, Camellia swayed her big belly and bent down to my eye level. Clearing her throat, her leaf-like lashes lifted. She whispered, 'Have anything to say? Mum's the word.' Her breath smelt of sweetened powder.

Suitcases trundled around us with their wheels rolling against tiles: dku dku dku dku. I had nothing to say. I spent every day leading to this trip trying to make up with them: I cleaned extra, boiled formula extra, wiped up nappies extra, helped with homework extra, shortened my showers extra. Still I landed here; unable to make up with myself.

Camellia's bough arms weighed on my shoulders; her paperbark skin glowing beneath the fluorescent lights of the airport. She grabbed me tight, pressing my skinny little frame upon her belly, and that's when it happened: My soon-to-be sibling kicked! Gasping, I placed my palms on Camellia's womb, feeling the baby through the fabric of Mumma's shirt. Clicking her tongue, Camellia sighed and smiled at me. 'Littlest One says, "Forgive, forget and come back clean slate."'

Pulling away, Mumma patted my accentuated collarbones with stick-like fingertips. This woman, who I called 'Mum' even though I never formed inside her, pecked me on the cheek and took in a deep breath, as though she was inhaling her daughter. I wondered if maybe there was room inside that epic womb of hers for me too.

♥

The plane to Auckland glided through sunlight and flitted between white tendrils that passed by a tiny double-paned window. Inside the plane, everything was grey and glistening. I was sitting next to Lahi, who was sitting next to Lotemi. An aisle separated me and Nana. The plane's felt and plastic ceiling was lined with spotlights and tiny vents that blew recycled air. On the floor, plush blue carpet ran down a single aisle marked with LED strips. On the back of each chair, little black screens played the same movie in sync, *The Lord of the Rings*, an excuse for Air New Zealand to show off its iconic landscapes. However, I couldn't concentrate on the film because being in the sky for the first time was so much more mythical to me than Mordor. Guests gurgling as they exited the tiny toilet rooms; small grey dunnies sucking down waste like a vacuum cleaner. *Far, where'd all the poo go?*

I also encountered the fanciest Fobs ever. They were all Brown women; all flight attendants. Each one was tucked into a light blue tunic which flared over their tight grey skirts and tan sheer stockings. Wide hips tucked into their waist belts and mahana hair gelled down into scalp-tight buns. *So posh!* It was here, up in heaven, that I saw how beautiful us Islander women could be.

Eventually, the flight attendants pushed a trolley full of food between the aisle. The attendant closest to us caught my eye – a blue mark curling under her bottom lip and down her chin like a seahorse's tail. She was skinny but not in the rib-stuck-out way that I was. Instead, her cheeks were taut from a sharp bone structure, accentuating the blue swirls across her jaw. She smelt of burnt coffee while she talked to a grey-haired pālangi in the row in front of me. 'Excuse me, sir, yew want anything?' The indigo ink on the flight attendant's chin twirled as she spoke.

Together, Tongans believed that tattoos were a sin against God. But Lahi, my encyclopedia, taught me that Tongans actually invented tātatau. We sharpened bones and strained koka sap to make needle and ink. With these tools, we marked the positions of stars on our hands and calves to traverse our vakas across the ocean. Closely examining the flight attendant, I crumpled my forehead, struggling to piece together the part of my brain that hated being Fob and the part that found this Fob so elegant, so above the earth.

Every time I tried to look out the window, Lotemi's oven-shaped skull blocked my view. Then, sensing my frustration, he'd turn to me and ask, 'Hungry, huni? Can get anything for you?'

Trying not to be laupisi, I sighed and spoke politely to my uncle: 'Just nervous. I don't know anything about Tonga.'

Fidgeting with her extension belt, Lahi promised she had booked me the window seat for our flight from Auckland to Tonga. 'Don't fuss too much, kernel. Soon you'll see the kingdom of light; the sun touches our people first.'

Before I could reply, Indigo Ink came to us with her trolley of goods. Lahi, like always, ordered a plethora of food: A packet of Twisties and a can of Creaming Soda for Lotemi. A sleeve of salted nuts and Coke for herself. She also offered to buy her mother something, but Nana declined, saying she had real food. Whatever that meant. Then Lahi bought a Coke and a small tub of Cookies and Cream New Zealand Natural ice-cream for me. It was the purest, creamiest dessert I'd ever eaten. With a blue plastic spoon, I slowly swirled around Oreo chunks; savouring sweetness. 'Yew enjoy, love.' Indigo Ink beamed at me – her intricate marks twirling and glowing

As Lotemi chewed and chuckled at the silvery elves on his screen with headphones in his ears, I leaned into Lahi's pillowy sides. So familiar and comforting to me that I almost fell asleep. But I couldn't, not before I asked her the questions that had been biting my tongue ever since her wedding.

'How have you been? For reals?' I whispered to her.

Lahi pursed her lips and shrugged. 'In Tongan, you say "Fēfē hake?" when you want to ask someone that. Good to know for the future.'

Biting into my last lump of ice-cream, I chewed on a large piece of cookie and responded, 'Yeah, but like.' Unable to form the words properly, I took more time, letting the cream melt on my tongue and starting again. 'Me and Kate spoke at your wedding.' Lahi's soft sides stiffened. She didn't say anything so I continued. Crushing my paper cup, I whispered softer still, 'How? How could you marry Lotemi if you love Kate? Love you and whoever you love.' Slowly, Lahi exhaled until she was soft again, but no answer came out of her mouth. On the screen in front of me, Frodo was traversing large expanses of green hills and rocky rivers with big, hairy feet. Clicking my tongue, tck tck tck, I psyched myself up for the most important question I ever asked: 'Meadow Fehoko, did you forget about me?'

At this, Lahi laughed and moulded me into her once more. 'How could I? You are me. We just Meadow.' I breathed in her manly perfume once more. Whole.

As the plane began to descend into Auckland, Nana reached out with her beak-shaped fingertips and tried to feed me Red Rooster stuffing, which she had smuggled onto the plane. When I shook my head, she muttered, 'No give bird, no take bird. Spoilt kids.' Then she turned back to her screen and began to giggle at the Hobbits.

Even though I was tired of her constant badgering, I couldn't help but smile. Underneath her tough and tired exterior, there was a child there, no different to myself, caught between two islands. I reached my hand out over the aisle and snatched the stuffing from Nana's fingers. Then I opened my mouth, tilted my head, threw the lump in the air, and felt it sail down my throat. My grandmother giggled again, but it wasn't at the Hobbits this time. Nana was giggling at me.

27.

*F*ar from the beach bonfires, tiki torches, grass skirts and leis on *Lilo & Stitch*, Tonga was sweat and mud. From Fuaʻamotu Airport (which was as big as a Bunnings Warehouse) to Malapo, I saw: Dust tracks filled with overgrown foliage, groups of stray dogs with rib cages for stomachs, drifts of pigs grunting in filth, and a single concrete strip for the main road at the centre of Nukuʻalofa. Even the quarters of Tonga's royal family were nothing but a simple palace made of red and white tin. All this confirmed to me what I already knew: Tonga was created from muck.

Real Tongans, who lived on the fonua, didn't make sense to me. Many of them were skinny. They were still broad-shouldered, big-bellied and thick-legged – but they were toned and muscular. Maybe because Tonga was one of the only countries in the world without a McDonald's!

On the streets, oldies wore plain tupenus and shirts while the younger ones wore raggedy jeans, Nike shirts, fluoro construction vests and oversized hoodies branded with dollar signs. And all of them, no matter what age, wore strapped jandals to their curved-toed feet. Pālangis, like our neighbour Shazza, had tricked me into believing that real Islanders were savages who lived barefoot and naked in the tropics. But most of the people here actually looked healthier than us. The schoolgirls walking to class surprised me most, with their mahana coils tightly braided to a scalp-shine: the children of Tonga were nit-free.

During the car ride to Malapo, we drove unbuckled, as it was legal not to wear seatbelts. (There weren't enough Tongans with cars for the government to care). This made it easier for Nana to stick her afro head out the front passenger window and yell to the people she recognised. (Over the next three weeks, Nana would systematically and discreetly distribute all the crap we lugged with us to these cheapos). The rush of air from her window was filled with saltwater and heat. 'Ah weh weh weh,' she chuckled, her gummy smile beaming like sand in the sun. And in response, the chillest Fobs I'd ever seen would fling up their arms, and holler back, "Oiauē!"

Uncle Lotemi chimed along in an ignition of vowels, laughing with his mother-in-law through the connection they shared: Tongans born in Tonga. He was sitting in the back beside me, and every so often he'd turn away from the window and give me a quick wink, just like he did at his wedding.

Lahi drove silently, one hand on her lap, one on the steering wheel, baseball cap turned backwards, like some kinda gangsta.

As we drove through each village, I realised that real Tongans had also given up on huts and now lived in fibro shanties that weren't much different to the housing commissions in Sydney. Every second home had a blue tarp strapped on its roof and every third house grumbled with the groans of generators. 'The prince uses all the power in Tonga for parties,' Lahi finally spoke in a sombre tone. Each fibro wall blended into the other. Together, it seemed, Tongans did not believe in fences.

What they clearly did believe in, however, was Jesus. The only stone structures to exist in Tonga were churches, be they Catholic, Anglican, Protestant, Latter-day Saints, Jehovah's Witnesses or Greek Orthodox. 'What Wogs live here?' I shrieked, the words accidentally blurting from my mouth.

Nana and Lotemi were too busy talking in Tongan to notice but Lahi rolled her eyes over at me. 'Rich as you are, know better.' It was a reminder: We may be Tongan, but we were also Australian, which meant we were richer than any Tongan-Tongan.

Finally, we arrived at Nana's family home in Malapo. Uncle Lotemi popped out of the van and opened a squeaky chain-linked fence, revealing a dirt path. Stray dogs barked. Lorikeets twittered. Palm trees rustled. The childhood house of my grandmother was a square concrete shoebox with a glass sliding door and glass slats for windows – a sign it was newly renovated. *So this where our money goes!* A thin stretch of concrete acted as a makeshift veranda and the crushed gravel walls hummed in the strong tropic sun.

The rental van was still rolling when Nana opened her door and skipped out. 'No, Fa'e,' Lahi shouted. Immediately, she stomped on the brakes. Schhhrt. The van staggered to a halt, creating a large cloud of dust. With her blanket-like arms outstretched, Lahi tried to reach across the gearstick and clutch onto Nana's soft backside.

But my grandmother was already on the ground, crying out, 'Ah weh!' Stumbling foot-to-swollen-foot, Nana pulled off her fluffy woollen socks and pressed the flattened arches of her feet on the earth of her birth. She leant her lemon-shaped body forward and used her melon palms to caress patches of green and brown grass. Her lush limbs, returning to the dirt like roots, reminded me of Warami, the warrior-poet in my Gifted & Talented class: 'You'll never know yourself until you know your land,' Warami used to say. And now I understood.

Slowly, Lahi followed in the footsteps of her mother, her pillowy frame draping over Nana's back. I stepped out of the rental van and onto Nana's fonua, mud soiling my soles. Then came Lotemi, lifting his wife and mother from the ground. The grease in my uncle's hair shone as he kissed both women on the cheek.

Turning to me, Lahi extended her cushion arms once more. 'Here is the patch of soil where your nana was born,' she explained. 'Let's go home.'

28.

*I*nside, the renovated shoebox was even smaller than it
looked on the outside. The whole abode was just two
squares separated by a single wall. In the first square was
the living room, where the concrete floors were lined with
mats woven with stringy coloured plastic. On the mats were
rolls of flimsy blue mattresses and a TV, which was so old
it still had dials. I asked where all four of us were gonna
sleep, and Lahi explained: 'Me, Nana, you; inside on the
mattresses; Lotemi outside on the veranda.' The humid air
thickened in my chest at the claustrophobia of it all, but at
least it would just be us women. It was tapu for my uncle
to sleep anywhere near me and Nana.

Crawling all over the ceiling were not cockroaches, like in
Sugar Drive, but little lizards called mokos. The lizards were
kinda cute except they were followed by the bzzzt bzzzt
bzzzt of mosquitoes. Lahi told me not to worry about this

either, showing me a bundle of green coils. 'We light this up like a little birdie boiler to keep them bloodsuckers away.'

My mouth downturned, I sniffed and scratched at the bloodsuckers in my head, completely unconvinced.

In the second square of the house was the kitchen. A sole black stovetop sat in the entire space, unconnected to any electricity or gas. Rubbing at the folds on her freckly neck, Lahi said that the cast-iron box simply needed coal or wood to start up, then we could make any mean feed.

My first evening in Tonga landed on a Sunday, which meant the whole island shut up shop. Since Sunday was the one day God rested, so too was it the one day Tongans chillaxed.

As Lotemi bobbed around in the kitchen, frying up corned beef on the stovetop, me and Nana and Lahi laid on our mattresses watching an illegally recorded Filipino drama series on a burnt CD. It was technically called *Sa Piling Mo* but Nana called it 'Tama Kui', which meant 'Blind Man'. From the subtitles, I gathered the show was about a love triangle over some guy who couldn't see. But I wondered how Nana could follow the story since she neither knew Tagalog nor much English. Then again, maybe it was easy for her to follow the whole show because it was so slow; filled with endless staring between the main characters beneath frantic piano music. Even the flashbacks were just lots of staring. Lots of staring in a show about a blind man . . .

To further ease my boredom, Lahi bought me junk food from the only stores open on the Sabbath, which were run by Chinese migrants. During a particularly dramatic scene where Tama Kui gained blurry vision, Lahi bobbed back through the sliding door with stacks of Chicken Twisties, cans of kapa pulu, a box of Mi Goreng noodles and soft yellow drink bottles she told me were Fanta. When I protested, she laughed at me, gold-tooth grinning. 'It's pineapple. You can't get this in Australia. It's a whole new world for you, Si'i.'

All through the evening, the yellow bubbles were nectar to my tongue. As it turned to night, Lotemi had smoked up the entire house frying canned corned beef. Then, wrapped in an apron, he distributed Styrofoam plates to the women. When I refused to eat, Nana didn't even blink, just sat next to me on the floor and ate her salty fill. With her afro bouncing in the corner of my eyes, I sipped my sugary fortune and leant on her soft side.

Circling the ancient television, like a little altar, were those green coils. Once lit up, they emitted streams of smoke that kept the mosquitoes away. The mokos above us, attracted to the television light, crawled down the walls as if they could understand Tagalog.

It was only when my grandmother nodded off to sleep that I felt a strain in my stomach. Quietly, I asked Lahi where the bathroom and shower were. Ever attuned to my laupisi ways, Lahi blew out her cheeks in preparation for the inevitable. 'Now, Si'i,' she started in a serious tone. 'Remember your humility.'

She led me outside to a little wooden shack just beyond the concrete veranda slab where Lotemi was snoring on a bundle of kafus. Inside the shack was a moss-covered and cracked porcelain toilet, which smelt like a bat was decaying in its dark, dark depths. To make matters even worse, a moko crawled across my bare toes – it was too hot in Tonga for me to wear socks. Flicking my jandals, I tossed the reptile onto the toilet seat and screamed. The moko hissed at me.

'Yuck, yuck, yuck, far no way never, yuck!'

Not even Pineapple Fanta could redeem this place anymore. Corn syrup swirled inside my stomach like a cyclone. Grrrrrrkkt. My insides moaned in harmony with the bzzt bzzt of mosquitoes. That first night, I laid on the thin mattresses with Lahi; just like I used to in the House of Fe'ofa'aki. Only this time, I kept as far away from her as possible. Groaning, I squirmed like a caterpillar in a cocoon as hot bile built up in the back of my throat. My bladder was engorged and my bowels were bursting with stuck-up stools. I moaned while humid air slopped in and out of my nostrils, my brain full of snot.

Lahi's clammy voice emerged from somewhere near my feet. 'Meadow, this is why you're here. Just go. No more fie pālangi or laupisi. Humility is what makes us Tongan.'

Tears mixed with my mucus as I curled in on myself and slowly sat up. Hiccuping, I tiptoed across the mattress, enlivening the mosquitoes that had gathered around the ashen coils. I grabbed the torchlight near the sliding door and lit it up. The mokos scurried towards and around and away from the light in confusion.

Outside on the concrete veranda, I avoided the shadowy mass of my sleeping uncle once more. Across the dusty driveway and into the outhouse. Like a horror movie, the cracked plastic seat of the toilet jumped into the grey streaks of my flashlight. Next to the ring of moss was a sun-faded bucket which once held ten kilos of Radiant washing powder. Lahi explained that we needed to fill this with water to manually flush the toilet. As bile coated my tongue, making me gag, I picked up the bucket and shakily stepped to the side of the outhouse. With the flashlight, I found the rainwater tap. There was a rustling in the dark, dark forest and the torchlight picked out many pairs of eyes. Trying not to scream, I filled the bucket.

On my tiptoes, I quickly tracked it back into the toilet. Whimpering as my biceps burnt from the large load of trembling water, I shimmied my trackies down and whined as my clammy behind grazed the fissured seat. Pinching my nose to block the dead bat stench, I pushed down phlegm. Scrunching up my face, I busted my hole trying to poo. I repeated the process over and over, becoming more and more bloated each and every time. *Ahh, crap.*

One week from the day of our arrival, I still hadn't kaka'd. Lahi left with Lotemi to complete newlywed duties. Or so they said. Any time they spoke to each other, they were always side-eyeing Nana to see if she was listening.

Apron in hand, Lotemi made his way to the rental car. I asked my mum-aunt where they were going, and she brushed me off; waving her sunburnt hand in my face. 'No more questions. Just let me show you later, yeah?' I nodded, even though my bowels knotted.

They left me with Nana; stuck watching Tama Kui as the island scorched. Clutching my tummy skin, I moaned, 'Gahgahgah.' All the while, I sipped on plastic-fumed Fanta as Filos forever stared at each other. I was sprawled on bedsheets trying to cool myself with an ī. 'Gah, gah.'

Nana clucked her tongue at me, turned off the TV and lifted her lemon-shaped frame from the ground. 'Gah, gah. So annoying you. Up. Up. You puke, you no come me, remember I say? But you still come me. Okay, okay then. No wrecking Tonga for me. I show how much the fonua loving you.'

My grandmother dragged me into a dusty Daihatsu midget, a squished ute Lahi tuned up in-between those so-called 'newlywed' duties. It was the perfect car for the dirt paths Tongans called roads.

As we drove, Nana ignored my groans. We passed roaming pigs, ragged dogs and lost chickens while the stiff-backed Tongans who lived in this tropical mess walked in jandals on the dusty nature strips.

Nana was driving me to 'Anahulu Caves. 'Fresh da wada, Si'i. You going kaka den. Me an' Hina making you betta,

betta.' I didn't really know what she was going on about; my backed-up bowels gave me constipation, which gave me cramps, which left me confused. Something about fresh water taking away my waste or something like that. *As if.* I sat with my arms crossed and my butthole clenched as we headed into bush.

Ferns hung across the dirt road and scratched against the windshield of the compacted ute. All the while, Nana was singing the words to "Ana Lātū', a lullaby for fussy and ungrateful children. 'Si kau tangata moe kau fefine, mou mātuku atu 'o mohe. Kae tuku keu 'au fia pe; he ko ho ma faka'osi pō e.' In English this meant, 'Oh men and women, retire and rest for now. For I cannot go to sleep; this night will be our last.' Nana swayed her shoulders from side to side as we bumped over gravel, her afro moving back and forth like a black cloud. 'Musie Si'i. 'Oiauē, all puke in you brain. Promise, Tonga making betta you.'

I shook my head and held my rib cage, right elbow poking Nana's breast. Brushing my arm away, she started singing again, louder this time, drowning out my laupisi'ing.

In front of a cave trail, we parked. One enormous rust-coloured man with a worm-like moustache approached our miniature ute. In a bright blue polo uniform, he reminded me of the police officers at Mounty Westfields. Only the badge on the Tongan officer's uniform looked different to Australia's. On Worm-Moustache's chiselled chest and swollen sleeves was a golden crown underneath Tonga's royal emblem, which was held up by doves. Underneath the emblem were golden stitches that spelt out Tonga's national motto: "Ko e 'Otua mo Tonga ko hoku Tofi'a' – 'God and Tonga are my inheritance'.

'Tulou,' Worm-Moustache said to my grandmother. He bowed his head with a wriggly smirk and their conversation began to flow. From what I understood, a young Tongan boy had drowned himself in the pool of natural freshwater found at the very bottom of the cave.

As Nana listened to the officer, she slowly stretched her melon palms towards my head and stroked the side of my face – leaving a thin film of sweat down my ear and cheek. At the end of the terse conversation, Worm-Moustache's enormous rusty muscles hardened. Wincing, he began to rub his thumb across his earth-coloured fingertips.

'Hckh,' Nana spat before digging around underneath her tea-stained lilac cotton shirt. She pulled a twenty pa'anga note from her bra.

'Mālō,' the officer's moustache twitched as he collected the money and stepped away from the driver's window.

Chucking a hard U-ey, Nana lumbered her eyes. There was no singing as she drove away. She slung about harsh Tongan words, soaring us over a mound in the gravel. All the while, I thought about a dead body in water. *We came from the ocean, and to the ocean we return.*

All of a sudden, I felt my bowels loosen and started screaming in perfect Tongan, 'Toileti, toileti, toileti!' Nana braked hard and I sprung from the van and straight into a bushy shrub.

'Ah weh,' Nana laughed in relief, her voice stretching long and hard through the leaves.

All the while, I squatted and soiled the earth beneath me. I had witnessed the worst in Tonga, just as Tonga absorbed the worst in me. We were now equals, trying to find the best in each other.

29.

Starlings shrilled in the blue-night hours before the sun touched Tonga. 'Wakey, wakey, kernel,' Lahi whispered in my ear, her breath full of rainwater and mint. Before I could even stir, she placed her cotton-soft hands over my chin, mouth and nose. 'Shhh, secret. Pop up but don't make too much noise.'

Sitting up slowly from the mattress on the floor, I absorbed Lahi's moon-shaped face and Lotemi's silhoutte behind the thin veranda door. Sliding the glass open, my uncle smiled at me and said quietly, 'Ha'u 'alu, huni.'

Swwwt swwwt went the starlings as Lahi and Lotemi piled me into the rental Tarago. Before long Lahi was driving us down the dirt paths towards Tāufa'āhau Road while Lotemi sat in the passenger seat speaking so fast that his Tongan sounded like whizzing fireworks rather than human words.

From the back seat I grumbled, 'What is he so excited for? Where are we going? Why so early?'

Sunlight rising from the horizon behind him, Lotemi turned around and peered at me through the space in the headrest. Then he gave me the wink. 'You know, *Talesi Island*? Pleasing book. Lopeti Stefensoni.' He meant *Treasure Island* written by Robert Stevenson; a pālangi who *wanted* to be Pacific Islander, or at least that's what Lahi told me.

'I didn't know you read,' I beamed.

Lotemi laughed warmly. 'Honi, lots don't know me.'

The light spilled out over Nuku'alofa and I saw pigs huddled half-asleep at the bases of banana and coconut trees. To Lahi I said, 'For real, Long John Silver? That's why you married him?'

My mum-aunt just chuffed from the driver's wheel. 'So many questions but no confessions. I heard you took the biggest dump at the caves yesterday. Wutta crack-up.'

I leaned into the space between the driver's seat and the passenger's front seat. Resting the side of my face on Lahi's upper arm, I clicked my tongue. 'So what?'

'I'll tell you "so what". Those caves are sacred,' Lahi chortled. 'It was where the goddess Hina bathed. It's not a toilet.'

Ten minutes later, we passed tiny shacks made of tin with blue tarp for roofs. The crude, slanted structures had jagged holes cut out of metal sheets to form doors and windows. Holding my breath, I tried not to whimper. My grandmother's concrete shoebox and moss-ridden outhouse in Malapo, just like her two-storey structure back in Mount Druitt, was a castle in comparison to this. Even in Tonga, there were layers to poverty.

But Uncle Lotemi was acting as if we were pulling up to the royal palace. With coarse fingers he gestured like a whirlpool, pointing at rocks and trees only his wife could appreciate.

The Tarago was strolling to a stop by the time Lahi said, 'This is the village your uncle was born in. Popua, which is named after an earthly woman. In ancient days, this was the place where 'Aho'eitu climbed up the toa into the heavens. But these days, Popua just sounds like "poor" because it is poor.'

Unsure whether to laugh or cry, and pointing directly at Lotemi this time, I asked yet again, 'So is that why you married him?'

Just as Lahi veered off the dirt path, I saw the other side of Popua. I hadn't realised that the shanties were all facing one way. Before us was a lagoon so vast that the crown of the world had emerged from its very depths. And in the vast expanse of water that met the horizon was standing a fakaleitī; transgender a thousand years before anyone had ever heard the word. The fakaleitī was swaying in a rainbow-patterned tupenu that hugged and softened their muscular curves. Turning to our car, they revealed a sweep of shoulder-length hair, arched cheeks framing wide nostrils and lashes as long as an ī. Little ripples of water lapped at their ginormous calves. Dawn turned into day, revealing wispy high clouds on a blanket of blue.

Even before Lahi could turn off the car, Lotemi jumped out and sprinted towards the fakaleitī. Immediately, they were in an embrace. Their arms, both thick and dark as stumps, strained against each other.

'Their name is Leitī,' my mother-aunt explained. 'Aren't they gorgeous?' Lotemi whisked his blocky fingers through Leitī's long hair. Leitī ruffled Lotemi's slick strands with elongated, sharply-filed fingernails. Through their expansive chests, the pair laughed loudly, fan-like lashes weeping. Cupping each other's square chins, Lotemi and Leitī kissed; stubble against stubble.

Lahi turned to me with a tender smile, her gold-tooth peeking. 'Come down and say hello.' She didn't have to explain anything further. All at once, I understood. Lotemi had his lover in Popua just as Lahi had hers in Mount Druitt. It was only together that my aunt and uncle could be truly free. And all this was just the messy, beautiful business of being a dirt poor islander.

30.

As Lotemi and Leitī disappeared into the lagoon, I could finally have a day alone with my mother-aunt. Lahi planned to drive me around various villages, recounting their milestones. 'Two hours to circle the whole mainland.'

Parrots trilled. Distant waves collected in a constant hum. Fronds bristled at the slightest of breezes.

Lahi crooned at me from above the hood of our rental Tarago, which shone bone-white. 'Ah weh, Si'i. Such a burden for you to carry our name.'

I took in a deep breath, inhaling all of Tonga. 'You carried me.'

Fourteen days into our trip, Lahi was full back to her boyish ways. Her baggy 2Pac t-shirt flapped in the wind, which rushed from the open windows of our van as soon as we hit the main concrete strip that led to Nuku'alofa. Straight black hair tied into a loose ponytail, Lahi tapped her knuckles on the steering wheel. Out the window, the dry dawn lit up shrubbery and fibro houses. Hard to imagine that just over a month ago, I was riding through the streets of Mounty in a stretch limo wearing a poofy white dress.

When Lahi saw my hands on the radio knobs, she tittered tentatively. 'Oh. No music today, kernel. Sunday.'

I laughed softly and elbowed one of Lahi's rolls. 'Oh yeah. Well, at least it's just us. No church, no husbands . . .'

'Shush.' My mum-aunt's cushiony cheeks rose into a wide gold-toothed grin. 'You know what I think? I think God knows love is love and doesn't really care.'

I nodded. After seeing Lotemi and Leitī's passionate embrace. I knew.

We parked in the village of Niutōua, which was the ancient capital of kings. First stop, Haʻamonga ʻa Maui – often referred to as the Stonehenge of the Pacific. The Haʻamonga was two vertical pillars made of coral rock, topped by another coral pillar laid horizontally. The earth around the natural structure was filled with overgrown grass and surrounded by the hush of a hidden ocean. Between each hole in the coral rock, fine fickle ferns poked through. A little way in the distance, a slanted stone made of the same coral sprouted from the ground. Old story said that a king sat on that slanted rock in order to protect his back against assassins. From his perch, the king flicked visitors' knees with a huge stick until they crawled towards him on their joints. My knees felt heavy: Our people had struggled for safety and security since the dawn of time.

Caressing the Haʻamonga with my fingertips, my hands became salt-encrusted and smelt of rain. I tried to climb the ancient monument. It scratched my palms and left me pockmarked – a punishment for my desecration. The shrush shrush shrush of the ocean swam in my ears. Lahi told me a woman named Fatafehi moved the ancient capital away from here because the land was too noisy. For the first time in two weeks, I laughed my Mount Druitt laugh. 'What a gronk, bro.'

I looped through the portal-like structure, which was keeping thousands of thousands of years in its sediment. It reminded me of my father's shoulders. I felt his biceps hugging me, willing me to love myself. Then I knew: Every Tongan, even while they were slowly eroding over time, had to be strong in order to carry their children into the future.

'It translates to "Maui's Burden",' Lahi explained in a whistle. 'We are looking onto the celestial plain of our Old Gods.'

Nana once told me I wasn't meant to know these tēvolo stories – the missionaries who brought the 'light' described them as the 'darkness'. But my mother-aunt taught me the true wealth of our people; weaving our tales into the wide and divine universe.

Second stop, three-headed coconut. Trampling through overgrown taro leaves, Lahi and I stacked it against rocks hiding in the underbrush. Meadow Senior became a saggy tomato as we trekked on; my forearms drying up and browning several shades darker. This difference in our skin revealed the messy truth of the 'half-caste'; it was never half-half. Lahi was as half-White as me but her sunburn was pink and peeled to reveal a lighter shade of fair. Meanwhile, my skin just soaked up the heat like toast – a reminder that I was just as much a Fob as I was a pālangi. Even though Tonga was taking the worst of me . . . this way of seeing myself . . . as half and never enough, *hafekasi* . . . it felt like a stain I would live with forever.

Three bunches of palm leaves, growing from one truck, forked out like a monster in an ancient Greek myth; a three-headed coconut tree twisted into the landscape and sharp sunshine. 'The three kings throughout our hundreds of islands became one kingdom,' Lahi explained between sips of Fiji water. Listening deeply, I wiped sweat from my forehead with my forearm, trying to catch my own breath, as Lahi went on: 'Only palm tree like this in the entire South Pacific, Si'i. It grew from a seed planted by our mothers across the ages – then it flowered.'

Squatting on the roots below, I looked back and forth between my paku skin and Lahi's bubbling skin. Sitting in silence under the shade of a frond, for what felt like an eternity, I finally mumbled to Lahi, 'That's why we're named Meadow.'

Lahi beamed at me. 'Always search for our mother's gardens.'

⁙

For our final stop, before we went back to Malapo, Lahi said we were going to see the blowholes in the village of Houma. She explained how waves sprouted from gaps in volcanic rocks, which were formed millions of years ago by lava. In our old stories, mainlands like Tongatapu were made from the fire god twins, Piki and Kele, playing in the moana; while smaller pieces of land were fished up by Maui Fusi Fonua. I stared wide-eyed at my mother-aunty, whose old knowledge made her as ancient to me as the island itself.

At the edge of the sea, just like Lahi promised, the waves met the sky. In Houma, we watched the rumble of the ocean spraying softly like confetti. It was here that I finally invited Lahi into Sugar Drive: the babies, the cockroaches, the holes my father left in the walls, the holes Mummy Le'o left in my heart.

Eventually, Lahi shifted my small waist from the blowholes until I was looking straight at her, and beyond, a stretch of fonua. Eyes drooping, she tucked a wind-swept strand of my hair behind my ear. 'I should tell you something . . . it will be hard to hear but I think it will help.' Then she pinched the semi-flat bridge of her freckly nose, squeezing her eyes prune-tight.

'Before Le'o died . . .' Lahi trailed off indecisively and started up again. 'Your mummy asked me to make sure none of you kids ever called anyone else "Mum". She made me promise.' Lahi wiped small drops of tears from her lashes. 'For a long time, I was angry at your dad for making me break my vow.'

Soaking in each syllable that bloomed from Lahi's lips, I listened against the shwosh shwosh shwosh of the moana. My mother-aunt pulled me into her folds and caressed my forearms, making sure I was still there.

'Then one night, I saw you, sitting in a grassy field. Big Sesi came up to you first and left a sprig of jasmine. Next, Aunty Heilala walked up and dropped on your lap a garcinia. Then Aunty Swa skipped over and gave you a lily stalk. On your head, Aunty Daisy placed a daisy crown. Then, Nana knelt in front of you and left roses at your feet. Soon after your mumma waddled up, pregnant like always, and from her belly button she pulled a shrub of camellias.' The freckles between Lahi's sparse brows clumped together as she added, 'And reeds popped up too . . . but I couldn't see who gave them to you.'

Tears flowing, Lahi took a moment to catch her breath. 'When I finally walked towards you, I was not alone. Your mummy Le'o was holding my hand. Then we sat in a circle around you, all us women, in the garden of mothers – held together by vines of bougainvillea.'

Families are made from all kinds of messy love and mucked-up feelings. Mine sprung, shwosh shwosh shwosh, from the soil of motherhood.

31.

This you last lesson, 'fore you go home,' Nana said as she picked up a chicken. The moa roamed between villages throughout Tonga and somehow each person knew which chick belonged to who.

Hot pink singlet. Beige shorts. Barefoot. Hazy afro. Nana was far removed from the layers of fluffy socks and baggy hoodies she wore back home in Mounty. Straddling a milk crate between her thighs, she sat straight-backed, as though she was on a throne. Gently, my grandmother cradled the fluffy chicken in the crook of her enormous elbow. Sulphur stung my lips as I observed; humidity muck-thick.

White and red feathers flitted from my grandmother's caresses. 'Name all my kitties, Angel. All da animal gifting God. Moa be Angel too, hmm?'

The sky sunk lower over my grandmother and the chook. Palm trees pulsated in growing wind while salt swam in the charged air – signs that a storm was coming. 'Last lesson, eating, den you Tongan,' my grandmother explained as mud swirled in her irises.

I sighed. By my third week in Tonga, I had lost a lot of weight. Weight I didn't have. My ribs protruded even when I wasn't sucking them in and my joints jutted and jostled like unburied bones. I had been living off pineapple Fanta, noodles, papaya and boiled taro, constantly mumbling to myself, 'I'll just eat Macca's when we get back.'

Clucking along with the chicken, my grandmother's melon palms wrapped around the moa's neck. 'Kai or die,' she commanded with her burning-bush glare whilst tightening her grip.

'Bawk-bawk-baw-baw-baw-baaaawwwk,' the chicken pleaded fiercely, clawing at Nana's forearms in a last-ditch effort to live. Scratches left little blood trails on Nana's forearms just like Aunt Daisy's self-inflicted scars.

'Bwakcrrek!' Nana bent the chicken's neck back, its spine curved like a question mark. Then, in a hooking motion, she tugged her wrist. The moa's head flicked upwards once, as if being pulled by a string, and then swept downwards, beak facing the fonua. Marble eyes turned glassy and milky. *Is that what it looked like when Maui pulled our islands from the sea?*

It felt like a butterfly was flickering in my throat, my eyes ready to blowhole burst. My grandmother was right. If I kept carrying on for Macca's, I was choosing a slow death. No one could live as half of themselves. To live, I needed to embrace Brown, pālangi, noble, peasant, Tonga, Australia – Islander.

Plucking curly feathers, Nana shook her head at me, afro waving back and forth. She refused to force-feed me this time. On the fonua, in front of Malapo Abode, Nana wanted me to embrace myself for myself.

I stepped slowly towards my grandmother. Her kafu frame dripped in sweat, as if she'd been unfolded. Broken sky. Rain turned to shower. The wind wept as the earth drowned. I yelled over the thrum of endless water for us to go back inside; last lesson and dead chicken be damned. I pulled at my nana's elbow, which was as hard as marble. I knew then where my father inherited his strength. Tonga poked through Nana's teeth as she laughed. Then she sung, 'Ha'u faka'uha.' Springing from her milk crate throne, chicken carcass tucked under her chunky chin, Nana lifted her wing-like upper arms and waved her hands to the heavens, repeating between the raindrops, 'Ha'u faka'uha.'

My first faka'uha – the kind of rain that invites us to play. The tropical storm was warm. Dashing around in the downpour, my grandmother and I pirouetted, skipped and chased each other. All the while, the water washed me inside out. Cleansed of Shazza, who called me a savage; cleansed of Ms Indigo, who saw me as an assignment; cleansed of Emma-Jane, who saw me as an object to be governed; cleansed of Bear Grylls, who saw me as a documentary for National Geographic.

Together, Nana and I plucked feathers and pranced. 'Ah. Weh. Ah. Weh.'

Then, a crack in the sky halted my grandmother mid-twirl. 'Look da wind change.' With the chicken curled between her chin and breast like an egg, my grandmother knelt before me on her knotted knees, swollen voice hurling above the storm: 'My girl. Almost time. Nearly Tongan.'

Nana and I continued to dance and pluck the chicken feathers. We blended our laugh-filled prayers in the hush and rush of the heavens. The faka'uha washed my spirit clean, and all at once, I was overcome with the thirst and hunger of a newborn child.

32.

The silence was deafening on our final trek across Tāufa'āhau Road. My grandmother and my uncle Lotemi were staying back for an extra month but they came to see me and Lahi off at Fua'amotu Airport. Parting ways was such sweet sorrow whether it was in the front yard of my grandmother's house in Mount Druitt or at the centre of the land she was born on. Usually, Nana's status meant she would take the front seat in any car ride, but this time she insisted on taking the back seats with me. I held Nana's warm and thick palms, tracing the sunspots on her knuckles, exchanging sweat from one hand to the other. I knew now that all the water and blood and skin my grandmother shed forever connected me to her, to Tonga. I didn't want to let go. 'Nana missing you too,' my grandmother sighed, pressing her withered lips to the top of my head.

Twirling a lock of his oily hair, Uncle Lotemi hummed from the front passenger seat, 'Oh, hunies. We go on because we no turn back. We together again soon.'

Yawning from the driver's seat, Lahi added, 'Just keep cooking for Mum and we'll never be parted.' This made Lotemi laugh as he caressed Lahi's ponytail.

Fua'amotu Airport was full of Whites, Asians and the occasional Māori waiting to depart. The enclosure was nothing but a grey storage unit with cracked concrete – China-imported cement was never meant for the salty air of Tonga. I took my time to breathe in the breeze. Thick as coconut juice. Fresh as the ocean. Mama'd by divine mouths to stay forever-warm. My belly was full.

Nana pulled me into her soft sides and pressed me into her bosom. Her afro tickled my ear as she whispered, 'My girl, Tonga always wif you.'

At the same time, Lotemi planted a kiss goodbye on Lahi's crown – Nana might have wondered why he didn't peck her on the lips, were it not for the fact that she knew we were all such good Christians.

Half an hour later Lahi and I boarded the plane to Auckland, from which we would then catch a flight back to Australia.

Brushing palm trees to a circle of coral to a tiny dot in a big blot of blue; I watched Tonga waving goodbye, reminding me to come back soon.

33.

The scent of McNuggets filled the air, and for the first time in my life, it sickened me. Mum and Dad were standing at baggage claim inside Sydney Airport, waiting for me and Lahi. I rushed towards them, dodging strangers and suitcases; dodging until my father's familiar forearms and Mumma's hard and protruding stomach engulfed me. I stretched my shoulders out of their sockets just to keep them close.

'Look at youse all tanned,' Dad beamed, pressing his sandy chin into my cheek. Caressing his square fingers across my jaw, he moved my face side to side, wide eyes taking me in. 'Youse sure this is my daughter?'

'Hug me any tighter and I'll pop,' Mumma laughed, her voice slightly out of breath. Releasing my parents, I pressed my ear to Mumma's rock-hard belly button. She smelt of milky soap, which reminded me of the bedsheets at 8 Sugar Drive.

I hummed, 'Littlest One still waiting for me?' I looked up into Mumma's leafy lashes and grinned – there was room for me in that magnificent womb of hers too.

'She definitely went back to her roots,' Lahi called out as she joined us, baggage in tow.

Pecking his sister on the cheek, Dad, his gaze on Lahi, said as sincerely as I've ever heard him speak: 'Thank *you.*' I suddenly saw my father and mum-aunt as children; searching for their own thankless father, dreaming of a better life for the next generation of Reeds.

Gently pulling away from Mumma, I discovered a sticky wet patch of goo had soaked into my pants. I looked up between Lahi's freckled folds, my father's shiny shale head and the purple rings under Mumma's eyes in confusion. *Have I peed myself?*

Mumma gasped, her breezy voice billowing out across the open space of Sydney Airport: 'Water's broke. She's coming!'

Stretched out in the back-back of the Tarago, Mumma rested her sweaty head on my lap. Her bark-like face was smooth as she closed her eyes and breathed steadily in-out, in-out, in and out again. Clutching onto her root-like fingers, I repeated over and over, 'What do I do?'

Lifting the corner of her mouth and twisting her nose, Mumma proclaimed, 'Ah, weh. Don't stress, nothing new. I've been through this how many times.'

'Turn, turn, turn,' Lahi directed her brother from the passenger seat. Then to us she yelled, 'How you two going back there?' As if I was pregnant too.

The motorway flushed behind us as the Tarago sped through specks of cars. Billboards advertised that Ronald McDonald was only using 100% chicken in his food. *What was I eating before?* Blue phone boxes spotted the emergency lane. Exhaust fumes spluttered. Before I could respond to Lahi's question, Dad's booming voice from the driver's seat shouted over a blaring car horn. 'No, youse move!'

Blood stopped flowing to my fingers, so tight was Mumma's grip. Under all that noise she screeched at me, 'I love having girls. A son is a son until he takes a wife. A daughter is a daughter all her life.'

Wiping Mumma's forehead, which was matted with hair, I asked where she got all her sayings from. Groaning, she replied, 'You didn't think you were the only one who reads, right? Gotta whole book full.'

What a shame – the questions that rushed through me about this woman who raised me, emerging at the worst of times. The car swerved and with a sharp gasp, Mumma's eyes cracked and jolted upwards. 'Jared,' she screeched, legs wide open; hand crushing my fingers. 'Just because we're Islanders doesn't mean one of my seven kids needs to be born in a Tarago!'

❧

Grasping the band of Mumma's cotton tights, I helped walk her towards the Emergency sign at Blacktown Hospital.

'Are you sure you don't want me to take her?' Lahi yelled through the driver's seat window.

'No, sis,' Mumma responded as she leant on Dad's sturdy frame. 'The bubs, please. Look after our other bubs.'

Leaving Mumma for but a moment, I ran back and kissed Lahi's cheek three times – one for each freckle that marked me out as Meadow Reed.

'What an honour for us to be the eldest sister to so many,' she reminded me before accelerating hard and taking off towards Sugar Drive.

As me and my parents limped through the emergency doors, a gust of air con hit my face – something I hadn't felt the entire time I was in Tonga. Finding a wheelchair, I helped Mumma settle in while Dad walked up to the reception desk. The Dettol-scented room was filled with rows of hard plastic chairs; patients wheezing, sweating, puffing and coughing. Scared of germs, I kept close to the handles of the wheelchair.

From the reception desk, a bulky woman in a purple and blue uniform with dotted spirals asked us, 'What mob you from?' This led to her and Dad having a succinct conversation about the cultural differences between Islanders and Blackfellas. Dad said, 'We big people, you first people.' Mumma stayed silent, whispering to her belly button and guiding my hand to rub her tummy mound. 'Cousins, we cousins,' the receptionist eventually concluded through a wad of gum. 'Let's bump up Big Mumma's priority and wheel her in. Emergency sucks.'

Moaning under her breath, Mumma waddled around the excessively sterile maternity ward between each contraction. I followed behind her with a water bottle, making sure she sipped every few minutes. To ease my anxiety, I tried to time my footsteps to each beep beep beep of the machines. Every now and then, women cried from neighbouring hallways.

Having already done this routine five times, Dad gave man-splainy advice to every other woman he could find in a white dressing gown. To a petite Viet woman who was a quarter of his size, he said, 'Just imagine a football coming out of a scrum and youse'll be all right.' And to the blonde-headed Bogan with the words 'Break Free' tattooed in cursive across her chest, he said, 'If youse lay down, the baby will never come out.' He then told a young Indian woman with cropped black hair, 'How can contractions be stronger than youse? They are youse.'

It went like this for hours until a bright pink sunset began to appear through one of the windows in the ward.

Sipping on the rest of the water bottle, Mumma breathed into her full height and stepped straight-backed into room number twenty-seven. 'Meadow, keep close.'

Stumpy legs bent. Knees stuck sideways. Swollen hips twitched. Limbs dampened. Walls, blankets and machines of white surrounded us, as if we were in a tight cloud. Mumma was really screaming now; so sweaty and red that the usual purple under her eyes had all but disappeared into the rest of her skin. Decked out in a plastic apron, blue surgical mask and yellow-gloved hands, a doctor draped a thick sheet of cotton lined with plastic over Mumma's thighs. The doctor's name-tag said 'Abeny', and she had the same dark brown complexion as Bruce, the West African boy in my class who could calculate large numbers without a calculator. I particularly admired Dr Abeny's long black braids, which were twisted into a bun.

With a quick peek between Mumma's wide-open legs, the doctor asked calmly, 'Soon but not quite. Did you want some pain relief?'

I held Mumma's left hand while Dad held her right. We stared straight at her from either side of the hospital bed as she wept and groaned. My mouth was dry and my heart was bleeding out of my ears.

'She's taken the epi a couple times and for sure nitrous with every kid,' Dad informed Dr Abeny in a self-assured tone. But even I could hear the underlying strain in his voice. Obnoxious as he may have come off, he was just worried.

Squeezing my fingers so tight I could already feel a bruise forming on the back of my hand, Mumma gasped, 'No! All natural this time.'

The whites in the doctor's eyes shrivelled from above her face mask, her braids twitching. 'Are you sure? From your records, this child is going to be massive.'

Mumma nodded, her cheeks squeezing tight. "Oiauē. I know.'

Soon after Dr Abeny left, a short midwife in fluffy pink slacks sat at the foot of the hospital bed. Her chubby cheeks doubled in size as she grinned and said to me in a thick Filipino accent, 'You mother like a great warrior.' Her name tag said Mrs Mariana.

Contractions growing closer and closer, Mumma directed her husband to stand by her shoulders, and me to stand at the bottom end of the bed. Rubbing at my knuckles, I rushed behind the midwife. What I saw between Mumma's legs made my skin cold with half-awe and half-disgust. Blood streaked down Mumma's thighs and calves; pooling all over white cotton. Soaked scent of sap and rust stinging my nose. Her pipi . . . no, her vagina . . . was dilated like a disc, covered in long black hairs. I clenched my thighs together in sympathy. From Mumma's dark, dark and mysterious depths, a patch of gold was crowning. It felt like forever, standing and staring into that universe until Mumma screamed, 'Ahhhh-weh!' And in a flush of light and dust, Kalmia Rose Reed came into this world wrinkled and reaching for air and milk – a full four and a half kilos.

Immediately, the midwife pressed Kalmia into Mumma's engorged chest. Dad was weeping, pressing his chapped lips on Mumma's head. It was the first time I had ever seen him fully cry, his hard stature melting away like clay. A big bang went off in every cell of my being – the man who came from those beautiful Brown men that toiled across the fonua. Still in tears, my father collected blood and mucus on the tips of his square fingers, and then said out loud, 'Be back, gotta call Tonga.'

Lactating and hyperventilating, Mumma clutched onto Kalmia as the midwife cleaned up and waited for the placenta. 'Biggest girl,' Mrs Mariana chimed as if she were talking about the weather. 'I'm no doctor but midwife long time. I knowing, if no natural, maybe you and bubba die.'

'I *know*,' Mumma said, holding my baby sister tight against her chest. Pressing my face into Mumma's chest as well, breathing her in, and breathing in my newest sister, all I could think was: *Mumma did know, didn't she? 'Oiauē, the things mothers know . . .*

That morning, I quietly vowed to converge with Mumma. This baby was our soil, our bark, our salt and our blood.

34.

*B*lood broken under my flesh. I pressed on the budding bruise on the back of my hand. Purple parallel pleats – the phantom of Mumma's fingers. The mark of Camellia and Kalmia imprinted upon my skin like tātatau.

A burning in the middle of my spine. Dad slowly dabbed an ancient Black & Gold packet of frozen peas on my knuckles. We were back home, sitting on our roach-bitten couch. It had been a day and half a night since my little-little-littlest sister was born. We were taking the rest of my siblings to meet her for the first time as soon as the sun rose.

'Oiya,' I hissed and then giggled. 'Why do we only use veggies as cold packs?'

Dad crushed coral in his throat as he laughed. 'That's being Fob for youse.' Since we were so busy at the hospital, the rest of my siblings had run amuck and turned the whole of Sugar Drive into a spiral before they all went to bed. The venetian blinds of our bay windows were dented; our overgrown backyard exposed. Between the gaps, heavy grey clouds within the shadows of midnight clung to our pop-stick fence. Underneath the window frame, our television set was topped with baby bottles, sippy cups and unused nappies. In the middle of some strewn shirts was a frayed pair of pink undies. Inside the undies was a pad, which had swollen to twice its size. The used cotton-like plastic had clearly been through a cycle in the washing machine; menstruation was stripped to nothing but a blot.

My father hummed and said, 'Youse know, I haven't forgotten what youse said before youse went to Tonga.'

Surprised, I opened my mouth to try and tell Dad that it was a lifetime ago, but he shook his head before I could speak. 'Let me finish.'

I snapped my mouth shut and stared closely into his eyes. His gaze was no longer the dark, dark story he once told me. Neither was his sight a burning bush, a severed worm in dirt, or even something we were cursed to share. It was deep and endless like the blowholes, known as 'whistle of the nobles', in Houma. 'One of the hardest things about us Islanders is that we are forced to grow up too fast. We born big so people treat us big. We grow up without our dads around. We have so many brothers and sisters to care for. We become parents when we still kids. We go through the pain of losing our first love.' Moulding the frozen veggies around my palm, I shivered at the messy truth of my father's words. 'We are scattered, that's why we stay together.'

The sky above Sugar Drive responded with a faint yet familiar crack. Through the late summer night hours, winds of change pelted at the windows. Faka'uha – the rain in which we play . . .

Slowly, I stood from the couch and gathered myself. Slower still, I bent over to press an 'uma onto my father's scalp, breaching the sacred space. My father's skin was as soft as sand. My father, the rock, fully eroded. I inhaled the smell of burnt cotton and tobacco, whispering, 'I was destined to have many strong mothers, but I am lucky to also have just one half-decent father.'

Dad's gaze upon me, I stepped through the sliding door and into the backyard; my spine no longer in pain.

Air and sod collided. I tipped my head, closed my eyes, and felt the raindrops fall onto my face. Washed again inside out. Beneath the soaking summer night storm, I felt the earth inside me. The last forbidden thing. What my nana called fonua. What my mum-aunt called a burden. What my mumma called lineage. What my dad called puke māhina. Mummy Le'o's final gift – the cycling of every speck of dust that made me.

Rain continued to pour as the universe coagulated between my legs and trickled down my thighs. My blood soiled like a seed spiralling into a new life. Period.

Ah. Weh. Ah. Weh.

Acknowledgements

A debt humbly repaid to those that invested: Creative Australia, Copyright Agency Ignite Grant, Writing NSW Varuna Fellowship, Red Room Poetry, The Leo Kelly Blacktown Arts Centre, Arts and Cultural Exchange and Sydney Writers' Festival.

A stack of leis to the Fobs that celebrated: Latai and Sēini Taumoepeau, Emele Ugavule, Hau Latukefu, Leo Tanoi, Meleika Vika Mana, Enoch Mailangi, Taofia Pelesasa, Eliorah Malifa, 'Ana Ika, Brian Fuata, Emily Havea, Vanilla Tupu, Didi de Graaf, Ayeesha Ash and Sela Vai.

A wealth of knowledge from the pages that inspired: *The Whale Rider*, *The Color Purple*, *12 Edmondstone Street*, *Inside My Mother*, *Beloved*, *Frangipani*, *Dominicana*, *Banana Heart Summer* and *The Tribe*.

A pot of gold to the pagemasters that believed: Fiona Hazard, Holly Jeffery, Vanessa Lanaway, Deonie Fiford, Lee Moir and double bills for Vanessa Radnidge.

A fortune for the caregivers that paved the way: Professor Witi Ihimaera, Professor Jioji Ravulo, Melissa Lucashenko, Evelyn Araluen, Professor Alice Te Punga Somerville, Dr Randa Abdel-Fattah, Lena Nahlous, Sisonke Msimang, Dr Jonas Ilocto and Debbie Viengkham.

A receipt of gratitude for the Sweatshop gees: Phoebe Grainer, Amani Haydar, Natalia Figueroa Barroso, Shirley Le, Shankari Chandran, Sheree Joseph, Gayatri Nair, Meyrnah Khodr, Raveena Grover, Janette Chen, Sara M. Saleh, Helen Nguyen, Patrick Cruz Forrest, Maryam Azam, Tyree Barnette, Adrian Mouhajer, Mark Mariano, Bruce Koussaba, Daniel Nour, Adam Novaldy Anderson and Elaine Lim.

A rare pearl for my moana sisters: Sela Ahosivi-Atiola, Christine Afoa and Anne-Marie Te Whiu.

A gem-filled hug for my favourite duo: Jane Worsley and Kahlil Isa Ahmad.

A call to charity for the strays: Brighter Future Cat Rescue. They saved Summer, who saved me.

A thousand apologies to those who were expended: My late grandmother, my late mother, my fahu, my mehekitangas, my grandparents, my parents, my brothers, my sisters and my nieces.

And lastly, infinite love to the one who treasured this dirt poor islander beyond measure: Mohammed Ahmad.

WINNIE DUNN

is a writer of Tongan descent from Mount Druitt, Western Sydney. She is the general manager of Sweatshop Literacy Movement and holds a Bachelor of Arts degree from Western Sydney University. Winnie's articles, essays, poems and short stories have appeared in *Meanjin*, *Griffith Review*, *The Guardian*, *Southerly*, *Cordite*, Red Room Poetry and *Sydney Review of Books*. She is the editor of several critically acclaimed anthologies, including: *Sweatshop Women* (Sweatshop, 2018), *Racism: Stories on Fear, Hate & Bigotry* (Sweatshop, 2021), and *Another Australia* (Affirm Press, 2022). Winnie is also the editor of *Straight Up Islander* (SBS Voices, 2021), which is Australia's first collection of mainstream Pasifika-Australian stories. In 2022, Winnie was the recipient of a literature grant from the Australian Government through Creative Australia. *Dirt Poor Islanders* is her debut work of autobiographical fiction.